UNBELONGING

A novel by

David J. Jepsen

HISTORIUM PRESS U.S.A.

This work is dedicated to my Mom and Dad

Prologue

1949

Joanne wondered how the tightly woven threads of her life deteriorated into a knotted snarl of fabric. First, it was the war. It took her life apart at the seams like a tailor working a pair of shears. She'd stitched it back together the best she could but her life appeared permanently frayed. Four years out, she could no longer blame her troubles solely on the war. But who else is to blame? She saw her reflection in the bus window. The sullen looking woman staring back at her was a good place to start. *You helped make this problem, so fix it,* she thought.

Headed to work, Joanne sat near the rear of the crowded Seattle Transit bus. She wore gray, pleated trousers, white blouse and light blue cardigan sweater. Outside she could see a cityscape reshaped even more than her life. Heavy downtown traffic crawled along Second Avenue in the morning rush hour. Pedestrians scurried to jobs in stores, restaurants and office buildings. The faces changed too. More Negroes, that's for sure. Dressed in work clothes and toting lunch boxes, they walked briskly, heads down. Department store salesgirls, secretaries and waitresses rushed along Second, eager to punch in at a job paying slave wages. On the east side of Second, striking telephone operators carrying picket signs chanted "an injury to one is an injury to all." Protests were everywhere. You couldn't pick up a newspaper without reading about one company or another dealing with disgruntled employees. Last week it was butchers, yesterday bakers. Who's next, she thought sardonically, candlestick makers?

She turned her attention to that morning's *Seattle Post-Intelligencer.* Beneath a front-page article about runaway crime, she read a piece about Boeing's new Stratofreighter. She sported callouses to prove how quickly Boeing can pump out aircraft. She'd riveted the skins of hundreds of bombers. She remembered the help-wanted ads when Boeing, desperate for workers during the war, started recruiting women. "Keeping America safe is just like keeping house," claimed one ad. "Driving a carloader is as easy as driving the groceries home on Saturday," promised another. *Yeah, right*. Rosie the Riveter bugged her the most. Posters of the fist-pumping woman were plastered on every factory wall and city storefront during the war. "We can do it," Rosie promised. *We can do it alright, if you accept wages less than men doing the same work. You can do it if you understand Boeing treats women like temps. And don't complain about groping from men with wandering hands. Boys will be boys, after all. Yes, you can do it, ladies. Just don't get mixed up in union business or with socialists. You'll learn fast what Boeing can do. Show you the door that's what . I learned that lesson the hard way. Yes, Rosie symbolized women's power but it disguised the limits of that power.*

Page two in the *P-I* included a story about her boss, Harry Bridges, president of the longshoremen's union. For the umpteenth time he faced criticism for socialist leanings. In this city, that meant you were branded a Communist sympathizer, or worse, an actual Red. Harry never backed down, though, God bless him. "We are left wing, but our union has no revolutionary plots and is not dedicated to communism," the paper quoted him as saying.

For more than two years, anti-Communist hysteria infected the city like the flu. A Commie hater from Spokane won a seat in the state house promising to root out anyone engaged in so-called un-American activities. He's now persecuting Americans for doing very American things, like questioning your government and holding it accountable. Endless hearings led to state government employees, writers, playwrights, actors, and college profs getting questioned, accused and blackballed. Refusal to cooperate promised jail time. Today it was a state employee sentenced to thirty days for his silence.

Joanne looked up from the paper. It started to rain, a brisk wind coming in from the south. Her dark mood matched the weather. Her marriage teetered on shaky ground for months. Actually it was longer than that. George came home from war damaged. The kind and gentle man she loved was damaged. He left a part of him – the part she loved the most – on some remote Pacific island. Her doctor called it battle fatigue but it was worse than that. She didn't know what to call it. Did it even have a name? His mood swings, his drinking, his self-pity came and went. The old George, the one she married, would show up for a while and then retreat into the bottle. His problems were her fault, of course, because she worked. She wasn't waiting with smile and dinner ready when he got home. She was neglecting their son, Danny, and their daughter, Natalie. They argued frequently. He often came home late, drunk. He'd eat whatever she'd left out for him. Afterwards, he'd plop down on the couch, drink in hand, and brood in silence before coming to bed. She could hear him enter the bedroom, stinking of booze. He'd struggle out of his clothes and stumble into bed. In seconds he was asleep, snoring. She didn't know what to do, but she needed to do something. But it has to wait. It was time to get to work.

She stepped off the bus at Second and Yesler and headed for the Alaska Commerce Building. The rain let up, sunlight streaming through gray clouds. The longshore union rented space on the second floor during the ninety-five-day strike against shipbuilders. Her union brother, Curt Jaworski, waited for her on the entry steps. They rode the elevator to the second floor and walked down the hall to the union's offices. She unlocked the door and they stepped inside. Overloaded filing cabinets and dozens of boxes were strewn everywhere. Picket signs were stacked haphazardly in one corner, office supplies in another. Work tables and office chairs, dusty from months of neglect, stood in the center of the room.

Joanne fretted over her marriage all morning while sorting through files and loading them into boxes. *I will confront George tonight. It will likely lead to another fight, but so be it. I can't go on like this.*

Jaworski was stacking boxes near the door. Later he would load them on the elevator. With the strike over, they no longer needed the downtown space so they were hauling everything back to the union's main office. Movers would be in later today.

It was nearly noon and Joanne was hungry. "You want to break for lunch before we go? she asked Curt. The big guy liked to eat. She'd made meatloaf sandwiches left over from last night's dinner.

"Sure, that would be . . ."

He never finished the sentence. Without warning, everything was in motion. Stacks of boxes tumbled over, spilling their contents everywhere. Tables and chairs skittered comically across the tiled floor. Fluorescent light fixtures rocked, then darkened. Joanne grabbed for Jarworski's arm to keep from falling but he stumbled towards the windows facing Second Avenue. From where Joanne stood, she could see buildings across the street swaying like tall grass in the wind. An ominous roar, insistent and unrelenting, assaulted them like a passing freight train. Suddenly the entire building jerked violently, slamming Joanne to the floor. It was like some vengeful god picked it up with one hand and shook it ferociously. A loud cracking and screeching came from above. She looked up to see the floor above her open up. It rained wood beams, cracked plasterboard, office furniture and dust. Joanne screamed and covered her head only to be met with pain and darkness.

Part 1 -- 1945

There is one front and one battle where everyone in the United States . . . will be privileged to remain in action throughout this war. That front is right here at home, in our daily lives, and in our daily tasks.

Franklin D. Roosevelt

Chapter 1

The sea of aluminum stretching hundreds of yards in all directions defied reality. It was mystical, almost unearthly, Joanne thought. Straddling the top of the fuselage of a Boeing B29 Superfortress, she lowered her rivet gun and looked out across the mammoth rows of partially assembled aircraft. On her first day at work, the enormity of Plant Two took her breath away. Fourteen months later it remained a wonder. Four rows of the flying monsters, each with a 141-foot wingspan, filled the cavernous forty-acre plant.

"Come on, Novak, pick it up! We're running behind," yelled her group leader, Derek Johnson.

She'd given up correcting the pronunciation of her married name, which Czechs pronounced Novak to rhyme with "walk," not "vac." With sweat dripping from her red bandana, Joanne adjusted her goggles and picked up the gun. Her shoulders and back ready to revolt as she resumed powering rivets into the skin of the long-range bomber.

Riveting has been around since manufacturers first needed to bind two metal parts. In aircraft, riveting demands masterful teamwork between riveter and bucker. Working from the outside, the riveter drives a solid steel rivet with a head on one end through a pre-drilled hole using a gun powered by an air compressor. To bind the rivet in place, a bucker positioned on the inside holds a T-shaped bucking bar flush against the hole. The gun's driving force smashes and flattens the headless end of the rivet, creating an unbreakable bond. Riveter and bucker dancing a two-step, drive and smash. Fred Astaire and Ginger Rogers tap dancing across an aluminum stage accompanied by the symphonic scream of a thousand rivet guns. Drive and smash, a thousand times an hour. A thousand rivets set one inch apart in a thousand perfect rows.

"Dammit!" Joanne could feel blood trickling down her left cheek. She put down the gun and wiped her face, applying pressure to the cut. Aluminum shavings nicked her just below her goggles.

Her bucker yelled up. "You alright, Joanne?" She'd worked with Anita Warner, a waitress from Yakima, for three months. Buckers rotated in an out, many promoted to riveting, and Anita was better than most.

"Yea, just a nick, she said." Aluminum shavings came with the job. It was everywhere, covering your clothes, your skin and invading your hair. It took ten minutes to wash it out at night. Staunching the bleeding, Joanne once more picked up the gun, and the tandem resumed their two-step of drive and smash.

Plant Two was a marvel of innovation and simplicity. When the United States entered World War Two in December 1941, Boeing faced two herculean problems, an avalanche of new orders for long-range bombers, coinciding with a hemorrhaging of experienced workers, literally all men. In a rush of patriotic fever following Pearl Harbor, they dropped the tools of industry and picked up the weapons of war. To meet the demand, the company began recruiting women, reluctantly at first and then aggressively.

The challenge was to simplify assembly for employees who, as Boeing President Phillip Johnson, put it, "had never worn trousers or gotten grease under their nails." To streamline production, engineers converted Plant Two and Plant Three in Renton from factories into assembly lines. Individual parts like wing panels, tail sections, stabilizers and bomb racks were constructed in new Boeing plants all over the Northwest. Like assembling a model airplane bought at the Five and Dime, it was as straightforward as opening the box to find individual parts ready to be glued, or in this case riveted, together.

The assembly line ran west to east, beginning near the banks of the Duwamish River. Planes lined up four abreast and placed on motorized tracks were assembled from tail to nose. Major parts were riveted in place as the craft rolled forward at a snail's pace. The lines never stopped. Nothing stopped in war. It was relentless but workers held up under pressure. By mid-1944, twelve ready-to-fly B29s rolled out the door over three eight-hour shifts.

Joanne almost didn't hear the whistle signaling the end of her eight-hour shift at three o'clock. She removed the goggles, ripped off the sweat-soaked bandana and headed for the women's locker in the basement complex below the factory. If she hurried, she'd catch the Boeing bus in time to get to her Capitol Hill home before Natalie and Danny returned from school.

As she worked her way down the crowded corridor leading to the lockers, thoughts of children were interrupted when someone from behind roughly grabbed and squeezed her butt.

"Nice ass, Novak. Don't flatten it sittin' on that plane all day."

"Buzz off, O'Malley," she shot back, annoyed. Many women endured catcalls, whistles and unwanted touching in the first months of the war. It was endemic, as if men thought they held license to fondle whatever they pleased. That women's bodies were just another toy they could play with at their leisure. It was more than a little irritating. Fortunately, it trailed off after men grew accustomed to working alongside women. She learned the best way to handle assholes like O'Malley was to return the guff.

"You know, O'Malley, you're going to lose that hand someday. The only thing you'll be good for is grabbing your own ass."

"I'm sorry, Novak," he said grinning, "but I just can't resist your femininity quotient," he said, drawing a laugh from the men around him.

That was the joke spreading around the plant. In 1943, with a workforce now approaching fifty percent female, Boeing faced public criticism for undermining American values and the family ideal, They were taking women from their proper place in the home. Young women should be schooled in "house-wifely duties," not making planes, protested one prominent minister. Boeing couldn't let that go, so the PR department issued a press release declaring their women maintained the perfect "femininity quotient." Boeing women displayed a picture-perfect balance of strength and softness, of muscle and makeup. She could carry her load at work and carry home the groceries on Saturday. The company offered classes on fashion, makeup, poise, and personality to help the girls in the Boeing family to enhance their FQ. They brought in a noted clothing designer to create a line of women's workwear, Flying Fortress Fashions, a military-style jumpsuit replete with the Boeing logo and chevrons indicating years of service. Boeing women were soldiers on the home front defending America in style. Joanne stuck with her pleated trousers and collared shirt.

During the 20-minute bus ride to Capitol Hill, she inventoried her aches and pains. She was physically spent, and hurt everywhere. Her hands, swollen with blisters in her first month on the job, now sprouted calluses matching a bricklayer's. Her feet complained about ten-year-old boots she'd worn shoveling cow manure on the family farm. What she needed now was a long, hot bath and to slip on a housedress. When the kids went to bed, she'd change into a robe, remove her bra and pour herself a bourbon, maybe two.

In spite of the toll it took on her body, Joanne loved the work. Yes, it was physically demanding, repetitive, mind-numbing, and not without hazards. But it was important. and she was good at it. She remembered recruitment ads in the first year of the war appealing to women's patriotism. "Join the workers at Boeing. Help our Air Forces pour it on the enemy." Joanne certainly wanted to do her part but there was more to it. She'd been alone with the kids since George quit his engineering job at Boeing, joined the Navy as a second lieutenant and shipped out, first to San Diego for training and then to parts unknown in the Pacific. Alone for the first time in her life, she worried about her husband incessantly. A job would offer some relief.

The interview at the Boeing Employment Office surprised her. It turned out that farm girls sporting a sturdy frame, accustomed to physical labor and comfortable working with tools, matched the profile for female workers. The joke was Boeing women could be as feminine as they wanted so long as they could "toss a varsity football tackle over their shoulders." Joanne didn't know about that but at five-eight she looked eye-to-eye with most men, and while lacking cover-girl looks, her high cheek bones, aquiline nose and thick dark hair drew the stares of men on the street.

The interviewer, a Mr. Ward Dobbs, was thin, balding and wore a suit that looked two sizes too big. His eyes wandered in all the wrong places. Behind him was a poster of a woman dressed in slacks and a blouse standing next to a B17. The caption below read "It's a short step from homemaking to plane making." Dobbs invited her to sit, smiling mischievously, eyes roaming from her face to her breasts. "Well," he said, stringing the word into two syllables. "Mrs. Novak, you certainly appear to have the physical attributes we're looking for. Tell me, do you think you have the endurance? This is demanding work, you know, eight-hour shifts, six days a week."

"Mr. Dobbs, farmers work twelve-hour shifts, seven days a week. It never stops."

"Yes, I imagine it doesn't, and I think you would be a fine addition to the Boeing family, but I have one concern, a question, really. How can you properly care for your children if you're working all day? The company doesn't want to contribute to the neglect of our employees' children."

Joanne expected this question. Her neighbor, Pam, was turned down because her three kids were all under age ten and hadn't found adequate childcare. The papers were full of news reports and irate letters to the editor about what the papers dubbed "latchkey kids," who came home from school to an empty house.

"Mr. Dobbs, I appreciate your concern for my children, but I can assure you they will not be neglected. Their schools are just a mile from our home. If I work the day shift, we'll all get home around the same time. If I'm late, Natalie is old enough to watch her younger brother."

That seemed to satisfy Dobbs. He stood, announcing the interview was over and handed her forms to complete. "Welcome to the Boeing family," he said lasciviously, once more letting his eyes roam where they shouldn't.

She stepped off the bus at Tenth Avenue and Mercer Street a few blocks south of her home on Federal Avenue. She checked her purse for ration coupons and headed to the Thriftway. On a weekday afternoon, no more than a handful of customers, all women, pushed carts up and down the aisles. She was putting a carton of milk in the cart when she spotted a familiar figure pushing a cart in her direction.

It was Mrs. Bloom, her next-door neighbor. She didn't want to get into a conversation with her, but it was too late to get away.

"Oh, Mrs. Novak, I'm glad I caught you. Doing a little shopping are we?"

Joanne smiled but didn't respond to the obvious. Mrs. Bloom, who was about sixty and a widow, complained about one thing or another since they'd bought the house nine years ago. With a war on protestations escalated – Joanne's unkempt yard (George kept an immaculate yard), her noisy children, and most recently, the baseball that found its way through Mrs. Bloom's kitchen window. The repair cost Joanne nearly two dollars. She wondered what Mrs. Bloom wanted now.

"How can I help you, Mrs. Bloom, I have to get home to the kids."

"Well, that's just the thing you see. I happened to look out the front window this afternoon and saw Danny come home alone from school. I didn't see Natalie anywhere. They always come home together. Not good for that boy to be all by himself in that house, you know."

Joanne looked down at her groceries. She wondered how to respond to a neighbor who turned looking out her windows into a fulltime job. More frustrating, was the unspoken accusation from someone who felt inclined to remind Joanne of her parental responsibilities. Well, she could get in line behind a growing list of so-called well-wishers. Her priest, Father Everett, Sister Theresa at Holy Names, and most of all her parents butted in. She resented insinuations she was a neglectful mother more interested in money than motherhood. But all that aside, Mrs. Bloom's query concerned her. Natalie picked up Danny at Stevens Elementary and they walked home together Where was she?

"Thanks, Mrs. Bloom. I'm sure Danny is okay. Now if you'll excuse me, I'll pay for these groceries and head home."

Federal Avenue, lined with maple and poplar trees, was part of a quiet, middle-class neighborhood at the north end of Capitol Hill. The Novak home had a large front yard and a detached garage. A third of their wages went to house payments. She unlocked the front door and stepped into the spacious, but sparsely furnished living room. A couch and two matching armchairs took up one side and a brick fireplace the other. Their Zenith console radio sat between the armchairs. The family spent many evenings listening to war news, President Roosevelt's Fireside Chats, and the Jack Benny Show. Danny liked the Lone Ranger. A large buffet that belonged to her grandmother and shipped from Czechoslovakia, took up most of the space. The only décor on the walls were a family portrait and a wood crucifix, a wedding gift from her mother.

Danny sat in the living room popping a baseball into his glove when she entered. "Where's Natalie?" she asked immediately.

"I don't know. I waited forever in front of the school but she never showed up, so I walked home."

Joanne walked into the kitchen, setting the groceries on the table. Unwashed breakfast dishes sat in the sink, another sign of her flagging housework. She hadn't polished the furniture, vacuumed carpets or cleaned the bathroom in two weeks, a level of neglect unthinkable two years ago. But she didn't lose much sleep over these minor failings. Nor did she have time for the endless campaigns of the home front. Thousands of volunteers spent their weekends on salvage drives, scavenging everything from paper and rubber to metal and glass. They planted Victory Gardens, knitted sweaters for soldiers and collected watches for Russian doctors and nurses. Well good for them but she had a life, a family and a job. She did, however, invest in war bonds because she didn't have a choice. The campaigns were incessant, the pressure substantial. Step right up, folks, it's nothing more than a loan. The boys are giving their lives, surely you can lend part of your paycheck. If you did all these things, if you rationed, and volunteered, and salvaged, and donated and loaned, you were awarded with a "V" for victory placard. You placed it in your front window, the sign of a true patriot. If you lost a husband or son in the war, you displayed it next to your gold star flag. Joanne didn't care about the former and thanked God she didn't have the latter. She contributed to the war in the factory, while keeping up with the laundry and being an attentive Mom. Her children were dressed in clean uniforms. They left for school on time carrying full lunch boxes and Pee-Chee folders stuffed with completed homework. She was doing her best.

She picked up the phone and called Holy Names. Not for the first time was she grateful they'd invested in a phone, although it took another bite out of her paycheck. Sister Theresa, who managed the front office, answered on the third ring. The Novak's were well known at Holy Names. George helped them with fund raising and Joanne sat on the parent's council.

"Sister Theresa, have you seen Natalie? She hasn't come home from school."

Several seconds passed before the nun answered. "No, Mrs. Novak. We didn't see Natalie today. Since you didn't call her in sick this morning, we assumed she skipped. We tried calling you but there was no answer. Were you working today?"

Joanne let the question go. Shit, she didn't need this. She thanked Sister Theresa, hung up and called the Stinson's. Their daughter, Sally, was Natalie's best friend. No, Louise Stinson said, they'd asked Sally. She said Natalie was not at school today. She got the same response from the parents of another friend of Natalie's. No one had seen Natalie.

Joanne decided the drink couldn't wait and poured two fingers of Jim Beam into a glass tumbler. Natalie's act of defiance didn't totally surprise her. She'd become increasingly troublesome in the last year, talking back, ignoring chores, forgetting homework. Last month, Joanne found a pack of Chesterfields in her room, which she and Sally stole from Mr. Stinson. Like everyone else, Joanne wanted to blame this latest trouble on the war. Natalie's Dad was somewhere in Asia. She was shouldering more responsibilities, a young adult in a girl's body. No, that wasn't right. Her body was no longer that of a girl's.

Joanne decided she'd give it another hour before calling the police. Following a dinner of leftover pot-roast and potatoes, she helped Danny with his homework, a page of long-division and writing a paragraph on "What it meant to go with God." A bright boy, Danny didn't need much help, but she needed to be physically close to him. A sweet kid, he was blessed with thick, wavy hair, dark eyes and prominent nose, must like his Dad. God, she loved him.

"Where do you think Natalie is"? he asked. "Is she in trouble?"

"Yes, I can promise you that. I don't know where she is, but she'll be home soon. Now let's get ready for bed." In his nighttime prayer, Danny asked God to watch over his Dad, a nightly ritual, and to make sure Natalie got home safe. Thirty minutes later, Joanne sat alone on the couch with drink number two. She looked up at the crucifix and prayed silently for the safety of her family. Two hours later, her worry erupted into something just short of panic. Natalie was missing fourteen hours. She called the police but they were of little help. Too soon to start a search, the desk sergeant advised, but he'd alert the units working Capitol Hill to keep an eye out. He told Joanne to call back in the morning if she hadn't returned.

She looked at the crucifix again. It reminded her of home, where a similar one hung in the kitchen in their Enumclaw farmhouse. Her parents, Jacob and Anna Dobrovsky, immigrated from Prague, Czechoslovakia, in 1910. They'd saved just enough money to buy a quarter of land near Sioux Falls, South Dakota. Dad, a good farmer, grew wheat and sunflowers. In 1923, he read a railroad brochure about the "Great Pacific Northwest." The brochure claimed crop failures were unheard of in the rich soil. Her father sold the farm and moved his family west. He was one of the lucky ones. He'd left the Great Plains before the skies dried up, the dust storms rolled in, and food prices dropped like a stone down a well. Mr. Dobrovsky made a down payment on a 100-acre dairy farm southeast of town. Joanne was thirteen years old and remembered the first time she saw Mount Rainier. She didn't think there could be anything that big. It nearly covered the eastern sky, hovering above the land, almost close enough to touch.

Joanne loved farming. They raised about thirty jersey cows and nearly two hundred chickens. Before school, she'd gather enough eggs to fill two large wire baskets. She'd carry them to the kitchen for washing and made ready for sale. On Saturday mornings she'd dole out scoops of feeding grain for the cows. Then she'd shovel up their dung, warm and steaming, into a wheelbarrow. The stench wafted over her. She cleaned milking machines, made silage, scrubbed the stinky chicken sheds, and spread fertilizer. She joined 4H and won a blue ribbon at the Puyallup Fair, getting her picture in the *Courier Herald* with Ingrid. Her jersey produced eight hundred pounds of milk that year. She learned to drive at thirteen. At sixteen she knew her way around cars, trucks, tractors and hay loaders. And it was all okay. She was part of something dear to her and her family. But sometime during her junior year at Enumclaw High School, Joanne sensed it wasn't enough. There was a fuller life for her out there, something promising and exciting. Her Dad said she had a good mind for engineering, but she wasn't sure.

The ear-shattering clang of the phone sent her heart into overdrive. She darted into the kitchen, picked it up on the second ring and said hello, obvious desperation in her voice.

"Is this Mrs. Novak, Joanne Novak?" asked a female voice.

"Yes, this is she. The questions came in a sudden torrent. "Who are you? Is this about my daughter, Natalie? Is she okay? Where is she?"

"Mam, this is Officer Woods at the Juvenile Detention Center. Natalie is currently in custody. She and several other teens, as well as two adult males, were arrested about two hours ago. They were found in Volunteer Park, in violation of the ten o'clock curfew, making quite a ruckus, apparently, drinking and what not."

Relief washed over Joanne like a spring shower. "Is Natalie okay?"

"She's feeling better, vomited in the back of the patrol car, I'm told. Officers were not too happy about that as you can imagine."

"Can I come and get her? We live nearby. I could be there in ten minutes."

"I'm sorry, Mrs. Novak, you can't. She'll have to spend the night with us. Judge Long deals with juveniles in court at nine every morning. He'll want to speak with you and Natalie. Be here by eight-forty-five if you want a seat. Juvie court has been pretty busy lately."

Joanne said she'd be there and hung up. "For the love of God," she said aloud. She didn't know whether to be relieved or angry. She couldn't imagine her little girl spending the night in a dirty jail cell. Add a wave guilt to the emotions flowing through her. She was to blame for this. It was her fault. Her parents, her husband, her nosey neighbors were right about her. She was selfish for not being home to greet her kids when they returned from school. She thought she held a firm handle on things, working a job she loved and caring for the ones she loved. For the first time since starting work, doubt sprouted inside her like a noxious weed. After a fitful night's sleep, Joanne made coffee and called her shift supervisor to say she wouldn't be in today. He didn't take it well.

"Novak, this will be your third missed day in a month."

He was right. She missed one day when Danny came down with the flu and couldn't go to school and another when the furnace broke down and she stayed home to meet the repairman. "What do you want me to do, Johnson? My daughter's in trouble. Should I let her stew in jail while mom builds airplanes?"

"Novak, I've been here twenty-four years and never missed a day. Tell me why you women seem to be gone all the time."

"It's simple, you ass. I don't have a wife."

Chapter 2

"You gonna get on the bus, lady? I ain't got all day."

The woman stood on the step inside the front door of his trolley, mouth agape, staring up at the operator like he was a dark stain on a white wall. She was the last passenger to board at First and Lenora on a busy Friday afternoon in April. The coach was nearly full with passengers returning from work or getting an early start on the weekend. The woman was about forty with stringy brown hair. Her black slacks and a long-sleeved, light blue blouse looked rumpled and disheveled. She held a black purse in her left hand and the ten-cent token in her right. She ignored the operator's question and turned back to look at the man with her.

"I'm not riding on a bus driven by a colored," she declared, turning around and stepping off the trolley, the man following closely on her heels.

"Suit yourself, lady," the driver said, pulling the lever to close the folding double door. He pressed down on the pedal, sending juice to the electric motor and continued his route, accelerating south on First Avenue, the whine of the motor streaming through open windows.

"God damn it," he mumbled, angered but determined not to let some bigot spoil a good day, a good week really. It was the last route on the last day of his first week operating a trolley without an observer aboard. It signaled the end of two month's training. As Seattle Transit's first Negro driver, his manager told him to expect offensive remarks from riders but today's was the first. In fact, many passengers, as they dropped their fare into the collection box, greeted him with a smile, a mumbled greeting, or even called him by name.

Lawrence Williams liked his job. At $1.15 per hour, it paid more than his delivery job before the war, and certainly more than his three-year stint in the Navy. He liked driving, especially the Twin Coach

Trolleys, built in Seattle. They were a pleasure to drive, steered easily, and packed enough electric power to climb Seattle's endless hills, especially on the Number Two run, easily the most challenging. It started at the bus yard at Fourteenth and Jefferson on Capitol Hill, wound its way downtown and then north to the Counterbalance at the summit of Queen Anne Hill, easily the steepest this side of San Francisco. From Capitol Hill to Queen Anne and back. Eight times a day averaging eight miles an hour. Yes, it was a good job, and challenging. He especially enjoyed dealing with the system of overhead wires and switches that guided and powered the trolleys. But it was also an important job, carrying no small amount of responsibility. His passengers looked to him to keep them safe and get them where they're going on time. They were in his care. He was in charge, the ship's captain.

Lawrence, with his outstretched arm wrestling with the over-sized wheel, turned east on Union Street when the trolley suddenly lurched to a stop. One of the two poles that delivered 600-volts of power from the overhead wires to the bus disengaged. Stray more than fifteen feet of either side of the wires and you lose power. Lawrence took the turn too wide. He opened the front door, stepped onto the street and walked to the rear. The bus, pale yellow with green trim, was thirty-five feet long and eight-and-a-half feet wide. With a roof rounded in the front and back, it resembled a giant loaf of bread. Lawrence reengaged the power pole and returned to the driver's compartment. Accustomed to these brief delays, passengers continued their chatter or looked out the window, patient. Their driver knew what he was doing.

The last of the passengers got off at Fourteenth and Madison, and Lawrence returned to the barn, done for the day. He checked out with the dispatcher, entered the locker room and changed into dark gray, pleated slacks and a short sleeved black shirt with a wide collar. He planned to return downtown to gift shop before going home. His wife's birthday was next week, and he'd seen some beautiful scarves at the Bon Marche. Anna Louise loved scarves. He boarded the Number Two, nodded a greeting to Bob Golinski, his replacement driver, and took a seat in the third row, relaxing in the mohair upholstery. At Madison, several passengers boarded, including the couple who'd refused to ride with him earlier. Only a handful of single seats were available, the one next to Lawrence and a few in the back.

"Hey, boy, why don't you move to the back so I can sit with my wife." The man hovering over him was around forty and stood about five-feet-eight. He was thick around the middle and sported a crop of unruly dark hair. He needed a haircut and a shower. Lawrence could smell the sweat practically dripping from the underarms of his stained white shirt. He looked at the man, expressionless, and turned to look out the window.

"Did you hear me, boy? I'm talking to you," the man said louder. The bus suddenly grew quiet as it headed to the next stop.

A man dressed in a tan gabardine suit seated in the row opposite to Lawrence spoke up. "Take it easy, mister. He's a driver."

"Well, he ain't driving now and he needs to go to the back where he belongs."

"What's the matter with you?" another passenger yelled. "He's a veteran for crying out loud. He was in the papers. He's a war hero." Other passengers nodded in agreement.

"Well good for him, but he still needs to know his place."

The man in the suit stood up, confronting the troublemaker. "If anybody's going to sit in the back, it's you, asshole. Now why don't you and your fat-ass wife go sit down or catch another bus." At that, the troublemaker threw a punch, missing wildly and almost falling into Lawrence's lap. At that point, Golinski, the driver, hit the brakes and rushed to separate the two men who continued to grapple. Heavyset and strong, he pushed his way between the two men.

"Everybody needs to calm down and take a seat," he demanded, pushing the two apart. He looked directly at Lawrence. "I don't need this kind of trouble, Williams," he said, like this was all his doing.

Lawrence looked at Golinski, disbelieving. In his two months at Seattle Transit, he'd faced little trouble with other drivers. Word quickly came from the top to treat their newest driver like any trainee. Most drivers seemed friendly, but they weren't exactly a welcoming committee either. Whenever he entered the locker room, the conversational buzz stopped. Few drivers looked him in the eye. He wasn't sure about Golinski, but it was clear now. He'd tolerate a colored driver provided he caused no problems, remained invisible and kept to himself.

He stared at Golinski for a good five seconds while he thought about how to respond. "There's no trouble, Bob," Lawrence said evenly. He stood, pushed his way to the front, and reached across the driver's seat to pull the lever that open the doors. He stepped out onto Madison and turned east without looking back at the retreating bus.

He worked his way up Madison heading for his home in the Central District, the late afternoon sun warm on his back. Shopping could wait. He hated walking away from that cracker. A year ago he'd put him on his ass, but this is no Honolulu dive bar. He worked here. He wasn't behind the wheel, but it was his job to keep order. So he left, in spite of Golinski's piss-poor attitude. In the four months he'd been home, one thing was as clear as ice water. Life for the Negro changed little during his three years at sea. Newspapers promised the Negro a Double V, a victory abroad and a victory at home. By serving their country, negroes would earn respect from fair-minded whites. Well so much for that crap. Yes he'd landed a good job but not because the white men at Seattle Transit suddenly saw the light. They caved to pressure from the Seattle Urban League and other rights groups fighting discriminatory hiring practices in public agencies. Beyond the passengers who came to his defense, he'd seen few victories for colored folks.

He knew from experience the asshole bigot on the bus wouldn't give a shit about color in a life raft. Not with his ship sinking, sharks circling, and the sea aflame with burning oil. Lawrence chuckled. *That cracker would have sat on my lap and kissed me. Other white boys took my hand as I hauled them out of the brink. They'd be happy as clams to share a seat while puking up oil and saltwater.*

It happened on November 24, 1943, aboard the *U.S.S. Liscome Bay*. The escort carrier was operating near the Gilbert Islands in the Central Pacific. It was Thanksgiving eve. His chief assigned him to help prepare one hundred turkeys and a thousand pounds of potatoes for nine hundred crewmen. The torpedo, launched from an undetected Japanese submarine, hit near midship just after seven in the morning. Generally, a single torpedo would have caused significant but not fatal damage. But this one struck the bomb magazine just below the waterline, instantly detonating two hundred thousand pounds of explosives. The massive blast ripped through the ship, spreading shrapnel in all directions. Aircraft lined up on the deck preparing to launch were flung a hundred feet into the air. The blast was so immense red-hot shrapnel rained down on the battleship *New Mexico* five hundred yards away. Sixteen miles to the north, the crew on the cruiser *Philadelphia* watched in awe as the explosion lit up the morning sky.

Lawrence knew he survived only because five minutes earlier he left the galley to take a shit. He was in the head when the force of the explosion launched him, commode and all, through the locked door of the stall and into the passageway. Disoriented, he tried to stand but tripped on the dungarees tangled around his feet. He fell into the foul water twice before he managed to pull up and buckle his pants. A piece of jagged metal opened a three-inch gash in his right side. The ear-splitting wail of the ship's siren – six short blasts followed by a long one – signaled the order to abandon ship.

The next few minutes was a swirling, pitch-black nightmare of pain and confusion. He stumbled his way in the dark, climbing over a jumbled wreckage of smashed sinks, urinals and bodies. He saw no other survivors. The passageway walls buckled inward like crushed beer cans. He could see a ladder that offered escape to the flight deck but it was partially detached from the bulkhead. It swung like a broken tree limb in the wind. His only escape route was climbing a heated steam pipe. He shimmied upward, burning his hands and the inside of his thighs.

The welcomed daylight topside immediately gave way to rolling billows of black smoke and flame. The ship listed to starboard making running almost impossible. He stumbled around parts of aircraft, avoiding bodies and burning metal. Breathing heavily and near panic, he made his way aft. Knotted ropes flung over the starboard side squirmed like worms on a hook. He frantically pulled off his boots, climbed over the side and worked his way slowly down. He jumped the last twenty feet into the oily water. Training taught him to stay submerged as long as possible. He swam away from the ship to avoid burning oil. Desperate for air, he splashed to the surface about fifty yards out. A life raft was heading in his direction, thank the Lord. He swam toward it. Large wood boxes, clothing and body parts littered the water. Thanksgiving turkeys bobbed around him like ducks in a pond. Two men pulled him aboard. Soon he helped pull others to safety. Chief Carson, in the shower when the torpedo hit, squirmed aboard buck naked.

The men watched in awe as the 512-foot *Liscome Bay* went down stern first, her bow pointing skyward. She hissed loudly as hot metal met tepid water. It gave off a last gurgling breath before disappearing forever. An American aircraft carrier sunk in just twenty minutes, taking with it 600 of her crew. It was one of the worst disasters in the Pacific Theater. All his galley mates were gone, including his buddy, Dorrie Miller. He was a genuine wartime celebrity. For his bravery at Pearl Harbor, Dorrie was the first Negro awarded the Navy Cross. The U.S. destroyers *Morris* and *Hughes* rescued 273 crewmen two hours later. Medics aboard the *Hughes* stitched the wound on Lawrence's side and treated the second-degree burns on his hands and legs. The injuries earned him a purple heart, early discharge and a trip home.

His memories of the rest of that day are as murky as the water that nearly swallowed him whole. But as he worked his way to the Central District, he knew one unmistakable fact. There were no coloreds in that raft. There were no whites. Just men flung together by fate and blessed by God to have escaped near certain death.

Chapter 3

Joanne parked her black 1940 Ford sedan at the King County Juvenile Detention Center at Broadway and Boren, two miles south of her home. The brick red Georgian Colonial looked like a college library, disguising the multitude of family troubles stirring inside. She entered the building and followed directions to the courtroom where a throng of men and women waited in the hall. The air smelled of sweat and cigarette smoke. One woman cried, wiping her eyes with a white handkerchief. Another argued quietly with her husband. Most parents sat silently, waiting to be called into court. The bench seats were full so Joanne stood in the back near the lady's room.

Beginning precisely at nine, a police officer called families into the courtroom one at a time. About every fifteen minutes, they exited, sometimes with their child, sometimes alone. Two hours later, Joanne heard her name called. She stood, entered the courtroom and took a seat in the front row. She radiated nervousness, teeth clenched, sweaty hands gripping the black purse on her lap. She'd never been in a courtroom let alone committed a crime. A man sat at a table to her right wearing a blue pin-striped suit, reading. A middle-aged woman sat below the judge's bench. Joanne assumed she was a court reporter, at least that's what they did in the movies.

The juvenile justice system in Washington State was decades past the practice of throwing kids in jail with hardened criminals. But it wasn't without issues. In recent years, public policy shifted to the progressive. It moved slowly from demanding justice to promoting rehabilitation, from punishing youth to protecting youth. With the onset of war, however, the pendulum began to swing in the opposite direction. There was an alarming spike in juvenile crime and teenage pregnancies. Front-page fodder for the papers, the spike in crime led to calls for cracking down on youthful lawlessness. At the root of the problem, according to conservatives, were Roosevelt New Dealers.

Hordes of outsiders invaded the city for war work. Working mothers shamefully chose wages over the welfare of their children. The city's precious children spent the day with strangers so Mommy can buy makeup or fancy clothes.

Judge William G. Long entered the courtroom, black robe trailing behind him, and took his seat on the bench. He was about fifty, heavy set with a high forehead and short, dark hair thinning at the top. He looked down at Joanne briefly and then read through the police report of the previous night's ruckus at Volunteer Park. Joanne didn't know it but she drew the lucky card getting Judge Long. He was a Roosevelt Democrat with a decade's experience dealing with youth. He'd built a reputation for his public service. The *Seattle Times* dubbed him the "Father of the King County youth center."

Progressive leanings aside, the increased frequency and seriousness of juvenile crime disturbed Long. Teen girls were a special concern. God blessed him with three daughters, who so far, God willing, stayed out of trouble. But today's youth was a different story. He'd seen far too many moral violations, disorderly conduct, vagrancies and sex offences in recent months. Men in uniform enthralled young girls. The press called them female sex delinquents, "Victory Girls" or "Knacky Wackers." In Tacoma last year, three sixteen-year-old Idaho girls married soldiers. The nuptials lasted ten days before their husbands shipped out, abandoning their brides without notice. Last April, the so-called "Wolf Pack" scandal made the front pages. Taverns in Renton sold beer and whiskey to minors. Underage girls partied with ex-cons and GIs in their homes while their mothers worked the night shift at Plant Three in Renton. Judge Long's crowded calendar this morning yet another sign of a society losing its foothold on morality. Why, he wondered are boys dying overseas for something that the people at home are letting go to hell?

"Mrs. Novak," Long said at last. "Police took your daughter, Natalie, and five other youth into custody last night in Volunteer Park. They violated the ten o'clock curfew for children under sixteen. Two adult males were also arrested. Most of them appeared to be intoxicated. Did you know the whereabouts of your daughter last night?"

"I didn't know anything until a juvenile officer called me, your honor. Natalie wasn't home when I returned from work. That's when I called Holy Names, and learned she'd skipped school."

"You work at Boeing, I understand."

"Yes, your honor."

"Mrs. Novak, I have tremendous respect for defense workers. They're doing a great service in this country's battle against tyranny. I've also come to accept, although reluctantly, that many women need to work these days. Unmarried women, divorced women, women who depend on a paycheck for rent and groceries. But I'm having a hard time understanding why you work. From what I can tell, your situation is far from desperate. You own a home in a nice neighborhood. Your children attend private school. Your husband is a commissioned officer in the Navy. He likely sends home most of his monthly paycheck. What do you need that is more important than your children?"

Joanne said nothing, looking at Judge Long. *There's that question again. One her mother made a point of asking almost daily. The fact is, I'm not sure anymore. Initially it was about patriotism, my love for this country, and a desire to support my husband. But I work now. I love it. I'm good at something besides cooking pork roast and cleaning house.*

"Mrs. Novak, are you okay?"

"Yes, your honor, sorry."

Long sat back and folded his arms across his chest. "So I ask again. Is money so important that your children have to return from school to an empty house?"

Why does he think this is about money? Yes, I earn more than most women. But it was never about money. This is another kind of need, a deeper one that I can't fully understand, let alone explain to a judge. Some internal force is pulling me away from the life I always wanted or thought I wanted. It was enough at least for a while, until I discovered the world outside. Until I saw the endless possibilities waiting to be picked like apples from a tree. The transformation has altered the landscape of my life. It is like the eastern winds that blow down the Cascades every summer, stirring the dust, bending the poplars. How can I explain that to this judge?

"Mrs. Novak! I haven't got all day," Long snapped.

Joanne looked at the judge and around the courtroom. How long had she been standing there? "Again, I apologize, your honor. I choose to work because. . ."

"Mrs. Novak, I don't care why you work. My chief concern is for the welfare of your daughter and the dozens of other youth I see in here almost every day. Whether you want to buy a new dress or pearl necklace. . ."

"Your honor! I'm not buying . . ."

"Don't interrupt me, Mrs. Novak. "You have a fine daughter here, why are you letting her out at night, getting into the backseat of cars with boys, or should I say men? She's a minor and . . . "

"I know how old my daughter is your honor."

"The facts say you don't. When you're at work, your children are coming home to an empty house. Some people think older kids don't need as much attention, so it's okay if Mom gets a job. But young people – these so-called eight-hour orphans – need someone to talk to about their day. They have problems at school, and need help with their homework."

"I help them with their homework, your honor. They're good students and good kids."

"I'm sure they are, Mrs. Novak, but this recent event is troubling. "

Long returned his attention to the report, tapping his fingers on the desk while reading through the facts one more time. "Mrs. Novak," he said, looking up. "As this is Natalie's first offense, we're going to drop the charges and hope we don't see her in here again. Meantime, I suggest you rethink your priorities. Natalie will be released to you in about an hour. You'll need to take her to the doctor to be tested for VD."

VD? Did she hear that right, venereal disease? The words wouldn't register. "Your honor, Natalie is a good Catholic girl. She'd never. . . "

"Mrs. Novak, do you know how many good Catholic girls I see in this courtroom? VD doesn't care if you're Catholic or Jewish, or where you worship. There's practically a VD epidemic raging in the city. For your information, when police arrived at the park, Natalie was in the backseat of a car with an adult male. He's now sitting in King County jail. Police waited until Natalie dressed before she could exit the vehicle. See a doctor, Mrs. Novak."

That afternoon, Joanne took Natalie to see the only physician she knew, Dr. Alex Demerchant in Enumclaw. He repaired Joanne's right arm which she broke riding a bike. Joanne waited in his office in the National Bank Building while Dr. Demerchant examined Natalie. He came out of the examine room looking grim. They'd have to wait for the results of the VD test, but he suspected Natalie indeed engaged in sexual intercourse. They were standing in the doctor's small office while Natalie dressed in the exam room.

"Are you sure about intercourse?" Joanne asked, a lump rising in her throat.

"No, but you'll know one way or the other in a month or two."

"Holy God," Joanne muttered, falling heavily into the visitor's chair.

A month later, Joanne heard Natalie throwing up in the bathroom before school. Her worst fears were all but confirmed. A month after that, when Natalie failed to have what Joanne's mother called the "friend," no doubt remained. On their next visit, the doctor said Natalie was due in December. The VD test turned out negative.

Chapter 4

"You what?"

"You heard me. I quit." Lawrence just returned from the barn on Jefferson. He'd handed his ID and locker key to the shift supervisor. He told him he was through and walked out. He sat at the kitchen table, cup of coffee in hand, looking at his Dad, Gerald. His Mother, Ida, and Anna Louise stopped their dish washing and turned around. They'd all been upset last night when he told them about the incident on run Number Two. Their anger turned to disbelief.

"Why would you do that? Gerald asked. "The first colored bus driver in Seattle and you quit? What's the matter with you, Son?"

"See, Dad, that's just the problem. I don't want to be a colored bus driver, just a bus driver. Why always first a Negro? A Negro driver, a Negro veteran, a Negro American. When passengers step onto the bus, they don't just see their driver, they see their Negro driver. 'Good for him,' they say. 'A Negro making something of himself, a credit to his race.'" He sipped his coffee and looked at Anna Louise. Her furrowed brow suggested worry, but so far she remained silent. He'll get an earful later.

"You're losin' sight of what's important, Lawrence. You're free, ain't ya?"

There's that again, Lawrence thought, Daddy's hole card. The son of a former slave was just thankful not to be shackled. His grandfather died before Lawrence was born, but Gerald talked about him often. He was born a slave in Biloxi, Mississippi. After the Civil War, he scratched out a living as a sharecropper, little more than a slave to white farmers. When Granddad got too old to pick, he moved his family -- Grandma Flow and his two children, Gerald and Winney -- into town. He spent the rest of his life doing repair work and odd jobs for townspeople. When Lawrence was ten, Gerald and Ida were fed up with Mississippi and all its ugliness. They moved to live with Ida's sister in Seattle. It was supposed to be better for colored folk. It was better, Lawrence knew. Seattle was no Biloxi. But by the time he graduated from Garfield High School in 1938, he learned better. Dad's generation believed the lie, but not Lawrence.

"I'm not free if I can't ride on my own bus without some son-of-a-bitch getting in my face. I can't even take my family out to dinner without being humiliated." Two weeks earlier he and Anna Louise took the boys to Daverso's Palace Grill at First and Yesler wanting to try their first pizza. There were no "whites only" signs in the window, or in any Seattle establishment for that matter, but there might as well be. The waiter seated them in the back near the kitchen. They waited twenty minutes to be served. Customers who came in after them finished their meals and left before they'd gotten their pizza. The check came with a note from the manager. "We served you tonight, but we'd appreciate you not coming back."

"You're never going to let that go, are you?" Gerald asked.

"Let it go! That's all we do is let it go," he said, getting pissed now. "When is it going to stop, Dad? Should I tell our boys growing up to let go every insult and injustice? Did I put my butt on the line for this country to live half American? I swore an oath to defend a Constitution no one else gives a shit about. I'm done letting go."

On Monday afternoon, Lawrence sat at the kitchen table going through help wanted ads in *The Times* when he heard a knock on the front door. Anna Louise answered it and returned to the kitchen. "It's a Mr. Swenson from Seattle Transit. He asked if he could please speak with you."

She watched as Lawrence went onto the porch and closed the door behind him. She could see the men through the front window. Mr. Swenson was talking, pointing back across the street. This wasn't the first time Lawrence's pride caused issues but this was different. There was more to lose now. She just graduated from Ruth Whiteside's Beauty School and worked at the Three Flowers Beauty Salon on Jackson. So they'd get by for a while but they needed his wages if for no other reason than to get their own place again. Moving in with Lawrence's parents was necessary after Lawrence shipped out but they couldn't stay indefinitely. Swenson spoke for another two minutes before shaking Lawrence's hand and walking off the porch. She watched him get in his car and drive away. Lawrence stood there motionless.

He came through the door and looked at Anna Louise.

"What did he want?" she asked.

"He apologized on behalf of Seattle Transit and asked me to come back."

"What did you say?"

Chapter 5

"Mom, if you're going to cry, just go, okay?" Natalie said petulantly. "I'll be alright here."

Joanne eyed her daughter, glad to see the return of her characteristic annoyance. It was an improvement over her defiance and self-pity over the last month. Joanne looked at her first born. Thick, dark hair touched her shoulders. Her brown eyes revealed only defiance. Her tanned face began to show the fullness of a woman in her first trimester. They sat in Connie's kitchen drinking iced tea. She arranged for Danny to spend the night with a friend in Seattle. Joanne could smell freshly cut grass through the kitchen window. Neighborhood kids played nosily in the street. Connie, her younger sister by two years, and her husband, Alvin, lived in a one-story home just off Kibler Avenue north of downtown Enumclaw. Farming was always too messy for Connie. She needed the tidiness of a small farming town, and stayed close to home after graduating high school. Alvin drove delivery for the Enumclaw Coop Creamery. They were childless, a source of sadness for both of them.

Joanne and Connie agreed the best course of action was for Natalie to live with her and Alvin until she gave birth. Losing Natalie, even for just a few months, was further punishment for her neglect. Fortunately, Connie didn't work and could stay with Natalie during the day. The doctor was close by. Joanne could visit weekends. Her parents, who were both unsympathetic and judgmental, accused her of allowing Natalie to ruin her life. Joanne had yet to write George with the news.

"Yes, I know you'll be okay here," Joanne responded. "Your Aunt Connie will make a good home for you, or I wouldn't have brought you here. It's what comes next that worries me."

"You don't think I can be a good Mom?" her daughter asked, incredulously.

Joanne worried less about how Natalie would care for her baby and more about the uncaring world around her. One minor blessing was the timing. Holy Names let out for summer before Natalie began to show, so she finished her sophomore year. Joanne wanted to get Natalie away from judgmental neighbors and friends all too willing to cast stones at the fallen. It didn't matter she was just fifteen. It didn't matter she was, and still is, a good girl. People would not appreciate what Joanne only recently came to understand about herself. In her behavior, Natalie did what she believed was expected of her. She wanted to be attractive, to comfort men, especially soldiers. She dreamed of getting married and having children, the path Joanne blindly chose for herself.

"No, honey, no. You're a smart, caring person and you'll be a great mother. I'm sure of that." Actually, she wasn't sure about anything, but she needed to express her concern without showing alarm. "When I was your age, my life was all planned out. I'd graduate from high school, maybe go to college. What I really wanted, what I dreamed about, was marrying a nice boy and having children. It would be perfect. But I realize now the life I chose wasn't a choice at all. It was a false choice because it was the only one I knew, the only one my parents, my teacher's our priest ever talked about."

Natalie sat up straight and folded her arms, not liking where this conversation was going. "So you don't like your life, is that what you're saying?"

"No, I'm not saying that. It's a good life. I love you and Danny and your Dad. I miss your Dad and can't wait for him to get home. But if the war has taught me anything, it's that there's more to life for us girls than making a family. I wanted to talk to you about that, to show you the world. I wanted to explain that you could be anything you want, do anything you want, choose any path. But I didn't, and now that choice has been taken from you, and I blame myself."

Natalie nodded, wanting to talk about her fear but not knowing how. She remembered reading a story in *Seventeen* magazine about a girl whose parents told her she'd ruined her life. She gave herself to a boy and had a baby out of wedlock. "It's not your fault I've ruined my life. I did this on my own," she said.

Joanne reached across the table and took both of her daughter's hands. "Your life is not ruined, Natalie," she said. "We're not going to let that happen, I promise. Your baby will not let that happen. A ruined woman, and you're a woman now, cannot be a good mother. Your baby will bring you joy. Just give it time; everything will be all right." Joanne knew this was a lie. If Connie raised this baby, Natalie would be a cousin, not a mother.

Connie finished her ice tea and looked at her watch, a signal it was time to go. They went out on the porch, Joanne fighting back the tears. She hugged Connie and then Natalie, squeezing tightly, not wanting to let go. She climbed into the Ford, started the engine, and backed out the driveway. When she turned off Kibler and drove north on Highway 169, the tears started to roll, unstoppable. She loathed the fact she worked and liked it. She ached for her daughter, and hated herself for not preparing her to make better choices. She was angry with the judge. She was angry with the boy, no the man, who'd taken her little girl. He was just eighteen, a Marine from Montana stationed at Fort Lawton. He's now facing charges for molesting a minor. She was angry with her husband for not being here to help her cope with this impossible mess. She was angry with the war makers, the Japanese, the Germans, the Italians, even the Americans. She loathed the whole damn bunch of them for turning her life upside down and dumping it into the manure pile.

So overcome with emotion, Joanne couldn't drive. She pulled over, stopped the car and got out. Bent at the waist, fists clenched against her knees, Joanne screamed. It was a deep, guttural scream from the depth of her lungs. She screamed at herself and her husband and the war. She screamed at the God deaf to her prayers. She screamed until she choked, bile working its way up, burning her throat.

As her breathing slowed and heart stopped hammering, Joanne looked around at the farmland of her home. The green fields were vibrant below the blue skies of late June. Mount Rainier was out.

With much of the snow melted, filling the thousand rivers and streams snaking through the Northwest, it had lost its springtime luster. She looked for the "deer's head," the prominent rock formation near the summit but the summer haze obscured it. Mount Peak and Mount Baldy stood in the near distance. They were upstaged by their colossal neighbor looming over them. Joanne stopped noticing her surroundings during her last years on the farm. She was more focused on the world she couldn't see. But now they were hallmarks of a less complicated life when mistakes were notations on a milk production report. She missed the days when choices were as clear as Rainier on a spring morning.

A group of Holsteins grazed near the four-foot barbed wire fence. The black blotches running from head to tail resembled spilled ink on a white tablecloth. They looked at Joanne impassively and returned to their business. Cows often tested the fence, getting too close, stretching their necks out too far to reach uncut grass below the wire. They sometimes paid for their appetite with cuts around the ears and neck, or worse, getting stuck. She remembered once helping her Dad disentangle a wayward calf that disregarded the barrier. Joanne wondered if she'd reached too far. Had she wanted too much? Would she ever break free from the fences entangling her?

Chapter 6

Dorinda Jones plugged a nickel into the newspaper box at Second and Spring, pulled out a copy of the *Seattle P-I* and climbed back into her black 1934 Ford. The day was overcast and cool. She leafed through the paper, scanning the help-wanted ads. As she hoped, there were many. Ads offered jobs for women and girls as waitresses. There were openings for housekeepers, taxi drivers, drill press operators and assistant service station operators. She glanced over ads for telephone operators, and stock clerks at Sears. Another sought a girl, "colored preferred," to cook dinner for a widowed professor and his two daughters. No thanks. Another needed thirty colored girls to learn power machines for night shift in a factory. The one seeking "attractive young colored ladies with nice personality to meet people" struck her as suspicious and moved on. Eventually she found the ad she'd been looking for. "Boeing needs one thousand women to help build Super Fortresses. No experience necessary. Clean, light, airy surroundings. Earn as you learn on the job." Dorinda tore out the ad, stuffed it into her purse and headed on foot to the Boeing Employment Office at Second and Union.

Dorinda arrived in Seattle the previous day and found temporary lodging at the YWCA in the Central District. The Y was a God send. It welcomed Negro women. They provided lodging for her and her little boy while she job hunted. Web, who just turned six, was there now in the childcare center. At her last job at Wilson and Company in Chicago, she packaged stew meat for the US Army. It was war work of a sort. GI's needed meat after all. During lunch breaks, she and her friends fantasized about moving to Seattle. It offered plenty of work in a booming city. Even better it was said to be a good place for Negroes. It seemed exciting. But talk about moving that far away from parents and friends was just that, talk. Until her life blew up. Until her husband opened a gash under her left eye. Until she ended up in the hospital with a two-inch scar. She met Edwin Jones five years earlier, shortly after graduating high school. They married that summer and had Web a year after that. Edwin, a butcher in the Wilson slaughterhouse. was the jealous type. No that was an understatement. He was crazy jealous. He flew into a rage if she so much as looked at another man. This most recent incident terrified her. He was not going to change. It would only get worse. She foolishly accepted his repeated promises to never hurt her again. She had to get away. Last week, when Edwin was out with friends, she made her move. She crammed a few things for herself and Web into a suitcase and walked four blocks to her parent's house on Chicago's South Side. They long feared for their daughter's welfare and didn't need any convincing. Yes, it was best she left, moved elsewhere. Her Dad gave her the keys to his Ford (he said he was about to trade it in anyway). He handed her a roll of cash, mostly fives and tens kept in a jar in a kitchen cupboard. and told her to go. So here she was in Seattle. She had $23 in her purse, a car she couldn't afford to gas up, and her sweet son. So far he held up well on what Mommy told him was "their big adventure."

About a dozen women sat in the reception area in the Boeing employment office filling out applications and waiting to be interviewed. Dorinda stood when her name was called, and a receptionist led her down a hall to the last office on the right. The name on the door read Ward Dobbs. He remained seated when Dorinda entered the small office. He told her to take a seat without a smile or eye contact. He wore a dark blue pinstriped suit. Sweat glistened on his forehead. He looked at her application, drumming his fingers on the desk. Neither person spoke for a minute. Second Avenue traffic hummed below.

Dobbs finally looked up, his eyes scanning Dorinda from head to toe, lingering on her breasts. She was dressed in dark gray slacks and a white blouse that couldn't conceal the fullness of her figure. Dorinda was used to men staring at her but for some reason Dobbs gave her the creeps.

"So, Miss Jones, why do you want to work at Boeing?" he asked without preamble.

"It's Mrs. Jones, and I need work. Your employment ad said you needed a thousand women to build bombers."

"Yes we do," he acknowledged, "but I'm not sure it's a good fit for you." He picked up her application and pointed to the front page as if that's the only proof he needed.

"Oh, why's that?" she asked. *Did this white man follow me from Chicago?* The needle in Dorinda's prejudice meter started to vibrate. She didn't want to prejudge this man but his brisk manner and initial dismissal of her application was concerning. The needle seldom moved without cause.

"Right now our biggest need is for buckers and riveters for Plant Two. It's dirty work and hard. I'm not sure you'd like it."

The needle inched toward yellow. "That's a surprise because your ad mentioned clean surroundings. I've got it right here in my purse if you don't believe me."

"No, no, I believe you. But you can't always believe those ads. Take my word for it, a girl without experience on a factory floor, especially in aircraft manufacturing, will struggle. We want newcomers to the Boeing family to be happy and fit in. This is important work. There's a war on, you know."

I wish I had a nickel for every time someone reminded her there was a war on. Her meter now quivered dangerously close to red, but she ignored it. She was determined to remain patient. *So much for learn while you earn.* "Mr. Dobbs, I understand that, but I can do this job. Your factory couldn't possibly be any dirtier than Wilson and Company. Butchering and packaging stew meat for our boys in the war isn't glamourous work. It's not as skilled as building planes, but I was good at it. I'm a quick learner and work hard."

Dobbs didn't respond, just rubbed his right hand over his balding head as he stared at her application. After a minute, he appeared to come to a decision. He sighed heavily and made eye contact for the first time. "Okay, Mrs. Jones, you have the job. An orientation meeting for new employees starts in an hour. It's on the seventh floor. Welcome to the Boeing family."

The seventh-floor conference room overlooked Second Avenue and Elliot Bay. Dorinda watched a passenger ferry slip into the Seattle Terminal. She marveled again at the beauty of the city. She decided a ferry ride would make another adventure for Web. About twenty women sat quietly in folding chairs. Dorinda took a seat near the back next to a woman who introduced herself as Florence. She just arrived from San Diego, where she worked for Consolidated Aircraft, riveting the B24 Liberator, a long-range bomber. Consolidated was losing ground to the more advanced Boeing B29, so Florence, unmarried and unattached, moved North.

Thirty minutes later, a woman stepped to the podium and introduced herself as Mrs. Schumacher, assistant employment coordinator. She was about fifty with graying hair. Behind her stood an American flag and a large photograph of William E. Boeing, company founder. He stood next to a bi-winged seaplane. Schumacher handed out a packet of materials that included everything newcomers needed for the month-long training starting Monday. "Once you've completed training most of you will work at Plant Two in Seattle or Plant Three in Renton," Schumacher said. She then introduced Elliot Carmichael, second vice president for personnel.

Carmichael stepped to the podium, wearing a blue, ill-fitting suit. *That boy should be wearing his fraternity sweater*, Dorinda thought. He cited Boeing's record of excellence, safety and commitment to employees. Most of all, he wanted to reassure the women they found a home at Boeing. "In fact, your place here is just like your loving home," he said. "Cutting airplane parts is just like cutting cookies. Working with blueprints isn't much different from ironing. Driving a car loader will remind you of vacuuming your living room. You'd be surprised how familiar it will all seem."

"What is he talking about?" Dorinda asked.

Florence shook her head. "Beats me. I don't think this ass has driven a rivet let alone cut cookies."

Concluding his remarks, Carmichael spread his arms wide like he wanted to give everyone a big hug. "Let me thank you all for doing your part to help us prevail in this war. Welcome to the Boeing family."

There's that word again, family. I doubt if everyone in this so-called family will welcome me with open arms.

Chapter 7

Joanne punched in and headed for her work station in Plant Two. Today they were assigned to attach starboard wing panels. Dorinda Jones, her latest bucker, was waiting when she arrived. She was paired with Joanne after Anita moved up to riveting a month ago. By 1945, dozens of colored women worked in Plant Two, but Joanne never teamed with one. It turned out, she and Dorinda made a good team. She liked her. They exchanged greetings, almost inaudible over the cacophony of rivet guns, loaders and forklifts, and took their positions. They quickly fell into the rhythm of riveting. The din of destruction overpowering Joanne's troubles.

When the whistle sounded at eleven signaling lunch break, the women headed for the cafeteria. It was a separate building north of the plant. Joanne looked up at a sky dulled by a giant canvas roof. Following Pearl Harbor, fear of another Japanese attack prompted Boeing to take extraordinary security measures. They erected a colossal camouflage over Plant II to conceal it from the air. Supposedly, incoming aircraft would see not a factory but an American neighborhood replete with houses, parks and tree-lined streets. In reality, it was twenty-nine acres of plywood, canvas, burlap and chicken feathers sitting atop steel supports. Joanne didn't think it would fool anybody even if the Japanese could reach the Pacific Coast undetected. It felt like walking under a circus tent.

Large enough to accommodate sixteen hundred hungry workers, the cafeteria was brightly lit and airy. It had a tiled floor and vaulted ceiling. They picked up their trays and made their way through one of eight serving lines. Today's fare included chicken a la king on a biscuit, peas and a salad bar, costing forty-nine cents. Joanne settled for a bologna sandwich and coffee. She could smell fried grease, cigarette smoke and the ever-present airplane fuel that wafted in from outside. The chatter of hundreds of men and women enjoying their meal and midday break filled the air.

As Dorinda headed for the tables where the colored employees ate, Joanne touched her on the shoulder. "Don't go over there. Eat with me for once, please," she asked, She nodded in the direction of a table half filled with men and women, all white.

Boeing struggled with the "colored issue" even before the war. Negroes worked mostly in service jobs, cooking and serving meals, cleaning corporate offices. They resisted hiring coloreds for skilled work even as production demands rose sharply in 1942, hiding behind the whites-only policy of most unions. But public pressure was unrelenting. First, A. Philip Randolph, president of the Brotherhood of Sleeping Car Porters, stepped into the fray. He promised to send "ten, twenty, fifty thousand Negroes on the White House lawn" if President Roosevelt didn't enforce Executive Order 8802 prohibiting discrimination in the defense industry. When Seattle District 751 of the machinists union bowed to the pressure, admitting Negroes for the first time, Boeing reversed course. The question was how. Segregating an assembly line wasn't feasible. They considered building a colored-only plant, but the idea was nixed for its impracticality. Most supervisors would refuse to head an all-colored crew and no coloreds were qualified. So Boeing grudgingly integrated its facilities. Whites who refused to work with Negroes were told to clock out and not return. Few did.

A corporation like Boeing can control who they hire and where they work. They can encourage teamwork and cooperation, and welcome people of all colors into the family. But they can't regulate hate and discrimination. They could make them work together but not eat together. Sitting elbow to elbow over chow with a Negro was too close for many white employees. When Joanne invited Dorinda to lunch with her, she hesitated. "I don't think that's a good idea. I'm not welcome there."

"Nonsense," Joanne responded. "I know these people, they're nice. Give them a chance, please."

Against her better judgement, Dorinda took the chair next to Joanne and picked up her fork. The lunchtime chatter quickly faded.

Everyone at the table suddenly interested only in their food. A minute later, a man slammed down his fork, picked up his tray and stood. It was O'Malley, the creep who grabbed Joanne's butt earlier this year. He started to leave the table and then turned to address the group. "God dammit, these sharecroppers have taken over this city in the last two years. The company says I have to work with them. But I sure as hell don't have to eat with them," he said, and moved to another table.

Dorinda poked at her mashed potatoes. *So much for Seattle being good for Negroes and one big happy Boeing family. Looks like there are two families, one white, one black. I like Joanne but she has no clue about what my life is like, the crap coloreds deal with every day.* She picked up her tray and turned to Joanne. "If you want to be my friend don't ever put me in this situation again," she said. She walked to the back of the cafeteria to join the colored workers. Joanne watched her friend walk away, stunned by what she just witnessed,. Appetite spoiled, she stood, plopped her tray onto the return stack and hurried outside. The incident horrified her. How could she have been so insensitive to put a friend in such an unfriendly situation? She was ashamed of her coworkers. She couldn't understand people who carried around hate like a lunch pail. Add another brick to the wall of guilt building inside her.

Chapter 8

War news was almost exclusively good in recent months. Last October, General Douglas MacArthur kept his promise and returned to liberate the Philippines. In February, U.S. forces prevailed in the five-week battle at Iwo Jima, immortalized by the photo of Marines raising the American flag on Mount Suribachi. In June, after a horrific three-month battle, Americans pushed the Japanese out of Okinawa, giving U.S. forces a launching point at Japan's backdoor. And then, starting last Friday, news reports, almost too good to be true, speculated the Japanese were ready to throw in the towel. The city was a cauldron of expectations, ready to explode all weekend and through Monday. On Tuesday, the lid blew off with news Japan "unofficially" accepted terms of surrender. That was good enough for Seattle as thousands took to the streets, honking car horns, drinking and celebrating into the late hours.

Joanne spent the night at home with Danny, playing Criss-Cross Words and talking about their postwar life and Daddy coming home. She celebrated with a drink, called her Mom and Natalie, but kept a grip on her emotions. Scheduled to work Wednesday, she went to bed early, but couldn't sleep. She looked at George's side of the bed. It was neat, pillows fluffed, covers undisturbed. For weeks after he'd left, she'd reach across to his side, expecting to feel his presence, hear his snoring. Now, she made that side of the bed only when she washed the sheets. She 'd grown used to sleeping alone and wondered what it would be like to share a bed again.

She remembered reading a letter in the *Saturday Evening Post* written by a woman whose husband was overseas. "When you come back to me," she promised, "you'll find everything just as you left it." She promised she'd put on the same blue dress she'd worn on the day he left. His children would be waiting at the door with shouts of joy and laughter. He'd find his house just as he left it. He could relax in his favorite chair, put on his slippers and read that day's newspaper. Joanne wondered what war that woman had been through. For the Novak family, everything changed. Nothing was left untouched in war. Nothing. She hadn't heard from George since writing him about Natalie. The papers said it could take months to bring everyone home so she wasn't sure when to expect him. She missed him, especially the last few months. But his pending return was nerve wracking. She spoke aloud, words only she could hear. "No, George, nothing's the same, especially your wife."

On Wednesday, dozens of Plant Two employees milled near the food trucks, enjoying their afternoon break. Two rows of completed B29s were lined up like sentries on the tarmac. Joanne and Dorinda shared a cigarette. The atmosphere was charged with hope, and promise and pent-up emotions.

"IT'S OVER." The Japs have surrendered! IT'S OVER." It was Johnson, the shift supervisor, running towards them, holding up a newspaper. The headline in the P-I covered the top third of the front page, PEACE! Suddenly everyone started hollering, shouting and jumping around. Joanne crossed herself and gave thanks. Then the kissing started. Men embracing and kissing women they knew, and some they didn't know. At least four men put their arms around Joanne and kissed her hard on the lips. Before she could dodge him, O'Malley grabbed and pulled her close. She managed to turn her face and pull away but not before he squeezed her butt yet again and kissed her cheek. He smiled mischievously. He was disgusting but she let it go in the excitement of the moment.

When the exhilaration abated, Johnson said they could take off the remainder of today and tomorrow. They could return to work Friday. Everyone was ready to celebrate but after last night's drunken ruckus, most bars and restaurants were closed. Joanne invited Dorinda, Anita and a few friends to her home, where a bottle of Jim Beam awaited.

It took two hours for the Boeing bus to make the five-mile trek to Joanne's Capitol Hill neighborhood. Joanne and the other passengers watched in amazement as their city exploded with joy. People dropped whatever they were doing and ran into the streets. Shredded paper rained down from office windows blanketing the streets like a winter snow. Horns honked. Sirens blared. Firecrackers exploded through the night. Men slapped each other on the back. Men and women embraced and kissed total strangers. Autos raced through town, horns blaring. Ten people at a time stood on car roofs, dancing and howling. Emergency vehicles sat hopelessly trapped in traffic jams. The joy was boundless.

At the University of Washington, students broke into Chimes Hall and rang the bells. Others paraded down Northeast 45th Street chanting "victory!" The mayor declared a two-day holiday. A Boeing B29 Superfortress, Seattle's triumphant contribution to the war, skimmed across the city skyline, lights blinking. Soldiers and sailors preparing for the deadly invasion of Japan's home islands wept in relief. Churches held special services. Mothers prayed, children prayed, almost everyone prayed. All gave thanks to the men in their lives who were at last coming home. Others prayed for loved ones lost in a war that took sixty-eight million lives worldwide.

When they finally reached Joanne's home, the group made short work of the Jim Beam and turned to chokecherry wine her mother made. Danny went to bed after charming the ladies and beating a couple of the guys at Criss-Cross Words. They danced to Glenn Miller, jitterbugged to Benny Goodman and offered up toasts to everyone from Roosevelt to Joanne's neighbor Mrs. Bloom. She came over to complain about the noise but stayed for a glass of wine. The firecrackers and honking horns were unceasing. They talked about the war and their plans now that it was over. Eventually the conversation turned to their jobs. They gathered around the kitchen table. The word was out. Boeing planned to cut back drastically when federal contracts dried up.

"That's fine with me," claimed Lucy, an Italian from New York. "I've done my patriotic duty and I'm ready to stay home."

"Me too. My husband wants a wife, not a career woman," agreed Mary Grace, one of the few women Joanne knew from Seattle.

"Hell with that," Anita said. "My job's in the plant. I'll work there or in another defense plant. I'm certainly not going back to slinging hash to smelly truckers." The women nodded in agreement.

"I thought you ladies wanted to go back to your beauty parlors and PTA meetings," said Johnson. Joanne worked with him for more than a year. He was a good enough guy if a little authoritarian.

Suddenly the mood turned tense. "Do you think I can afford a beauty parlor without a job, Johnson?" Anita asked disbelievingly.

"All I know is the men are entitled to get their jobs back."

"That's precious, Johnson, Anita shot back, a little drunk. "I can just hear it now. 'Thanks for your contribution to the war, Warner, but you're being benched. The men are home and they want their jobs back.'"

"That's just the way it is, Warner."

Anita looked at her drink, unsure how to respond. "Yeah, maybe you're right, but I tell you what. They'll have to throw me out before I quit."

Everyone was focused on this exchange. Dorinda snuffed out her cigarette and finished her wine. She didn't doubt where she stood. She and all the coloreds would be the first to go. She stood, kissed Joanne on the cheek and left.

Joanne pondered her own situation. She didn't fear losing her job. Management recognized her skills, she was told. It also helped that George belonged to the Boeing family before the war. In fact, George was the problem, not her bosses. In his letters, he acquiesced to her working, realizing he was in no position to stop her. But he would expect to return to the life he left three years ago. He'll want to see the prewar Joanne, the one who saw him out the door in the morning and greeted him every evening. Good luck with that, she thought.

Friday morning she rode the bus to Plant Two. The only people visible were merchants clearing the streets and sidewalks of shredded paper, empty beer cans and broken glass. She stepped off the bus and joined the parade of workers headed inside. The thrills of yesterday had faded, but workers stepped a little lighter this morning. She could hear men whistling, women chatting. Dorinda was waiting for Joanne when she reached her station. Before they started working, Johnson walked up and handed each a sealed manila envelope.

"What's this, Johnson?" Joanne asked.

"It's your termination papers, Novak. Clean out your locker at the end of your shift. This is your last day."

Chapter 9

" Keep Seattle for white people."

"Banish Japs from the USA."

"Expel the yellow devils."

Takashi "Frank" Sasaki ignored the racist graffiti scrawled in red paint on the boarded up businesses on Jackson Street in Japantown. Each reminded Frank that the war may be over, but the battle for justice for Japanese in America was not. He worked his way down Jackson to Maynard Avenue on a Monday morning in early September. The summer sun had yet to reach the southern edge of downtown.

The Tokyo Restaurant, or what remained of it, had been in the Sasaki family since 1930. But the thriving business where his parents worked fourteen hours a day was all but gone. It was unrecognizable from the place where Frank and his siblings worked after school. The storefront looked like a truck rammed through the front window. The front door was buckled at the middle and wouldn't open. To get in, he must climb through the front window which, too, was smashed. Glass shards were strewn along the sidewalk. He could make out fragments of the restaurant's sign on the sidewalk, "Tokyo Restaurant." His sister, Toyome, artfully painted it on the window. The mess at his feet another indicator of their shattered lives.

Businesses on both sides of Jackson Street and all of Japantown, or *Nihonmachi*, were as broken as his restaurant. It was hard to believe that before the war the neighborhood, albeit a ghetto by some standards, was once a thriving community. Nearly eight thousand Japanese lived in or around the district. Centered around South Main and Jackson streets, and between Fifth, and Seventh avenues, Japantown teemed with life and vitality. Visiting dignitaries, businessmen, dock workers, laborers and travelers found accommodations at dozens of hotels and boarding houses. Doctors, dentists, bankers and attorneys hung their shingles offering their services. Higo's Ten Cents Store sold every good imaginable. Flower shops displayed their products on sidewalk stalls. Dozens of restaurants were packed during lunch. The smells of grilled beef and chicken and every kind of fish Puget Sound offered wafted onto the streets, enticing passersby. But that was four years ago, a lifetime, ago. Now only the smell of rotten vegetables and decay hung in the air along deserted streets. Japantown was a ghost town.

This was Frank's second trip from Camp Minidoka in Hunt, Idaho. The last eight months was a whirlwind of hope and fear. Everyone was relieved when the Supreme Court ruled that the defense department could no longer detain "loyal" Japanese. In January, the government officially ended the internment, ending thirty-two months of forced incarceration of more than one hundred and ten thousand Japanese on the West Coast. It began in April 1942, when the Sasaki's were transported to Camp Harmony on the Puyallup Fairgrounds. Months later they moved to Camp Minidoka in Hunt, Idaho. It was a concentration camp in all but name. His Father, Sanjiro, his Mother, Toyo, and their four children shared a fifteen-by-twenty foot "apartment." The walls didn't reach the ceiling. The crowding eased when his younger brother, Fukashi, volunteered for the Army. He was now serving as an interpreter under General Douglas MacArthur in Tokyo. In 1943, his baby sister, Aiko, was released from the camp along with most other Nisei, or second generation Japanese. Born in the United States, these U.S. citizens, were deemed non-threatening. The release was conditional. Detainees must enroll in college or find a job, and not return to the West Coast until war ended. Aiko was now studying sociology at Earlham College in Richmond, Indiana. Frank and Toyome, his younger sister by two years, remained behind to help care for their parents. Frank, the oldest son, was duty bound to stay.

The exultation that followed the official end of internment soon gave way to anxiety and uncertainty. Where would they go when the camp closed? Most Japanese lost their homes and businesses, their meager savings exhausted. Did they dare try to start over in a city that cruelly cast them aside? Instead, many moved to the East or Midwest, areas more accepting of Japanese. Fears about Seattle grew when rumors of hate crimes, mostly untrue or exaggerated, reached the camps. By June, less than half of the detainees had left Minidoka. When the camp closed in October, two thousand remained. Like a prison parolee who'd adjusted comfortably to the bars he once hated, many Japanese feared returning to the free world. Many stubbornly remained in their dwellings even after the government shut off the water and electricity.

To help clear the way, Frank obtained permission to return to Seattle in April to check on the status of their restaurant and their home on Fourteenth and Yesler. He was relieved to learn about a drop-off in violence against Japanese. But with war still raging in Asia at that time, anti-Japanese sentiment was ever present. At the invitation of his pastor at the Japanese Congregational Church, he'd attended a public hearing at Seattle City Hall on resettlement. Seattle Mayor William Devin and Washington Governor Mon C. Wallgren presided. They sat behind a table on the stage flanked by three members of the city council.

Organizations opposed to allowing Japanese to return before war's end dominated the discussion early. Frank sat quietly in the back. Fallacious accusations and groundless speculation alarmed him. Particularly offensive was the Remember Pearl Harbor League. They represented the interests of white farmers in the Kent Valley who took possession of fields once leased to Japanese. The speaker was the League's president, Ed Phelan, who appeared to be about fifty. He stood and looked at the crowd of two hundred. "From my experience, you can't trust these Japs," he declared. As he spoke, he seemed to zero in on Frank, one of the few Japanese present. "During the Depression, they worked for a buck fifty a day in the fields and turned around and gave twenty-five cents of that to some Jap who is now a captain in the Japanese army. Those two-bit pieces are now punching holes in our boys."

A member of the equally despicable Japanese Exclusion League stood and called for an amendment to the U.S. Constitution to deport all Japanese who were noncitizens. Another criticized the court ruling that only "loyal" Japanese were to be freed. "Sure, most Japanese are loyal, but one out of a hundred may not be. You can't tell if a Jap is loyal just by looking at him. The only way to be sure is keep them all out. Let them go back to Japan or move off the coast."

"If they're not American citizens, throw them out," one woman demanded. "The only people who will benefit are the social reformers with their impossible aims."

The barrage of hate speech droned on.

"The Japanese have been indoctrinated with sadistic philosophy of emperor worship."

"For every Japanese our soldiers destroy, you shield and protect the fanatically dangerous here at home."

"Humanitarian gestures in behalf of the Japs is parallel to the historical Trojan horse."

"My grandfather fought to take away this land from the Indians, and now the Japs are trying to take it away from us."

Suddenly a man seated in the front stood and raised his right hand. "Mr. Mayor and Governor how long do we have to listen to this nonsense?" The speaker was Arthur Barnett, an attorney with the Seattle Council of Churches. The Council and multiple other civic organizations vigorously opposed internment. Since then the council remained a constant source of support for the Japanese. They traveled to Minidoka repeatedly to deliver supplies and offer legal services. He looked directly at Mayor Devin and Governor Wallgren, both of whom showed only lukewarm support for resettlement. "I ask you, sirs, what other group on the home front has suffered more than the Japanese?" He looked around the suddenly quiet hall. "They've been deprived of their civil and constitutional rights. They've been socially and economically ostracized, and treated with unwarranted suspicion. They've lost their homes and businesses. The least we can do is help them to get back to normal." The crowd appeared split on this notion. Some nodded in agreement, others shook their head, shifted in their seats.

"You bring them back, we won't be responsible for how many are hanging from lamp posts," yelled a man from the back.

"Where is your decency sir?" Barnett pleaded, looking back at the man. He turned to face the men on the stage. "Have we not learned anything from the atrocities in Europe? he asked. "The thing most lacking in the early days of Hitlerism was civic righteousness." He stretched the word into three syllables, *right-eous-ness*. "The atrocities committed against the Jews were tolerated for years by groups that feared to speak out until it was too late. Where is our civic righteousness? We must speak out now on behalf of our fellow citizens and Christians before it's too late. "Surely, Mr. Mayor," Barnett concluded, "Seattle will respond as a truly American city. They will grant the returning American-Japanese citizens all the rights to which they are legally entitled."

Frank remembered leaving the meeting torn. He was impressed with the obvious support of Seattle's Christian and civil rights groups. But they were outnumbered. The fear and loathing among much of the general public disturbed him. When will it ever end?

He picked up a rag and wound it around his right hand for protection and began to remove the glass shards lining the front window. When it was safe to peer inside, he could see overturned tables and broken chairs. The cash register lay in the middle of the floor littered with debris. The large wall mirror behind the counter was shattered. Fortunately most of the movable items and valuables were removed before evacuation. Iron pots, serving bowls, glasses, teacups and dishware were stored in the basement of his church. It was yet another example of Christian kindness. Frank threw his right leg over the windowsill to step inside when he heard a car pull up behind him.

"Hey, Jap, what are you doing?"

He stepped back onto the street and turned around to see three men climbing out of a dark sedan. They were sailors in dress whites. They stepped onto the sidewalk and stared at Frank, eyes glassy, unfocused. They looked to be in their early twenties and obviously were on the tail end of an all-night bender.

"You trying to break in, steal something, Jap? You people have taken enough from Americans. Go back to where you belong, the tallest one demanded."

Frank looked at them impassively. "I belong here, in America. This is my family's restaurant," he replied evenly. The deserted streets closed in as he eyed the menace facing him.

"He's one of those no-no boys," the other sailor declared.

"Is that right, Jap? You hate America? Won't fight for her?

Frank said nothing.

In December 1943, the defense department required all Nisei men to take a loyalty test. Question twenty-seven asked if he was willing to serve in the armed forces. He'd answered no because of his duty to Mother and Father. Question twenty-eight was easier to answer. "Will you "swear unqualified allegiance to the United States." To that, he answered yes. He believed in the righteousness of America. He held no sympathy for the militants in Japan who caused so much pain for so many millions. But the government, and soon the press, weaponized the test results. Nisei who answered "no" to both questions were labeled "no-no" boys and deemed disloyal. He was tagged as a "No-yes" boy, and considered suspect.

The tallest of the three nodded and grinned. "You come to America, get rich on our land and now won't defend her? I gotta tell you that pisses me off. I watched too many of my buddies get killed because of you people." At that point, with arms out to his sides and chest puffed up, he moved in.

Frank stiffened, unsure how to respond. What would father do? he asked himself. Four years ago, a tidal wave of fear washed over Japantown following the attack on Pearl Harbor. Father was one of dozens of Issei men rounded up by the FBI. They were questioned and detained for weeks. The FBI found no evidence of espionage. After he was released, Sanjiro, returned to the restaurant, stoic as always. He acted like nothing happened. "*Shō ga nai*," Father said. It was a Japanese catch-all philosophy suggesting life isn't always pleasant. "At times we must suffer, embrace reality, live in the present," Father declared.

Weeks later, Frank experienced one of the saddest nights of his life. With war hysteria in full bloom, Issei feared appearing sympathetic with their home country. To demonstrate their loyalty to

America, families burned or destroyed all personal belongings that were Japanese. The Sasaki's family photos, magazines, sheet music, books, poetry, toys and dolls were all reduced to ashes. When Frank refused to burn his Japanese flag, a gift from his grandfather in Kumamoto Prefecture, Father cautioned, "*shō ga nai,*" it can't be helped. Frank wept as he watched the symbol of his ancestral home go up in flames.

Things only got worse. In March, when the government announced that all Japanese on the coast were to be imprisoned, not just immigrants, Frank was shocked and outraged. He was Nisei, born in America, a citizen. He had constitutional rights. In America you can't arrest someone without cause. "*Shō ga nai,*" Father repeated. "It is what it is. Let it go."

These men threatening him now seemed to mean business. Frank took a deep breath, tightened the rag wound around his right hand and picked up a large glass shard. *Shō ga nai*? Not this time. Not today.

Chapter 10

Frank could have handled one of his attackers, maybe even two. Not three. He slashed the tall guy's left arm and put the second down with a kick to his right knee before the third man joined the attack. He punched Frank from behind, slamming him to the sidewalk, knocking his eyeglasses to the pavement. His only choice was to curl up and cover his head as the blows and kicks rained down. Sharp stabs of pain pierced his sides and back. Just when he thought he'd pass out, the attack suddenly stopped. He looked up to see his attackers turn their attention to a colored man rushing toward him.

"What the fuck's going on? the man asked. He was tall, lanky and quick on his feet. It was Lawrence Williams

"You stay out of this, Nigger," the tall sailor demanded. "It's none of your business."

"Three on one. You must be tough guys," Lawrence shot back.

The tall guy threw a wild punch at Lawrence but missed. He took a vicious punch to the kidneys for his troubles. The attacker buckled, his knees colliding with the sidewalk. A second man lunged at Lawrence. He sidestepped and pushed the attacker face down on the cement. He followed that with two brutal kicks to the man's ribs.

The man flinched in pain as Lawrence helped him to his feet. "You guys double-time it out a' here before I lose my temper," he growled.

The fight had gone out of all three men. He helped them to their feet and the trio limped to their car and climbed in. The man in the front passenger seat leaned out the window. "Just like a Nigger to help a Jap," he yelled as the car sped away.

Lawrence turned and helped Frank to his feet. "Sorry to spoil your fun. I'm sure you could have handled them," he joked. "I thought the war was over, for God's sake."

"Apparently not for me," Frank said shakily. "But thanks for stepping in." He looked at his rescuer, recognizing him. "I know you. You're Lawrence Williams."

Lawrence looked quizzically at Frank. "How do you know me? he asked.

"You played ball for Garfield. You were a senior. I was a freshman. I'm Frank Sasaki What brings you to our neighborhood?"

Japantown lay just west of the Central District, two communities separated only by race. Lawrence occasionally shopped for food there before the war. He looked up and down Maynard, shaking his head. "This place is torn all to hell but the food is still good if you can find it. My wife is making gumbo. I'm getting sausage at Tahara Meats." Tahara's lay just around the corner from the Tokyo.

Lawrence looked at the broken glass covering the sidewalk. "What whitey did to your people ain't right, man. Is this your family's restaurant? Can I help you clean things up?"

Frank carefully brushed glass shards from his clothes and looked around for his glasses. "That's very kind, Lawrence, but I'll be all right. Thanks again for stepping in. If I can ever help you with anything, please ask. You'll find me here if we can put things back together."

The two men shook hands and Lawrence continued heading up Jackson. Frank found his glasses among the mess on the sidewalk. The frames were broken, lenses cracked. Great, he thought, and turned to climb in through the window to begin clearing the debris and cleaning. He'd have to repair the front door. This weekend, he planned to return to Minidoka to bring his family home. They couldn't see this mess.

. . .

Four hours later, Frank sat in the front seat of a gray 1941 Chevy sedan. The headache eased but pain still throbbed through his back

57

and ribs. Arthur Barnett from the Seattle Council of Churches was driving them to the Sasaki's family home on Nineteenth Avenue. It was commandeered as a boarding house for war workers. Like most Japanese families, the Sasaki's lost their property when imprisoned. They were now fighting to regain possession. Frank visited the house twice in April to speak with the woman running the place. She wouldn't speak with him or let him in. This time he took help, the attorney Barnett.

As he drove up Jefferson, Barnett thought about his work that morning. Frank wasn't the first victim of random violence he'd helped today. He'd called the police on behalf of a Filipino tavern owner. He was mistaken for Japanese and beaten by drunken soldiers. Later, he counseled a family whose daughter was refused admittance for an operation because the hospital wouldn't tap into their limited blood supply for a Japanese. He met with a nurse who worked at Harborview Hospital before the war and now couldn't get her job back. He took a call from a restaurant operator denied a lease to a building he previously occupied. He wrote a letter to the owner of a pharmacy who promised to rehire a Japanese pharmaceutical assistant but reneged due to public pressure, Since news of the impending release broke, literally every Japanese he met or spoken with lost personal property. That was just in Seattle. Hate flourished everywhere. He'd heard reports of white resistance to resettlement in Kent, Auburn, Puyallup, Bainbridge Island and Vashon Island. Hate-filled men torched three Japanese-owned houses on Vashon.

The Sasaki home was a six-bedroom affair set back from Nineteenth near Jefferson in the Cherry Hill neighborhood. After a decade of penny pinching, banking nearly all the earnings from the Tokyo, Sanjiro secured a loan from Pacific Commercial Bank in Japantown. The Sasaki's moved into their new home in 1938, the year Frank graduated from Garfield. Renting out the two back bedrooms helped with monthly payments.

As they pulled up in front, Frank saw the un-mowed lawn, the gravel driveway overtaken by weeds. Such neglect would disturb Mother to no end, he thought. They walked up the steps onto the porch and Barnett announced their presence with three hard knocks. A minute later, a woman of about forty opened the door a few inches and stuck her head out. It was Mrs. Simon Herbert, who apparently ran the place. A short-sleeved faded red dress covered her thin frame. A navy blue bandana rapped around her brown hair suggested she was cleaning.

Barnett introduced himself and Frank, and explained what they wanted. Could they please come in?

"Well, I don't know. I'm cleaning now, and I got people here, war workers. Some of them work the late shift and are sleeping."

Barnett removed his hat, leaned in close, his six-foot frame hovering over her. "This won't take long, ma'am, and it's best we talk inside." She hesitated a moment, nodded and opened the door. She pointed for them to sit on the couch in the front room and took a seat in an armchair on the other side of a mahogany coffee table. She looked tired and stressed but made eye contact. They heard people talking and washing dishes in the kitchen. Music played on the radio. Two boys about seven years old ran down the stairs and out the front door.

"Mrs. Herbert," Barnett began, "we're here to inform you that we're prepared to take the necessary legal action to return this property to its rightful owners. We hope to avoid that but only if you agree to move out voluntarily. It will save all of us time and expense if you do. We're prepared to give all the renters thirty days' notice."

"That can't be right," she said. "Japs can't own property. The city let us move in here."

Barnett opened his briefcase and pulled out some papers. "Mrs. Herbert, I'm aware of the property ownership restrictions on immigrants, but if you look at this copy of the deed of trust, you'll see it's in Frank's name. He was born in America and has all the constitutional rights afforded every citizen." Many Asian Americans adopted the practice of putting property in their children's name to skirt restrictive laws. He placed the paper on the coffee table and pushed it towards her.

She looked at the paper, but didn't pick it up. She crossed her legs and sat back, pointing upstairs. "Look, we got eight families living here," she said, turning to look at Frank for the first time. "I'm sorry for you people, but it would be a lot easier for you to find a place to live then it would for everyone else." Hearing the discussion, four people came in from the kitchen. A man and a woman descended the stairs. They all stood behind Mrs. Herbert, now looking more self-assured.

"Mr. Barnett, we're not going to stand by and let Japs take over this neighborhood again. We got a petition going to keep them out. We've already collected signatures from our neighbors." A woman standing behind Herbert held up a clipboard. Barnett could see the bold heading "Keep Japanese off Cherry Hill."

"We're here to work, said a broad-shouldered woman, about twenty years old, dressed in coveralls. "We don't have time to run around looking for a place to live. Plus there's nothing available. It could take us weeks to find a place." She pointed to a woman on her right about the same age. "We moved out here from Minnesota. If we can't find a decent place to live, we'll just go home. You can't expect people to work here if they don't have a roof over their heads."

Barnett understood. The housing shortage was acute, even desperate. Nearly a hundred thousand workers from all corners of the country converged on Seattle since the war began. The city couldn't match the demand. Lumber shortages worsened the problem. More than two thousand war workers were living in public housing originally built for low income families. The fact that eight families, some with children, were crammed into a six-bedroom house spoke loudly about the need. Nonetheless, the injustices had gone on long enough. He looked up at the group and saw only resentment and anxiety in their faces. Nothing would get settled today.

He returned the papers in his briefcase, closed it, and stood. "Thank you for your time, Mrs. Herbert, you have my number if you change your mind." With that, he and Frank left the house, walked down the driveway and got into the car. "That went about as I expected," Barnett said resignedly.

Frank promised Barnett he'd keep quiet but he was livid. It was like a playground bully who punched you in the face before snatching your lunch and eating it in front of you. *I wish I'd screamed at those squatters. Told them what I thought of their so-called right to occupy my home. It was an insult on top of an assault. Seeing strangers lounging on our furniture, eating off Mother's dishware. Shameful.*

"What am I going to do?" Frank asked. "The war authority is closing the camp. They said they're going to shut off the water and electricity in a few weeks. Where can my family live?"

"We have places they can stay temporarily while we sort this out," Barnett promised. The Seattle Council of Churches directed all its pastors to appeal to their parishioners to open their homes to the Japanese. The response was encouraging. Hundreds of Christians welcomed in families who had neither homes nor jobs. The Japanese Language School was just up the street at Rainier and Weller. For decades, Issei sent their children to learn Japanese culture and traditions. It was now converted into a boarding house. With a touch of irony, they called it the Hunt Hotel, after Hunt, Idaho, where Minidoka was located. Thirty families were crammed into fifteen classrooms, living in quarters not much bigger than those in the camps.

Barnett turned to Frank who was staring back at the house. "Look at me son. You're not alone in this. Christians have been with you from the beginning. We're not going to turn our backs now. You know that don't you?"

Frank wanted to believe but faith and hope were fleeting things in the face of seemingly endless adversity. "What are we going to do now?" he asked.

"We're going to do what I do best. The next time we see Mrs. Herbert, it will be in court."

Chapter 11

For the first time in nearly four years, Joanne felt whole. Her family was together, safe and secure. The whole business of war was in the past, and best of all, God answered her prayers. Her husband returned home in one piece.

This was turning out to be a wonderful Christmas. They were at her parent's farm in Enumclaw. Joanne sat near the fireplace, its warmth and pine scent enveloping her. Opened gifts were piled under the tree and strewn around the living room. The Andrew Sisters were singing Jingle Bells on the record player. Her Mother, Anna, and George's mom, Margaret, were in the kitchen washing dinner dishes, their chatter audible from the other room. The family fittingly gorged on turkey, dressing and all the trimmings. They followed that with prune and poppy seed kolaches, a Czech pastry. Her son, Danny, and her Dad, Jacob, played checkers on the coffee table. George fell asleep on the sofa, holding a half empty beer glass perched precariously on his stomach. Connie, Alvin and Natalie fussed over little Michael, three weeks old today. The only missing family member was George's Dad, Bill. He was killed when his tractor overturned in '36.

Joanne watched Natalie with satisfaction and pride. She finally agreed to let Connie and Alvin raise her baby but only after some tough talk and difficult soul searching. She recalled the conversation back in June. She and Natalie were gathering eggs. It was a cool, misty morning and they could see their breath. The familiar stench of chicken poop filled the air. Natalie followed her mother holding a basket nearly full with eggs against her growing belly.

Joanne placed an egg in the basket and stopped to look at her daughter. "What are you going to do, Natalie? You need to make a decision." This was round three of the make-a-decision conversation, the first two ending in tears. "Ask yourself, what's best for the baby?"

"I know what's best for the baby, to be with its mother," Natalie retorted. "I can be a good mother."

"Yes you can, but at what cost? Do you have any clue what your life will be like? You'll have to drop out of school. Forget your plans for medical school and being a doctor, something both your father and I dreamed about. Your teen years are supposed to be a special part of your life. But how many of your friends will want to come over and watch you wash dirty diapers? Do you think the boys will line up to take a girl and her baby to the movies? Think, Natalie. Only you can make this decision."

Natalie eventually came around. Little Michael will be raised by good parents thrilled to adopt. Joanne's grandson will be surrounded by loving grandparents, aunts and uncles, and cousins Danny and, yes, Natalie. A life-altering event that began at a drunken party in Volunteer Park would not ruin her daughter's life after all. She made a mistake but not a fatal one. Everything was going to be okay, for which she thanked God profusely.

Suddenly George yelped and sat up, the glass slipping from his hands, spilling beer on the carpet but not breaking. That happened more than once since George returned home in November. She watched as he stood and left the room to clean up his mess. She thought about his first day home, a cold, rainy Saturday afternoon. The entire family gathered at King Street Station to meet the train arriving from San Diego. Joanne spent hours that morning deciding what to wear, changing her mind three times. She brushed her long, dark hair, thick and wavy, and showing touches of gray. Should she wear it up or down? She settled for down, letting it hang around the padded shoulders of her waist-length jacket. The cherry red jacket and black skirt cost a small fortune. Joanne, creeping up on forty, would not have thought so, but she looked stunning.

Four months following VJ Day, servicemen and women returned home in droves. The station was a beehive of humanity. Soldiers, sailors, marines carried suitcases, or duffle bags slung over their shoulders. Men, women and children flush with excitement, waiting to greet them. Joanne noticed a young attractive blonde, not much older than Natalie, sitting alone on a bench. A small suitcase lay at her feet. She looked frightened, nervous. Her rumpled skirt and sweater looked like they'd been worn for days. She was watching the station's front entrance not the platform like everyone else. *She must be one of the war brides I read about in the paper. Welcome to America sweetheart. I pray you find what you're looking for.*

Joanne turned her attention back to the platform. She was a wreck. The nervous anticipation that spawned inside her weeks ago mushroomed into near panic. Perspiration dotted her forehead, the nausea rising. Standing on her tip toes, stretching to spot her husband, hands shaking, She thought she was going to throw up.

"There he is! I see him! I see Daddy!" Danny yelled.

Joanne spotted him emerging from the throng of servicemen stepping onto the platform. George dropped his sea bag and ran towards his wife. She met him half way and literally flew into his outstretched arms. The nervousness and nausea suddenly dissipated. She kissed him hard on the mouth and then buried her face into his neck, her tears staining his shirt. The joy was undefinable, the embrace exquisite. She held her husband at arm's length and looked at him. He'd lost weight. His Navy whites hung loosely around his shoulders. The bars of a Lieutenant Commander, which George wrote proudly about, shined in the overhead lights. She embraced him again, more tenderly this time, the symbolic end of years of embracing things she neither wanted nor understood. She embraced the reality of war, rationing and loneliness. She embraced a very real fear her husband was in danger and may never come home. And she embraced the metamorphosis that transformed a once dutiful farm girl and housewife into something more, something bigger. She embraced.

His first days home turned out just how she dreamed. Everyone was thankful to be together in their Capitol Hill home, sharing meals and catching up on their lives. A week later, she began to notice changes in George. Generally a taciturn man, he grew even more quiet, except when he barked at Danny for not cleaning up after himself. He had yet to confront Natalie about her pregnancy. He complained about headaches and stayed up late, drinking. When he came to bed, he slept fitfully and often woke in a sweat. He spoke little about his war experiences. She knew he built airstrips on a succession of islands in the Pacific, the last one on Okinawa. She couldn't possibly understand what that experience was like for him. He worked as an engineer in the Seabees. Presumably, he wasn't in the thick of it, but she didn't know. She'd gone to confession prior to a weekday mass at Saint Joseph's in Enumclaw. She shared her worries with Monsignor Farrelly. It was battle fatigue, he said. It was perfectly understandable and common for men who saw action. Nothing to worry about. It would go away in due time, he assured her.

The family was going to Midnight Mass, a Christmas tradition in the Dobrovsky and Novak families. As she donned her coat and hat, she reflected back on 1945. It was a year of embracing the wanted and unwanted, a year of sin and salvation, a year marked by fear and relief. It was also a year of growth and new horizons. At Mass, she would pray for her husband and for brighter horizons in the new year.

Part 2 – 1946-47

"It's a sad fact of humans that we often gain a sense of belonging in a group by denying access to another."

CJ Dearlove

Chapter 12

The gun John Jacobson pointed at the store manager felt all wrong – foreign and leaden. That was curious because the .38-caliber Smith and Wesson revolver with its two-inch barrel weighed a mere three pounds, nothing compared to the M1-carbine he carried in France in the war's waning months. The M1 felt right. It was a part of him, always pointed in the right direction, at the enemy. It was a force for good, if there was such a thing in war. But there was nothing good about the killing machine in his hand now. It wasn't pointed at some Fascist or Nazi but at an American, just another Jimmy trying to feed wife and kids on a buck and change per hour.

Suddenly, irritated with misplaced empathy, John wanted to put an end to this. But the 23-year-old struggling veteran, who returned from the European theater just four months earlier, knew it was too late to pull out. The store manager looked about forty. He was short, balding, thick around the waist and, understandably, scared. His nametag read Norman, Safeway Store Manager.

"Norm, open the safe," John demanded. He pointed the pistol at the small office behind the manager. The safe was the size of a kid's lunch box set into the back wall of the office. Not the first time he'd been on the wrong end of a holdup, Norm just nodded, turned around and started working the combination.

While John watched Norm, his partner, Louie Smith, rounded up the four other employees. He locked the front entrance and turned out the lights. He waited in the back near the meat counter. He held a gun on two butchers, a cashier and a stock boy. Luckily, the store was empty of customers.

Norm opened the safe and stepped back to reveal a gray bag, the kind merchants used to deliver cash to the bank. It looked to be about half full. "Take the bag out of the safe, set it on the desk and step back," John instructed. Norm did as told, and John picked up the bag and waved Norm over to the meat counter where the others waited.

While John held his gun on the employees, Louie took the money bag, hurried to the front of the store and raided the three tills. He stuffed the bills into the bag, leaving behind the rolls of coins. Pedestrians walked by the storefront in both directions on Fremont Avenue, hands stuffed in pockets, heads lowered to ward off the January cold. They were oblivious to events inside. One woman stopped at the entrance and tried to open the door. It rattled but didn't open. Cupping her hands around her eyes, she peered inside, wondering why her grocery was closed at six in the evening. After a few seconds she hurried away.

The only light came from the meat counter. Steaks, chops and sausages were lined up on a field of ice like soldiers on a winter march. The two butchers wore white aprons, soiled from cutting meat. The cashier, a woman of about fifty, looked terrified. The stock boy, a pimply kid of about sixteen, chewed gum like it was his last piece. They all looked at John.

When Louie returned with the haul, John waved the gun back and forth at the group. "This is what's going to happen," he said, pointing at the oldest butcher. "You, open the meat locker and then everyone will go inside."

"You're nuts," the older butcher said incredulously. "It's thirty eight degrees in there. We'll freeze."

"It's warmer than it is outside. Now get in and move to the back."

The younger butcher, who looked about twenty-five, was built like someone who lifted heavy meat boxes all day. He glared defiantly at John, his weight on the balls of his feet, fingers of both hands flexing nervously. Was he going to do something stupid? Was John going to have to shoot this guy? God, he didn't want that. Fortunately, John and Louie stood too far away for him to make a charge. He might subdue one without getting shot, but not both. Realizing the hopelessness of the situation, the young man shook his head, turned around and followed the others into the dark locker.

Louie quickly shut and locked the door and both men hurried out of the store. No one was in sight.

Earlier, they decided to split up before walking to Louie's apartment about two miles south on the northeast end of Queen Anne Hill. Louie would take Aurora Avenue, the main northern route into and out of Seattle. John would walk the more direct route, following the backstreets to the Fremont Bridge. Louie patted John firmly on the shoulder with a look of triumph. John smiled but didn't feel triumphant. They could see their breath in the frigid night.

"It's too damn cold to walk, I'm going to catch the bus on Aurora," Louie declared.

"No bus, Louie!" John shot back, irritated. "We talked about this. That woman who looked in the window bothers me. She might have called the cops. They always check local buses."

Louie nodded, but didn't look convinced. With the money bag stuffed under his coat, he headed north on Fremont. John turned in the opposite direction, cutting over to the backstreets paralleling Fremont. A heavy rain earlier that week followed by freezing temperatures made walking downhill precarious. As he picked his way down the icy sidewalks, he thought about what they'd just done. The recklessness of it now seemed painfully obvious. What would happen to him if he were caught? What would his wife Ellie say? His parents?

Harold and Margaret Jacobson were missionaries, prominent members of the evangelical Assemblies of God. Its roots traced back to the Holiness Movement of the late Nineteenth Century. The Jacobsons moved from Courtland, New York, to the Pacific Northwest during the Great Depression to open a new church in Seattle. Deeply devout, they let God guide every aspect of their lives, especially how they raised their three sons in their modest Phinney Ridge home. It was a Christian life – church services all day Sunday. Harold sermonized about his literal and narrow interpretation of the Bible. Margaret played the organ, leading the congregation with classics like "How Great Thou Art." and "What a Friend We Have in Jesus." John and his brothers took turns collecting the offering. The family prayed four or five times a day: morning prayer and Bible study, evening prayer and more Bible study, grace before every meal, and finally bedtime devotions. It was a suffocating life for three boys whose mother spent every waking hour determined to insulate her sons from the sinful temptations of a rapidly decaying world. In four years at Ballard High School, John didn't date, go to parties or attend dances. He saw his first movie after he joined the Army in 1943. On senior prom night, he snuck out and met his date in the school gym. Afterwards he and several friends parked along the Lake Washington Ship Canal in Ballard and drank Rainier Beer into the early morning hours. When he got home, he vomited in the toilet, and then staggered upstairs to his bedroom, relieved to have avoided a confrontation with his mother.

To John's surprise, she heard him come in. Standing at the bottom of the stairs, wrapped in an ankle-length robe, her long, black hair tucked under a net, Mrs. Jacobson yelled up at her wayward son, the source of most of her troubles. "The wages of sin is death, John!"

That was all she said about that night. Three years later, he wondered what the wages were for the sin of robbery. As he headed into the Fremont District, thoughts of regret bounced around his head like tumbling pins in a bowling alley. What kind of death awaited him? It was certainly the biggest sin of his life, scaring those people. Yes, he'd acted wildly in Europe, not unexpected for a young man socially smothered growing up. But what choice did he have? Ellie, his British war bride he'd met while on leave in London, arrived in Seattle just four months ago. Like the other British girls he'd dated, Ellie held grand expectations about life in America, expectations he so far was unable to meet. Now she was expecting a baby. That would have been okay until he was fired from his truck driving job at Rainier Brewing. He was seen handing out a Teamsters Union flyer – "Fight for a living wage" – at the brewery south of downtown. Just one month later he was out of money and options. His parents, who lived off church tithings, couldn't help. His army buddies, Louie included, were as broke as he was. Robbing a small Safeway in a quiet North Seattle neighborhood seemed doable, and would stave off the crisis.

As he made his way down the hill, he could see the Fremont Bridge looming ahead like a draw bridge to a medieval castle. Spanning the ship canal, the bridge was only about five hundred feet long, but as he made his way along the walkway, he felt naked, exposed. Bridge traffic was constant but not heavy. The repetitive hum and clunk of vehicles driving over the bridge deck agitated him. Suddenly the clatter was drowned out by the piercing whine of a Seattle police car. Red lights flashing, it sped north across the bridge and up Fremont. John's heart jumped, but he kept moving until he reached the relative safety of a narrow, unlit Fourth Avenue. The streets were deserted. As he climbed the hill and turned onto Nob Hill Avenue, he began to relax for the first time since entering the store. They just might pull this off.

He could see Louie's apartment, the lower unit of a duplex facing west. The lights were on, which was odd. Louie took the longer route home and should have arrived after John. He must have ridden the bus, the asshole. Less than an hour after leaving the store, John climbed the stairs to the front porch. He opened the door and stepped inside. Louie was there alright, standing in the living room. Flanking him were two uniformed officers, guns drawn.

"Oh shit!" John spurted. He looked at one officer and then the other, shook his head and slowly raised his hands. The woman must have called the cops, and Louie took the bus.

Chapter 13

Eleanor Jacobson arrived in America carrying a suitcase bulging with expectations but she didn't count on feeling so utterly alone. Sure, she was lonely for her mum and family, but that was in the suitcase packed with all her other emotions. On some days, the snaps would pop open and her longing for home would unfold and wrap itself around her like a shawl. But that was expected, the feeling of abandonment was not. She wasn't one of those GI brides who glamourized America, who thought every girl owned a closet full of fashionable clothes and spent five minutes deciding on shoes. John tempered her expectations about life in Seattle. When he got out of the Army, he'd work for wages while going to university on the new GI bill. He wanted to study psychology. Money would be dear, but they'd manage just fine, he said.

But they weren't fine. John was going to prison and she was on her own months after arriving in a new country with no friends and a family she didn't know. Her in-laws moved to Oregon to join a new church, and Ellie lived alone. She checked herself in the bedroom mirror one more time before leaving the house. She didn't like what she saw. She'd lost the fresh youthfulness from her wedding day. Lines of worry and stress rimmed her eyes, her cheeks puffy and red. She felt fat all over. The doctor said the baby would come in September. What was she going to do?

She locked the front door of the Phinney Ridge home they rented from John's parents and walked north on Second Avenue to Northwest 65th Street, the spring air refreshing. She was headed downtown to visit John at the Seattle jail where he's been held for three months. Tomorrow he was being transferred to the state prison in Walla Walla, and God knows when she'd see him again.

Phinney Ridge was a middle-class neighborhood north of the city. Green Lake and the Woodland Park Zoo lay to the East. Sixty-fifth ran west down the ridge into Ballard, a predominantly Scandinavian community and home to one of the largest fishing harbors on the West Coast. Ellie turned east on 65th and waited for the bus on Phinney Avenue. It was warm, sunny and, unlike London, free of smog.

The bus arrived within a few minutes. She boarded, dropped a dime in the coin box and took a seat on the right near the front. The bus entered the southbound lanes of Aurora Avenue towards downtown and picked up speed. As they crossed the George Washington Bridge, the city's natural beauty was in full display, so different from London. To the south she could see the Smith Tower, and in the distance, Mount Rainier, still burdened with snow in April. The Cascade Mountains to the east and the Olympics to the west framed this beautiful watercolor, like sentinels guarding Shangri-La from intruders. John was right about that. On days like this, Seattle was other worldly.

She'd met John a year ago in London shortly after VE Day. The shroud of uncertainty and war wariness that burdened the city for six years began to lift. She and two girlfriends were in Kensington Gardens near Hyde Park. Three GIs, sporting smiles and an easy manner, began to chat them up the way only Americans did. They soon paired up into couples, strolling through the gardens, making small talk. Rows of daisies, daffodils and tulips were in full bloom. Mostly spared from war damage, the gardens were a showcase of tree-lined walkways rimmed with perfectly manicured hedges. Scores of Canada geese waddled in Round Pond. As they walked, Ellie could see John was different from other GIs she'd met or dated. Not cocky or self-absorbed, but easy to talk to and with movie-star looks. He reminded her of a young Gregory Peck. She mostly remembered his smile. Perfect white teeth and an ocean of thick, wavy hair pushed the boundaries of Army regulation.

He apparently was attracted to her, too, because he asked for a date. He lived on base but could see her on Saturdays. The dating was fun – taking in movies, walking in Hyde Park and lunching on chips at a pub near Hooper Square in Whitechapel, a working class neighborhood where Ellie grew up. At every turn, he was polite, courteous and interested in what she had to say. He made her feel important. Yes, like most men, he tried to get into her nickers, but she managed to hold him off. The war led to a less restrictive social climate for young British women, but Ellie was not ready for that.

Things were going so well it was time to meet her parents. Edward and Maud Walker lived in a fifth-floor flat on Stutfield Street. John arrived in uniform carrying gifts; nothing extravagant, a block of butter and a can of Spam from the base for Maud and a pack of Lucky Strikes for Ed. GIs were known for overspending and throwing their money around, but not John. Ellie thought the gifts perfect.

John was surprised by the parents' ages. Ellie was the youngest of ten and life took its toll on both Maud and Ed, especially the last six years of war. Maud wore a faded blue dress over her heavy frame. Ed was about fifty but looked seventy, stooped after thirty years working the furnaces in the Whitechapel Bell Foundry. The dinner of roast lamb, potatoes and peas was pleasant enough. Her parents were polite but understandably reserved. John was on his best behavior. He offered no rude comments about bland British food, Cockney accents, or driving on the wrong side of the road.

Edward didn't add much to the dinner chat, he seldom did. He tried to take full measure of the American sitting across from him. Many Brits viewed GIs as pushy, immoral or scandalous. They wanted nothing more than to seduce British girls. As one of his mates put it, GIs were "over paid, over sexed and over fed." The Walkers mostly asked about John's experiences in the war, but eventually the conversation turned to his future. What were his plans now that the war was over? Maud asked.

"The war may be over in Europe, Mam, but it isn't for me or America," John said. "It won't be until we put down the Japs."

Of course, Maud thought, annoyed with her thoughtlessness. She'd read in *The Daily Mail* that the imminent invasion of Japan would take a million men or more, including British boys. John's uncertain future worried her, because she knew where this was going. Eleanor was obviously smitten with this GI and wanted marriage.

Perpetually doted over by older siblings, her baby girl knew how to get what she wanted. She was manipulative, often mischievous. She'd have her way even if it meant leaving her family and living in America. So it was a relief for the Walkers – and the entire Western world – when Japan surrendered on August 15, VJ day.

Eleanor Walker and John Jacobson married in June. It wasn't a girl's dream wedding. War and rationing saw to that. They held the ceremony at Saint Luke's Church in the Borough of Islington. Their home parish, the historic St Paul's Cathedral, was heavily damaged during the Battle of Britain in 1940 by the German Luftwaffe. This was an unforgivable sin in the minds of Londoners. But Ellie felt and looked very much like the perfect bride. She looked radiant in a long-sleeved, white satin dress borrowed from her sister, Vera. John was dressed in full uniform, a single row of medals pinned on his topcoat. He cast the image of the perfect American soldier. Armed with an electric smile and easy manner, he charmed the Walker sisters. Her brothers, on the other hand, struggled to hide a long-held mistrust and resentment of American GIs.

Their honeymoon consisted of a night at a small hotel on Hanbury Street. The sex was pleasant enough. She enjoyed cuddling with her new husband – but she wasn't sure what all the fuss was about. The following week, John left for Germany and then America, where he'd be discharged from the Army. It would be four months before they'd spend another night together.

Brides immigrated to the United States under the 1945 War Brides Act. The Defense Department and Red Cross were overwhelmed by the tens of thousands of GIs who married women from around the world. Unlike immigrants from most other countries, brides were not fleeing from social and political upheaval. Between 1945 and 1950, more than 70,000 young, newly married women and their children arrived in America.

Ellie lost count of her visits to the U.S. Embassy and the Red Cross office at the Rainbow Center in London to secure a visa. She attended Red Cross classes on adjusting to life in America. Today she sat at a metal gray table in the embassy undergoing questioning from a fortyish sergeant wearing dress greens, her dark hair cut just over her ears.

The questioning was endless. "Why do you want to go to America? How will you support yourself? Where will you live? Do you have the funds to get by on the journey? Ellie looked at her interrogator, unsure what to say. *She seems to think I'm one of those promiscuous girls enthralled with GIs. My friend, Ruth, was like that. She chased after GIs, interested only in getting to America. No, I'm in this for love. America, Australia, Zambia, I don't care. I want to live where my husband wants to live.*

Her veneer of confidence, though, covered a growing fear that the lengthy absence from her husband would sour their relationship. Finally a departure date was set for the second week of October. Her parents, five brothers, four sisters and a gaggle of cousins gathered for an emotional good-bye at Waterloo Station. Over tea and biscuits provided by the Red Cross, Ellie hugged everyone, leaving the last for her Mum. She would miss her most. Would she ever see her again?

The three-stage journey, fully funded by the Army, began with the train ride to Tidworth at Southampton Port on the south coast. What was to be a two-day stay turned into five due to delays in the arrival of the "bride ship." She made friends with other brides, including some with babies. Nearly all brides from the United Kingdom in 1945 and '46 crossed the Atlantic on the HMS Queen Mary. It was a one-time luxury liner converted for troop transport. Ellie shared a berth with five brides and two infants. Good food, spoiled only by bouts of nausea, and entertainment provided by the Red Cross, made the eight-day trip tolerable. Mostly she enjoyed lounging on the deck chatting with other brides. Lines of diapers, or nappies were strung from bow to stern. The conversation often turned to fears over their reception in America. Some brides hadn't received letters from their husbands in months. Others shared stories about husbands rejecting their wives upon arrival in New York. Some renewed relationships with old girlfriends. Still others, according to these reports, filed for divorce before their brides arrived. They hadn't even bothered to tell their wives. The anxiety, fueled by uncertainty and fear of rejection, sometimes overwhelmed Ellie. She'd retreat to her berth in tears.

Arrival in New York Harbor was a riot of frantic wives, anxious husbands and harried Red Cross volunteers trying to keep order. Ellie was among the last to deboard, watching from topside as brides struggled to find their husbands on a dock jammed with people and luggage. A few couples connected straight away. Others waited nervously for husbands delayed in traffic or who showed up on the wrong day. Many were bussed to the Red Cross Center downtown where their husbands waited anxiously. The Red Cross drove Ellie to a hotel near Grand Central Station. The next morning she'd begin the third leg of her journey – a four-day train ride to Seattle.

The overland journey, with countless stops, including transfers in St. Paul, Chicago and Spokane, opened Ellie's eyes to the vastness of America. As they barreled steadily west, she marveled at the uncountable miles of rolling wheat and cornfields. Through the train car window she saw a succession of meandering rivers. The mountains, first the Rockies and then the Cascades, took her breath away. They were a wondrous sight for a girl who'd never been outside London. No wonder America is so rich, she thought. It's blessed with so much God-given wealth. Her chief worry, beyond the rapidly approaching union with John and his family, was running out of money. She'd spent almost all of her small allotment from the Red Cross, even eating just one meal a day.

At a stop in Spokane, a bride panicked, refused to get off the train. "What in the world have I gotten myself into?" she asked, in tears. "No way am I getting off. I'm going home." Ellie and two other brides literally pushed her off the train.

As they pulled into King Street Station, Ellie fixed herself up as best she could, her nervousness palpable now. The wool, plaid skirt and cotton sweater she'd worn for two days was wrinkled and soiled. She deboarded, found her luggage, entered the station crowded with travelers and found herself surrounded by elegance. The building's architects, the same firm that designed New York's Grand Central Station, envisioned it as a grand portal through which visitors entered a thriving American city. It was all of that. Its twelve-story clock tower stood guard over the city. A high ornamental ceiling, marble columns and ornate tile floor spoke of richness and promise. But all that was lost on Ellie. She cared only for what she couldn't see – her husband. The Red Cross and a throng of newspaper reporters and photographers greeted the first brides to arrive in America. The bride story brought a human touch to the war. The papers featured photographs of hugging couples and quotes about how wonderful it was to be in America. None of that awaited Ellie. The story quickly became old news. Not seeing John, she looked around, self-conscious in her soiled and out-of-style attire. She sat on a bench and waited, her lone suitcase at her feet. A family gathered nearby waited anxiously for someone to arrive. A handsome woman with long-dark hair and wearing a red jacket over a black dress looked wound tighter than a wall clock. Suddenly everyone started to shout and point in the direction of the platform. The woman ran ahead and literally jumped into her husband's arms.

Sitting alone on the bench, Ellie wondered what welcome was in store for her. The next twenty minutes was the longest of her life. *Could this really be happening? Why wasn't he here? Were the stories and rumors about unwelcome wives true? Have I come this far only to be abandoned?*

"Ellie!" It was John rushing towards her. She screamed in delight, literally launching herself into his arms.

"Where were you? I've been waiting, it seems like forever!" This was the little Ellie now, petulant and pouting when things didn't go her way. "I was so worried you wouldn't come!"

"Of course, I'd come. You think I'd leave you? I'm here now. It's okay, it's alright. Welcome to Seattle."

Chapter 14

That shaky welcome at King Street Station hinted at troubles ahead. As Ellie stepped off the bus at Second Avenue, she tried to focus on the present. She wanted to visit the Bon Marché on Pine. The Bon was a place to dream, and she needed to dream if only for a while. The fashionable art-deco architecture, full of odd geometric angles reminded her of Harrods. It shouted wealth and sophistication. Even though she couldn't afford to buy anything, Ellie entered on Pine and wandered around the main floor with other shoppers. She inspected the costume jewelry, sampled cosmetics and perfumes, tried on leather gloves and admired the designer purses. *Why am I torturing myself with these bloody trinkets. I can't afford them and likely never will. Your husband is going to prison. Focus Ellie!*

She exited the Bon on Third Avenue discouraged and annoyed with herself for her useless daydreaming. She headed north on Third, crowded with shoppers and workers on lunch break. Ellie thrived on the energy of this American city. It felt alive and full of promise. But the bloody hills and angled streets were tricky to navigate on a busy weekday morning. She walked north with a growing sense she was headed in the wrong direction. *Where in the bloody hell am I going"*

She stopped walking and tried to orient herself. Her mother in-law told her about a helpful way to remember street names. The city's founders named the streets in matched pairs beginning with the same letters. From south to north, the main east-west streets were Jefferson, James, Cherry, Columbia, Marion, Madison, Spring, Seneca, University, Union, Pike and Pine. Taken together they made the letters "JCMSUP," or "Jesus Christ Made Seattle Under Protest." *Bollocks. The planners must have been real wankers.*

She turned around and walked south on Third to Yesler Way. She was looking for the Public Safety Building at 400 Yesler. On her left, the thirty-eight-story Smith Tower, which Seattle liked to boast was America's tallest skyscraper outside New York City, cast its shadow over the city's south end. She was more taken with the four-story Public Safety Building, whose trapezoidal design looked like a giant wedge of Swiss cheese. She entered the station and was directed to take the elevator to the fourth floor, which housed the jail and a visiting area where prisoners could meet with families or lawyers. The afternoon sun streaming through barred windows brightened an otherwise lifeless room.

While waiting to see John, she tried to pinpoint when her marriage turned sour. Life on Phinney Ridge unfolded neatly in the couple's first month alone. Ellie did her best to keep the house clean and have dinner waiting when John got home. The food was eatable if unexciting. John ate everything put in front of him and thanked her for the meal, but Ellie sensed his disappointment. Determined to do better, she found a recipe for spaghetti in one of her mother-in-law's cookbooks. She made a list of ingredients and walked to the Thriftway, where she bought ground beef, tomato sauce, fresh tomatoes, onions, garlic and spaghetti. It was an extravagance she'd never imagined. In the afternoon she cut up the vegetables, browned the beef and garlic without burning them, miraculously, and placed them in an ancient cast-iron pot. She then added the sauce, oregano, salt and pepper, and let the concoction simmer for two hours. When she thought it was ready, she took a spoonful and tasted it. Not bad, she thought, and sat at the kitchen table, smoking and drinking coffee waiting for her husband.

When John got home and entered the kitchen, Ellie could barely suppress her excitement and nervousness. "I made spaghetti!" she said.

John kissed her on the lips and then moved to the stove. He looked curiously into the pot, nearly over flowing with the simmering sauce. "Are we having a party, Ellie?

"No party, why?"

"Well there's so damn much of it." He looked at the recipe in the cookbook still open on the counter, and understood. "Ellie, this is a recipe for 20." After a silent moment, they both broke out laughing. It so happened the spaghetti was more than edible, for which John was thankful, because they ate it three nights straight.

Things began to turn dark when John was fired. Their first big row occurred a week later. He came home after ten, grumpy, smelling of beer and cigarettes. Normally, Ellie wouldn't mind but tonight she cooked lamb chops, his favorite. He promised to come straight home. He entered the kitchen, but before he could say a word, she threw the pan of chops at him. "You bastard!" she yelled, and hurried into the bedroom, the frying pan and chops skidding across the floor.

After that, the nights out became more frequent. He'd saunter in after she'd gone to bed, wanting sex, undeterred by her growing belly. On Saturdays, John's best mate, Louie, came over with other friends, partying well into the night. Sometimes the guys brought girlfriends. Ellie hoped to befriend them, but she quickly discovered she held little in common with young American women. They complained about how the war upset their daily lives. Rationing, food coupons, gas shortages were so tiring. You couldn't even buy nylons. You know nothing about war, Ellie thought. *You haven't been rousted out of bed, air-raid sirens piercing the night. You never ran in terror for the shelter of the underground, huddling with your Mum in the damp cold until the skies cleared. I'll keep those stories to myself. They're too good for you.* So Ellie stayed clear, smoking and drinking coffee in the kitchen or reading *True Confessions* magazines in bed. In the morning, she'd clear away the beer bottles, empty over-flowing ashtrays and clean stains off the carpet.

A month later, she was home alone when someone wrapped loudly on the door. She rushed to put on her robe as the knocking became more forceful. When she opened the door, two uniformed policemen were standing on the porch. One was tall and lean, the other a thickly built Negro. She'd never seen a Negro policeman.

"Mrs. Jacobson,?" the white policeman asked.

"Yes. What is it?" Ellis asked, alarm in her voice. "Has something happened to my husband?"

They asked if they could come in. They sat in the living room, their leather gun belts protesting the movement. "Your husband isn't hurt, Mrs. Jacobson, but he's in jail."

This wasn't good news, but at least he was okay. Probably taken in for fighting or drunk driving. "Why was he arrested?" she asked.

"He and an accomplice, a Mr. Louis Smith, were arrested for armed robbery around seven this evening."

She didn't remember much about that night, but by the next day, shock gave way to anger. That ass was in jail and she was alone and expecting a baby. He wasn't even a competent crook, apparently, getting nabbed inside an hour. The store employees they locked in the meat locker escaped within minutes and called the police. A woman walking by suspected something was amiss and she too called the police. According to the papers, Louie was captured on a bus headed into the city. He quickly surrendered and told the cops where he planned to meet John. "I guess you got me, boys," he said.

Ellie waited thirty minutes before John came through the door accompanied by a guard.

"You've got fifteen minutes, Jacobson, and no touching," the guard warned, retreating to the far corner.

John looked pale and apparently underfed by the looks of the dungarees bunched around his waist. Ellie, the anger long gone now, felt her attraction to her husband creeping to the surface. Damnit, she loved this bloke in spite of the last hellish three months. He pled guilty at his arraignment. He faced sentencing weeks later. She sat in the front row of the courtroom right behind John when the judge announced his ruling. John was to serve no more than twenty years, but eligible for parole in two with good behavior. Given John's shenanigans over the last year, she didn't hold high hopes for that. Louie received a similar sentence.

They sat on the opposite sides of the table closest to the door. "How are you, Ellie? How's the baby?" She was fine, she said, and the doctor told her everything was coming along nicely. She shifted her weight in the chair and laid both hands on her stomach to underline the point. *God he looks awful.*

"Ellie, I want to say something, so, please, let me finish before you speak. I know an apology isn't going to help now, but I want to apologize anyway. I did something really stupid and hurt you and our baby. In defense, I'd say I did it for us, but I've had three months to think about this, and there's no defense. It was wrong, and now we're both paying the price."

"You're right, an apology doesn't help," she countered sharply. "You've had three months to think about what you've done. Well I've spent three months carrying your baby and wondering what in the hell I'm going to do."

"I think you should go home, Ellie. Go back to London with the baby. You'll be better off with your family. I'll give you a divorce if you want."

"Oh, that's grand, John. That's just what my family wants, to say they were right about you all along. That you were just another over-sexed GI, a lay-about who wouldn't amount to anything. What about my friends? What do you think they'll say? 'There goes Ellie Walker, couldn't even make it in America.'"

"I can't help what your friends think. All I know is I can't take care of you from prison. Just tell them your American dream didn't come true."

"American Dream!" Ellie snapped, angry now. "Do you think I was some starry-eyed girl chasing a dream? This wasn't about America. I would have gone anywhere. I gave up everything to build a life with you, didn't I? That was my dream. What have you given up? You still have your family, your friends. You didn't have to give up your country."

"Okay, but I've lost my freedom."

"Yeah, you have," Ellie responded, "But I didn't ask you to rob a bloody Safeway, did I?"

"Time's up, Jacobson. Let's go." The guard's interruption put an end to the exchange, but there wasn't much left to say. John started for the door, but turned around as Ellie stood. "Go home, Ellie. You can't make it here on your own," he said, before the door closed behind them.

On the ride home, Ellie wished she'd been more sympathetic. He was the one going to prison and was probably scared. It saddened her to think she made it worse, but she needed to think about herself now. What was she going to do? Contrary to what she told John, she considered returning home. It was the safest choice, all humiliation aside. But the thought of returning to London with its rubble and rationing depressed her. Compared to Seattle, it felt old and worn out. As it so happened, Ellie wasn't the only bride needing help. The Overseas Brides Club, which met at the Downtown YWCA, provided support for war brides. Women contesting divorces, coping with abusive or alcoholic husbands or troublesome in-laws found respite at the Y. They could meet other GI brides dealing with similar problems.

As the bus crossed northbound on the Aurora Bridge, she could see the Olympic Mountains once again. The late afternoon sun turned them a rosy pink, beams of sunlight shafting through grayish clouds. The tableau was a striking reminder of what attracted her to this city. No, London was in the past. She would visit home someday, but for now she'd move out of the Phinney Ridge house and share one of the flats on Capitol Hill the Y told her about. She could take care of herself, thank you. She'd have this baby, on her own if need be. She would make a life in America, and make it in Seattle.

Chapter 15

"I look beefy," Joanne said into the mirror. No that wasn't right, she looked chubby, but that wasn't right either. She was trying on a dress George bought, an apology gift following their first fight since his return. It was a beautiful dress, what her friend Dorinda would call an "I'm all yours dress." It was black, sleeveless, and ran from her breast line to mid-calf. At the middle was a peplum, a piece of fabric that flared at the waist, designed to create a touch of elegance and grace. Except her figure was more pear than flare, the consequences of bearing two children. Her bare shoulders and biceps were well defined growing up on a farm and driving a five-pound rivet gun for two years. She looked chubby, certainly not elegant.

That was it, she looked pudgy. The woman in the mirror resembled the renowned female weightlifter Abbye "Pudgy" Stockton, Queen of Muscle Beach. Recently featured in *Look* magazine, Pudgy reportedly could bench press a hundred pounds. "I could be a competitive weightlifter," she said aloud. "Call me Joanne Novak, the Rugged Riveter."

The argument with George broke out after informing him she was returning to work at Plant Two. Seven months passed since being let go following VJ Day. She pledged to devote her life to her family like most women who worked during the war. Isn't that what she always wanted, dreamed about, a home, husband and children? But a quiet unease with home life mushroomed into something more disturbing, something she couldn't understand or make go away. It came to a head two days ago when housecleaning. George returned to his old job in Plant Two. The kids were in school, Danny at Stevens Elementary, and Natalie, wanting a change after having her baby, transferred to Garfield. Joanne mopped the kitchen floor moving sluggishly, her mind not on the task. She washed the windows with vinegar water. From there, she vacuumed the living room carpet and polished the end tables, every task feeling more laborious. She took a deep breath and trudged up the stairs. She stripped the three beds and laundered the sheets. When dry, she pulled them out of the dryer, placed them in the laundry basket and headed upstairs. She was making Danny's bed when a sense of emptiness washed over her, drowning her, threatening to pull her under. She sat on the bed and began to cry silently, tears streaming down both cheeks, staining her apron. She felt utterly exhausted, empty. She'd lost her appetite, picking at last night's dinner and breakfast this morning. And she felt alone, friendless. She missed her friends. Dorinda was rehired at Plant Two. Anita worked the late shift in Renton. They promised each other to keep in touch but hadn't. Giving up work meant giving up friends. Spending the day alone felt like solitary confinement. *What was wrong with me? Why did something that once seemed important now seem meaningless?* She didn't especially enjoy cleaning, few women did, but she'd always taken pride in the cleanliness, the orderliness. She prided in being a good wife and mother. That sense of accomplishment and pride sustained her. But when war broke out, Joanne, took up arms on the home front. Within weeks after starting work, the sense of accomplishment was derived not from inside the home but from the outside. For the first time in her life, she wanted more than what her mother wanted, what almost every other woman she knew wanted. The ancient proverb, "the home is where the heart is," was her mother's favorite. But Joanne's brain was crying out for more. She needed the fresh air and endless possibilities of the outside world.

She wiped her tears, walked downstairs and picked up the phone to call Derek Johnson at Plant Two. The papers reported that Boeing was gearing up for a forthcoming government contract for the B29. It had something to do with Russia causing mischief in Europe and tensions ran high. She started to dial the number and then stopped, placing the receiver back in the cradle, her hands shaking. She was torn, unsure. *Do I really want to do this knowing the trouble it will cause? It will upset George to say the least. The kids enjoyed having me home after school. What would they say? I know what my family wants but what about me? Have my needs ever mattered? Where is it written in scripture that a woman shouldn't put her needs first? Will I forever be the self-sacrificing wife?*

"Damnit," she said aloud, picked up the phone and dialed the number. It was a short conversation. "When can you start?" Johnson asked.

As she feared, George did not take the news well. "Why would you do that?" he asked, looking befuddled.

They stood in the kitchen, Joanne washing dinner dishes, George hovering close. She waited until after dinner to break the news. Natalie and Danny retired to their rooms presumably doing homework.

"I don't understand, Joanne. What about us? You have responsibilities here, the kids, me. Is it that awful here?"

She put down the dish cloth, placed her wet hands on the edge of the sink and turned to her husband. "No, George, it's not awful for God's sake. I love our home. I love you, I love the kids. It's just that, that . . ," she hesitated, the right words elusive.

"It's what? Tell me," he demanded, his voice rising, anger showing.

"I JUST NEED MORE! OKAY?" she shot back. There it was, out in the open, an admission previously shared with no one.

"You're being selfish, Joanne. You're telling me you can work fulltime and still manage this house, the kids?

"Look, George, I did just fine alone here for three years. It will be okay, I promise."

"Okay? You think things were okay? I've got a grandson, for crying out loud, who has a fifteen-year-old mother. If things were fine, if everything was so okay, why did you allow our daughter to run around with G.I.s like some whore?"

His words hit hard and she hit back immediately. "You son of a bitch!" she screamed. She shoved him hard with both hands, knocking him against the counter, tattooing wet handprints on his white undershirt. She turned and stormed upstairs.

That was two days ago, and tonight George came home with his gift. It was wrapped in gold paper topped with a red bow. The sales clerk at The Bon must have wrapped it for him, she thought. He stammered an apology, He was never very good at apologizing, and kissed her on the cheek.

She took one last mournful look into the mirror. "Yep, that's me. Joanne Novak, the Rugged Riveter." She left the bedroom and descended the stairs, her black heels clopping against the hardwood. George looked up at her. His furled brows and pinched lips confirmed that he knew this dress was all wrong for her.

Joanne placed one foot forward, and cocked her hips, mimicking a movie star. "Come, darling, why don't you buy me a drink," she whispered in the gravelly voice of Betty Grable.

"You look ravishing," he joked back, "I'd love to buy you a drink." They both laughed, the tension evaporated.

"Seriously, do you think I look good in this?" she asked

He hesitated, not sure whether to be honest. "Not really," he admitted.

Joanne was touched by his thoughtfulness but she wanted to make a point without sounding ungrateful. Enough hurt feelings, she thought. "This was very sweet but even if the dress was right for me, it's not what I need right now. If you want to get me something, buy me boots."

"Boots?"

"Yes, honey, work boots. I've been wearing those clodhoppers from the farm for three years. I need new boots with steel-tipped toes."

"Men don't buy their wives steel-tipped boots."

"Okay, but maybe they should. I'm not your kitten anymore. I'm no longer that farm girl who dreamed only about landing a good husband and having babies. Can you see that?"

"I don't know. I just want my wife back."

Joanne wrapped her arms around his neck, looked him in the eye and spoke softly. "The dreamy girl you married is gone, George. She's not coming back. This working mom and housewife is all you've got. I need you to accept that."

When he didn't respond, she took his hand and gestured for him to sit next to her on the couch. "George, I need you to hear me out so please don't interrupt. For the first few months after you shipped out it was lonely here and frankly dull. I spent too much time sitting around and worrying about you, terrified you were hurt or worse. When I saw the Boeing ads it was a perfect opportunity to do something important. I could support the war effort, to support you."

"I was proud of you for that. But the war is over. Most women who worked have given it up, content to stay home."

"I'm not like most women, you must know that. All my life, I've been dependent on men, first Dad and then you. Work gave me independence. I was good at my job. Men respected me for what I did. It took a while but instead of seeing a lady riveter they saw a riveter who happened to be a lady."

George was not surprised by his wife's stubbornness. He sensed for some time that this was a losing battle. She wasn't going to let this go, and besides another paycheck wouldn't hurt. He let go of her hand and sighed heavily, not looking directly at her. "Okay, I can see there's no changing your mind. Take your job if that's what you want and I'll try to help."

"You will?"

"Yes, but I'm not buying you boots."

Chapter 16

"Sir, that's my arm."

He looked down at the dismembered limb he held in his right hand, a bloody tangle of torn ligaments, severed muscles, leaky arteries. He didn't remember picking it up. He looked at the man who spoke to him. It was Corporal Angelos, blood spurting from his right shoulder, obscured by a thick haze of dirty smoke.

He offered up the arm. "You alright, Corporal?"

Using his left arm, Angelos took possession of the recovered limb. "I'm fine, sir, just a flesh wound."

"Where are the others?"

"Look around you, Lieutenant, they're all dead."

That's when he saw them, bodies strewn across the airfield, contorted unnaturally, motionless. He could taste metal and smell burning flesh. "What happened?"

"It was the Japs, but you killed them, sir. It's your fault."

"It is?"

"Yes sir. We were in condition red. You should have ordered us to retreat to our bunkers, Lieutenant. The Jap bombers were right over us We didn't have time to take cover."

He stepped closer to his men. Rossi, Wojcik, Walters, and three others he didn't recognize – all dead. Impossibly, all six died with their eyes open, unblinking. Their bluish, blotchy faces revealed no emotion, no pain, nothing. Except there was something. He could see it now. Like a prosecutor pointing a finger at a guilty defendant in the courtroom. All the dead-eye stares pointed squarely at him. "He's the guilty party, your honor," the eyes said. "That's the man who killed us, Lieutenant Novak."

"I didn't," he stammered. "I DIDN'T!"

"George, wake up." It was Joanne, shaking George's shoulder.

"I didn't!" he pleaded again. He suddenly sat up, nearly clipping Joanne's chin. He looked around, disoriented, sweat running down his cheeks, his pajamas top soaked.

"What didn't you do?" she asked.

George looked at his wife but didn't understand the question.

"You were crying in your sleep, moaning that you didn't do something. What didn't you do?"

"It was nothing," he said, not looking at her.

"Don't say that, George. Don't shut me out. These nightmares are happening more and more. You're not sleeping. You're not yourself. So don't tell me it's nothing."

Without responding, he climbed out of bed, slipped on his robe and slippers and headed for the bedroom door. "I'm alright," he said, quietly closing the door behind him.

He went into the kitchen, retrieved a glass out of the cupboard, picked up the bottle of Jim Beam from the counter and headed for the living room. He sat in the middle of the couch and poured three fingers of the bourbon.

Joanne was right, he admitted to himself. The nightmares were getting worse. He hadn't slept well since getting home. He couldn't concentrate at work. The only respite at home was staying busy and the booze. When he returned from work, he'd attack one chore after another in the garage or backyard. At dinner he said little, the family chatter a distant buzz. After dinner, he'd plop down on the couch with a drink, feet up on the coffee table, and doze off. On the Fourth of July he scared the whole family when Danny set off a string of firecrackers. The machine-gun patter triggered an internal alarm, making him jump and yell at his son. It transported him back to Guadalcanal if only for an instant.

That's where it all started, of course, Guadalcanal. During his three years in the Pacific Theater, he'd led construction crews in the

Solomon Islands, the Mariana's, Iwo Jima and Okinawa. But it was the hellish six months on Guadalcanal in the Solomon's, early in the war, that nearly did him in.

Guadalcanal, one of the largest of the Solomon Islands, lies about two thousand kilometers northeast of Australia. George attended briefings about the island's hellish nature. Two thousand square miles of steep mountains, dense jungles awaited his company. Unrelenting heat, intolerable humidity, swarming mosquitos, deadly malaria, and the dreaded dengue fever awaited them. But an otherwise unlivable mass of land featured one redeeming value. Its airstrip was a perfect launching point for Allied Forces to leapfrog from one island to another towards Japan. Just a couple of minor problems, the briefer noted. A Japanese carrier force and 31,000 heavily armed fighters determined to fight to the death to retain control of their airfield.

On August 7, 1942, eight months to the day following Pearl Harbor, Allied Forces launched Operation Watchtower, its first major offensive in the Pacific. It began with the First Marine Division's amphibious landing at Lunga Beach on the northwest side of the island. A heavy cloud cover limited Japan's ability to detect Allied movement. Five-inch guns on U.S. destroyers protected a contingent of eleven thousand marines. They encountered little resistance on the beach. Their initial objective was to take the airfield near Lunga Point. That was relatively easy as well. The U.S. command considered the airstrip, later named Henderson Field, the center of gravity for Allied operations. Losing it threatened to set the Allies back six months.

Taking the airfield was one thing, holding it and keeping it operational were all-together different. While U.S. forces controlled the Northwest part of the island, the Japanese remained entrenched on the southcentral coast. The enemy also enjoyed superior airpower and controlled much of the straits surrounding the island. U.S. ships clashed with Japanese naval forces. Planes engaged in dogfights. Marines fought hand-to-hand combat in the jungles. For six months, U.S. Forces took on an enemy willing to accept horrendous casualties and refusing to surrender.

The Sixth Naval Construction Battalion (SeaBees), to which Lieutenant Novak was assigned, arrived on Guadalcanal in late August. George's first impression, beyond the stifling heat, was the thousands of fallen coconut and palm trees, evidence of incessant Japanese and Allied bombing. Job one was to keep the airfield operational. But there was more. George's company, mostly recruits who'd worked in construction before the war, accomplished nothing less than building a fully operational military base. They were part of a one-thousand man force that constructed roads, bridges, docks, railways, sawmills, fuel depots, quonset huts and buildings of all sizes. They dug tunnels to protect heavy equipment and fuel stores. They erected a radio tower, a power plant and a cherished ice plant that provided refrigeration. But what the Americans struggled to build, the Japanese easily destroyed. It was an endless cycle of construction and destruction. Build and rebuild. The Seabees would no sooner fill in bomb craters on the airstrip when Japanese dive bombers swept in and blew it all to hell.

For three days beginning on October 12, the Japanese threw everything at the Allies with coordinated naval, air, and ground attacks. With the goal of retaking Henderson Field, Japanese cruisers and bombers tore up the airfield and destroyed dozens of planes and fuel stores. U.S. Marines engaged trail-weary Japanese troops desperate for a victory. Over two days, more than two thousand Japanese were killed in action, compared to less than a hundred Marines.

An alarm system alerted Seabees of impending air raids. Condition Yellow, three siren blasts, meant bombers were thirty to forty-five minutes out and crews should begin heading for safety. Five blasts of the horn, signaling Condition Red, meant an air attack was likely within minutes. Crews often worked through Condition Yellow, and sometimes into Condition Red, especially if they needed to clear bulldozers and tractors. But the alarm system wasn't foolproof. On day two of the battle, George's company was twenty minutes into Condition Yellow when two things happened at once. The Condition Red alarm sounded and George looked up to see several Japanese carrier bombers almost directly overhead. The roar of their engines drowned out the alarm.

"Let's go!" They're here! Go! Go! Go!" George yelled. Everyone in the crew spotted or heard the incoming bombers and began sprinting towards the bunkers a hundred yards away. George brought up the rear to ensure none of his men were left behind.

The Japanese D3A1 bomber, what the Americans called the Val, carried a single 250-kilogram bomb and two sixty-kilogram bombs. It carried sufficient firepower to heavily damage a runway, especially one composed of compact dirt and gravel. Dive bombing to attack a ship at sea required the pilot to engage in a steep dive and drop his load from two thousand feet or lower if he hoped to damage or sink the moving ship. But a stationary airstrip was easy pickings. Cruising at around two hundred knots, the pilots released their loads from five thousand feet setting off a chain of explosions and unleashing volcanos of flying dirt and rock.

Knowing all his men were ahead of him, George ran hard. He played running back for Enumclaw High School, scoring ten TDs in his senior year. He could outrun most defenders but not the blast wave of a 250-kilogram bomb. The force of the wave swept George off his feet and sent him rolling down the runway like dice on a craps table. He tumbled for about twenty feet before he collided with a tractor parked in the middle of the strip. The collision knocked him out.

It's difficult to overestimate the damage an explosion can wreck on a human body, even from fifty yards away. It sprays shrapnel, rock and flames in all directions. But the serious injuries are often internal, invisible to the naked eye. The force of the blast slammed George's brain against the back of his skull. Called a blast brain, it causes a serious and sometimes fatal concussion.

George was severely concussed but alive. He came to slumped against the tractor. He bled from both ears. It felt like someone smashed a sledge hammer to his chest. He was confused, unsure what happened, or where he was. He saw a man standing ten feet away, but unrecognizable through a thick layer of smoke and dust. The man said something but the thunderous ringing in George's ears drowned out the words.

The man stepped closer. "Sir, are you all right?" It was Corporal Angelos, bleeding badly from his right shoulder.

George ignored the question, staggering to his feet. He looked around, saw bodies strewn everywhere. He counted six. They looked familiar, but he couldn't pull up the names. That bothered him. *I trained and worked with them for God's sake. I know these guys. Why can't I remember their fucking names?* The next thing he knew, medics took him by the arms and lowered him onto a stretcher. They carried him to an ambulance and drove to the make-shift hospital north of the airstrip.

Three months later, George sat at the bar in the crowded canteen, nursing his third whiskey and water, oblivious to the buzz and chatter behind him. The attack in October was Japan's last major offensive on Guadalcanal. Sporadic fighting continued but by February it was clear they could not retake the island and began to withdraw. Objective complete. The United States now maintained a permanent foothold in the Pacific. The men enjoying themselves that night deserved R and R.

George spent one night in the hospital and returned to duty the day after that. The medics gave him aspirin but he downplayed the headaches. His hearing improved but the throbbing persisted. He learned that six of his men died in the raid, Tony Rossi from Philadelphia, Alvin Wojcik from Buffalo, and Christian Walters, the son of a cattle rancher in Fort Worth, Texas. The remaining three, Patrick O'Leary, Eric Anderson and Bernie Smyth had just joined his company. He wrote letters to the families praising their service to their country. Doctors amputated Angelos' right arm and transferred him to Pearl Harbor for rehab. These men, all under age twenty-five, were killed or injured under his command. It was a first for him. He disregarded the air raid warnings and they followed his lead without question. He was never given an explanation why the warnings came so late. He didn't blame reconnaissance. He blamed himself. Six of his men were in the ground because he would not give ground. A Marine officer he chowed with said he lost nine men in jungle fighting. Get used to it, he said. But there's no easy out in death. He couldn't turn off the guilt, any more than he could bring his men back, or stop the throbbing pain in his head. He found an ounce of relief only from multiple ounces of whiskey. He downed his drink and ordered another.

Chapter 17

"*It don't mean a thing, if it ain't got that swing.*"
"*Doo-ah, doo-ah, doo-ah.*"

Lawrence watched as Anna Louise and the nightclub audience responded to Ernie Lewis and His Girls belting out the Duke Ellington hit.

"*It don't mean a thing, all you got to do is sing.*"

"*Doo-ah, doo-ah, doo-ah.*"

The jazz pianist and his vocalists held the audience in hand but Lawrence's attention was on his wife. Her flowered shirtwaist jacket with padded shoulders, and A-line skirt that came down to her knees created that hourglass look he loved. Her hair was made into an intricate pattern of curls and braids with a white flower pinned at the top. It looked stately, almost regal.

"*It makes no difference*
If it's sweet or hot
Just give that rhythm
Everything you've got."

"*Doo-ah, doo-ah, doo-ah.*"

They sat at a table near the front entrance of the Bebop Rendezvous, an unlicensed nightclub on Jackson. Anna Louise held a champagne cocktail in one hand and a filtered cigarette in the other. She rocked in the chair, her head bobbing to the music, looking lively and ready to dance. She took a drag on her cigarette, the white smoke curling slowly away. She even smoked with elegance, Lawrence observed. She held the cigarette between her long, delicate fingers Their painted red nails glowed under the club lights.

"*Doo-ah, doo-ah, doo-ah.*"

On this cool spring evening in 1946, couples filled the dozen or so tables below the stage. Cigarette smoke hung over their heads like a morning fog. Uniformed soldiers sat on stools at the long, curved bar that filled one side of the room. Three bartenders in white jackets provided "set ups." Selling spirits in the city limits violated prohibition laws. Patrons brought their "bottle bags" and the club collected a fee for the setup, basically a glass, ice and mixer. In the back, patrons gathered around two poker tables, playing pokeno, a combination of poker and bingo. Their discordant shouts blending with the music.

The Bebop Rendezvous was one of several licensed and unlicensed clubs and auditoriums in full swing six nights a week in the Central District and downtown. Jazz gravitated to Seattle like the hordes of defense workers that filled the clubs. The Civic Auditorium at Fourth and Mercer hosted a who's who of jazz greats. Bandleaders Count Basie, Duke Ellington and gravelly-voiced trumpeter Louis Armstrong played to sold-out audiences. So did vibraphonist Lionel Hampton, Jimmy Lunceford, the "King of Jaznochracy," and Jay McShann, "the band that jumps the blues." Go to Finnish Hall at Thirteenth and Washington and take in Arthur "Buddy" Banks and His Buddies, or the do-wop vocalists the Ink Spots. Earl "Father" Hines, the swing maestro, blended jazz with church hymns. Ernestine Anderson, a local product and Garfield High School graduate, launched her career at Finnish Hall.

"Doo-ah, doo-ah, doo-ah."

Lawrence made watching Anna Louise a national pastime. "It don't mean a thing if I ain't got Anna Louise," he whispered to himself. He laughed at the failed rhyme. He was glad to see her having fun, letting go. Between her job at the beauty shop and caring for the boys, she needed to let loose even for just one night. He needed the release too after taking extra routes in the last two months. He'd returned to Seattle Transit, of course. He took a small ounce of pleasure watching that suit from headquarters standing on his front porch, hat in hand. How often does some white man apologize to a Negro? More important he needed the job. He loved his parents but he'd been home for almost a year. It was time to move on. He closed his eyes and gave into the music.

"It don't mean a thing, if it ain't got that swing."

"Doo-ah, doo-ah, doo-ah."

An ear-splitting explosion ended the reverie. A line of uniformed and plain-clothed police burst open the doors and stormed through the entrance. They screamed for everyone to stay where they were. There must have been twenty of them, Lawrence thought, alarmed. The first wave swept their nightsticks across the bar, sending glasses and bottles skittering along the bar and onto the floor. Soldiers leaped off their stools to dodge the flying glass. The second group ran through the tables, smashing bottles and striking anyone who got in their way. Panicked men surreptitiously discarded knives, handguns, and bags of drugs, tossing them carelessly across the floor. Two officers jumped over the bar and handcuffed the bartenders.

"Let's go!" Lawrence yelled, grabbing Anna Louise and pushing her towards the entrance.

"I can't. We gotta get Lanelle. She's playing pokeno!" Lanelle worked with Anna Louise and accompanied them to the club. She pulled away from Lawrence and rushed towards the pokeno tables and stepped right into the path of a swinging nightstick. It struck her on the temple putting her flat on her back, head banging against the hardwood floor.

"Fuck!" Lawrence screamed, rushing forward and kneeling over his stricken wife. She lay there, unmoving, semiconscious, eyes unfocused, arms spread like wings. Blood ran down her right cheek into her ear. As the panic welled up inside, Lawrence felt someone pull him by the collar and scream "Get her out of here!"

"What the fuck did you do, man?" Lawrence screamed back.

"It was an accident, she got in the way, that's all. But I can't deal with this shit right now. She'll be okay, just get going."

"But she's unconscious. . ."

"You will be too if you don't move your ass right now!"

Lawrence sensed what was going on. This cop didn't want to deal with having struck an innocent woman, accident or not. Anna Louise let out a groan and tried to sit.

"Shush, baby," he said and bent down. "It's okay, it's okay." He placed his hands under her armpits and hoisted her over his left shoulder. Known in the navy as the fireman's carry, it affectively distributed the weight of an unconscious body. Inelegant but effective. With her hundred-and-twenty pound frame balanced evenly over his shoulder, Lawrence walked into the cool night air, his wife's arms hanging limply against his back.

Chapter 18

Lawrence wasn't sure when he decided to move out of the Central District, only that he must. The fiasco at the Bebop Rendezvous was the last straw, but he blamed himself for that. It wasn't the first time police raided an unlicensed club. He'd been lucky Anna Louise wasn't seriously hurt, or among the seventy arrested that night. She recovered enough to walk home where he dressed her wound and put her to bed. No it wasn't the biggest straw, just the latest in a serious of warning signs that told him they needed to find a better neighborhood to raise their boys. Gerald, was about to turn fifteen and Elijah, eight. The temptations on the streets of the CD could seduce teenage boys. And the crowding continued to worsen. By his figuring, the population of the twenty square blocks of the CD tripled since the start of war. It was time to get out.

He sat in the lobby of the Madison Street office of the realtor John L. Scott. He booked an appointment with agent Robert McNally. As the wait stretched from fifteen minutes into thirty, he thought about the last few months. The CD was rotting from the inside out. Everywhere he turned he saw problems, old ones and new ones. Prostitutes plied their trade day and night. Drug peddlers loitered along Jackson and Yesler, homeless people asking for handouts on every corner. War workers occupied the Yesler Terrace apartments ostensibly built for poor folk. The grounds were reduced to a garbage dump, trash littering the yard and sidewalk. The health department threatened to take action before residents organized a cleanup party. Thousands of colored workers descended upon the city in the last five years. It seemed to Lawrence every damn one of them squatted in his neighborhood. But it wasn't the crap in the street but the danger crossing the street that convinced him it was time to go.

He was walking his youngest son, Elijah, to Bailey Gatzert Elementary School at Thirteenth and Yesler Way in May. He started doing that since switching to the swing shift in January. Gerry walked with his friends to Garfield High School. The walk to Bailey took them through mostly residential streets except to cross at Yesler and Broadway. The previous night's heavy rain eased but persisted, the southerly wind buffeting their faces. As they approached Yesler, several parents and their children waited to cross. With no stoplight or crosswalk, traffic streamed by, oblivious to pedestrians. A previously safe crossing transformed into a death trap. Yesler Way was now a speedway jammed with commuters, delivery trucks and busses, all ignoring the thirty-five-mile speed limit. They huddled to shield themselves from the wind and rain. Cars splashed muddy water and gravel at their feet.

"When in the hell are they going to put up a light here," yelled a woman, holding the hands of two girls about ten years old.

"The city said it's on their schedule but God knows when it will get done," Lawrence yelled over the roar of traffic."

"It's been a year since they promised to fix this, for God's sake. Is someone going to have to die before they get off their asses?"

A milk delivery truck drove too close to the curb, spitting gravel and muddy water, soaking Lawrence's shoes. "Dammit. that's enough," he said. "Elijah, stay here and don't move until I tell you to." With that, he stepped off the curb and into the street, avoiding the rush of water flooding the gutter and spilling over the sidewalk. He saw a brief break in the traffic and stepped into the westbound lane waving his arms. Three vehicles zipped by before a car braked ten feet in front of him. With westbound traffic halted, he stepped into the eastbound lane. He waved his arms, yelling at drivers to give way. When both lanes cleared, Lawrence beckoned everyone forward. Women with children in tow scurried across the two lanes. Older children carrying lunch boxes and notebooks ran ahead of them. The woman with the twins ushered Elijah to safety. Just as the last of the pedestrians crossed Yesler, Lawrence heard a screech of tires and an ugly thump and scream. He turned to see a small boy lying in the westbound lane sprawled in front of a gray sedan.

"Elijah, stay with this lady until you get to school." He rushed back across Yesler, dodging traffic. He knelt in front of the fallen boy, the heat and exhaust fumes wafting over him. A woman, who couldn't have been much more than twenty, presumably the boy's mother, kneeled over her son, wailing. The driver of the sedan climbed out of his car and ran around to the front.

"He just ran out in front of me! It wasn't my fault!"

Lawrence ignored the man's protestations and looked at the boy. He was unconscious but breathing. Blood ran from the back of his head onto the street, turning the rainwater a muddy pink. He needed to get the boy out of the street. Against his better judgement, he picked him up and stepped onto the sidewalk, the mother's cries irrepressible now. He laid the boy gently onto the sidewalk, removed his overcoat and placed it over the boy. Another man removed his jacket, shaped it into a pillow and placed it under the boy's head. Lawrence pulled a handkerchief from his back pocket and applied pressure to the head wound.

"Someone go find a phone and call an ambulance!" Lawrence yelled. The man who gave up his jacket ran north on Broadway towards the nearest house. Unobserved in the commotion, the sedan's driver slipped into his car, slammed the door and sped away, spewing exhaust fumes and gravel in his wake.

Sitting in the realty office, thinking back over the incident, Lawrence got pissed all over again. A cop heading west on Yesler stopped and radioed for help. An ambulance showed up fifteen minutes later. The boy spent two days in Harborview Hospital, but survived. The whole thing, Lawrence thought, was FUBAR, Fucked Up Beyond All Recognition. The hit-and-run driver, who was never identified, FUBAR. The city, which unapologetically installed the light and painted a crosswalk two weeks later, FUBAR. The Central District, where he'd attended the same grade school as his sons. Where he played basketball at the Boys Club. Where he hung out with friends eating candy and lagging for pennies outside Kay's Ten-Cent Store. Where he'd attended Sunday services at Mount Zion Baptist. Where his mother wept and father brimmed with pride when he'd walked up the aisle in the Garfield gymnasium to receive his high school diploma. And where he'd met and married Anna Louise. The neighborhood he once loved was damaged beyond repair. FUBAR.

"Mr. Williams, Mr. McNally will see you now. Come with me, please."

Lawrence looked up, surprised. He didn't see her approach. She led him down a hall to the last office on the left. McNally was sitting behind a desk. He stood, shook Lawrence's hand and made eye contact. "Good to see you, Mr. Williams, please sit down." The metal desk, painted military-green, was clear except for some papers in front of McNally and two framed photographs. One was of McNally with his wife and three children, the other showed McNally in Navy dress whites, replete with cap, lieutenant bars and two rows of ribbons.

"I've taken the liberty of identifying some homes currently on the market. They're in your price range and ideal for your family," McNally said, handing the paper over to Lawrence.

Three homes were listed. A two-story affair on East Fir priced at $4,200, a two-bedroom bungalow on South Jackson asking $5,300 and a three-story Elizabethan at Sprague and Sixteenth, the most expensive at $6,350. Lawrence looked at McNally. "These are all in the CD. When we spoke over the phone I told you we want to buy in the Capitol Hill neighborhood or Madison Park."

McNally sat back in his chair and folded his arms. "I remember, but don't you think your family will be happier in the neighborhood where you grew up, surrounded by your own people?"

"That's the point, Mr. McNally, I don't want to be surrounded by my own people. We want a fresh start in a new neighborhood."

McNally took a deep breath and sat forward in his chair. "I'm sorry, but I can't show you houses in those neighborhoods. I'd violate real estate board rules and my company's policies."

Lawrence looked again at the photo of McNally in uniform. "You made lieutenant, I see. What ship?"

"*The Vigilance*, a mine sweeper, Philippine Sea."

"I was on the carrier *Liscome Bay*. Went down near the Gilberts. You remind me of my LT, James Watson.

"I do?" McNally sat up, interested.

"Yes, except he watched out for his men. Had our back."

McNally grimaced. "Mr. Williams," he responded, his voice rising. "Do you know what would happen if I showed you homes in those neighborhoods? I could be fined, even fired. No realtor would hire me. I'd be blackballed, out of the business. These neighborhoods have real estate covenants that prevent owners from selling to a, to . . . ," he struggled to find the right words.

"Selling to coloreds, you mean? Aren't Jews and Japanese on that list, or anyone who ain't white?" Is that what you're trying to say, McNally?"

"Look, I didn't make the rules, Williams," dropping the Mister now. "These covenants are enforceable in court. As much as I'd like to support a fellow vet, I can't put my job and my family at risk."

Lawrence remembered a story in the *Northwest Enterprise*, Seattle's black owned newspaper. It was about a twelve-year-old girl in Columbus, Ohio, who won an essay writing contest. Entrants were asked to describe how Adolf Hitler should be punished for his crimes against humanity. "Paint him black and make him live in America," she wrote.

The girl was on to something, Lawrence thought. So is this how it's going to be? I was afraid it would come to this. The folks at Christian Friends were right. I was stupid to think a fellow vet would help me break through the bullshit. Looks like I'm on my own, again. "Thank you for your time. Mr. McNally. "I certainly wouldn't want to put *your* family at risk but I have my own to care for." With that, he stood, shook hands with the agent and walked out of the office.

Chapter 19

Two days later, under a hazy afternoon sky, Lawrence and Anna Louise parked on East Mercer Street near Seventeenth Avenue in his father's 1940 Chevy. The for-sale sign posted on the fence said to call Robert E. Bailey, MacPherson Realtor. It was a narrow, two-story home with large dormer windows on the second story. The ad in the *Post-Intelligencer* listed it at $7,500, above their price range but manageable, Anna Louise thought. Between their two jobs and help from Lawrence's Dad they saved $1,000 for a down payment. Anna Louise looked at the house hopefully. White with blue trim, it looked inviting but she didn't feel invited.

This was a fool's errand, she thought, but went along due to Lawrence's insistence. "Let's do this," she said resignedly, climbing out of the car and slamming the door.

Lawrence's knocked on the door. A woman about forty answered. She wore a green housedress, her hair rolled into large curlers. She opened the door just wide enough to lean her head outside. "Can I help you?" she asked hesitantly.

"Ma'am, my name is Lawrence Williams and this is my wife Anna Louise. We'd like to talk to you about buying your house."

The woman looked at Anna Louise and back at Lawrence, her grip firmly on the door. "You need to speak with my realtor about that. That's what I pay him for."

"Yes, ma'am, I understand that. But from what I can tell, your home has been up for sale for a month or more. Don't seem like Mr. Bailey is doing a very good job."

"Ma'am?" Anna Louise interjected, "I really love what I've seen of your home. It's perfect for me and our two boys. Can we please see the inside?"

Opening the door a little farther, the woman appeared to consider Anna Louise's request, but then stopped. "I'm sorry, you seem like nice people but I can't let you in. My husband is at work and I have an appointment in town. You'll have to call the realtor." With that she closed and locked the door, the click of the lock sounding an abrupt end to the encounter.

Lawrence also liked the look of the house on Twentieth and Lenora. Set back from the street, it featured a two-foot brick fence protecting a large front yard. A concrete sidewalk and staircase led up to a large covered porch. He pictured himself lounging in an easy chair, drink in hand, enjoying a warm summer evening. A woman in her sixties answered their knock. Lawrence introduced himself and Anna Louise and stated their business.

"I'm sorry the house has been sold," the woman said abruptly.

"Is that so?" Lawrence said, sounding surprised. "How come you haven't taken down the for-sale sign?"

"It just sold yesterday. The realtor is coming to take the sign down," she said and closed the door.

It got worse at the third house, a three-bedroom, New England Colonial on Twenty Second and Prospect. The owner, a man of about fifty with thinning white hair and a firm build, interrupted Lawrence before he could finish the introduction.

"You know what, pal. I wouldn't sell to a Negro for all the money in the world. This is a good neighborhood. We don't want your kind around here. Now get off my property before I call the cops," he said, slamming the door in their faces.

Back in the car, Lawrence, gripped the steering wheel with both hands, seething, his face flush with anger mixed with humiliation. *What will it take to get some respect? I got a good job. I'm married and have children. I'm a vet. Why did I put my ass on the line only to be treated like a criminal?*

"Look at you," Anna Louise said. "You're about ready to explode. How long are you going to do this to yourself, to me?"

"I don't know. Whatever it takes. All I know is I can't quit. I have a right to live anywhere I want."

"Yes, you do, but it takes seller and buyer. No one is going to sell to you in these neighborhoods. How much humiliation will it take before you accept that? It hurts me to see you trampled on like this."

Lawrence looked down at the steering wheel, running his fingers around the Chevy logo, trying to calm himself. "It isn't the first time I've been humiliated and it won't be the last. Sooner or later somethings got to give."

"Well, if you want to keep banging your head against the wall, be my guest, but I'm done with this."

The following Saturday, Lawrence sat alone in the Chevy outside a two-story home on East Republican and Thirty First in Madison Park. At $8,550 it was out of his price range, but the ad said "owner leaving town must sell." Brownish moss overtook the roof, creeping up from the gutters and around the chimney. The siding, once a cheery yellow, looked washed out and blotchy. A broken-down picket fence, cracked sidewalk and overgrown front lawn showed further signs of neglect. Lawrence got out of the car, opened the creaking front gate, walked up the brick path and knocked on the door.

The man who answered looked to be in his early forties. He wore the uniform of a Navy Chief, his perfectly creased khaki trousers just touching well-shined, dress black shoes. The polished gold buckle on his khaki belt glistened. The short-sleeve khaki shirt, open at the collar, revealed a white T-shirt perfectly tailored at the waist. Four rows of ribbons over his left breast suggested he was one well-decorated, buttoned-down sailor.

"Hey, Chief," Lawrence said, smiling and extending his hand. "My name is Lawrence Williams. I'm Navy too. I'd like to speak with you about your house."

The man ignored the proffered hand and looked out at the street, first one way and then the other. "Come inside," he said, "quick." He ushered Lawrence inside and led him into the dining room. He offered Lawrence a chair and then sat opposite him.

The man introduced himself as Chief Bernsten. The house belonged to his parents, who since passed away. Bernsten grew up in the house but not lived in it since joining the Navy in '34. He was now stationed at the shipyard in Bremerton, but was transferred to D.C. for what he called "a shit desk job." He needed to sell the house, as is, and furnished, before leaving at month's end.

From the dining room, Lawrence could see both the living room and kitchen. Everything about the house looked and felt old. Two tattered armchairs and a sofa with frayed arms filled the living room. The flowered wallpaper was faded and peeling along the corners. Knick knacks and figurines cluttered the end tables and bureau. Dust was everywhere. The kitchen looked right out of the last century. A two-burner wood stove, blackened with age, took up one corner. Next to the stove stood an old-fashioned sink, the kind set into a stand-alone table rather than built into the cabinets. The closest thing to a modern appliance was a small refrigerator. The house smelled of mothballs and mildew. Faded curtains covered dirty windows, and the walls begged paint.

This is a dump but it's perfect, Lawrence thought. *We can make a life in this house, I'm sure of it. Madison Park was a good neighborhood. Fine schools close by. Lake Washington beaches just down the hill. No view of the lake but we can't afford that anyway. The boys will love it.*

"You in a position to move on this, Williams?" Bernsten asked. "Down payment, financing? I don't have time to mess around."

"No messing around, Chief. I have $1,000 for a down payment, good credit and a FHA loan all lined up. The paperwork is all done. My banker at Washington Mutual will submit it as soon as we settle on a house."

Bernsten nodded, looking satisfied. He showed Lawrence around. The three small bedrooms and upstairs bath were as worn out as the downstairs. From a bedroom window, he could see the fenced backyard. It, too, was overgrown. The picket fence sagging in all directions. A frayed rope swing hung from the lower branch of a large maple. When they returned to the dining room, Lawrence was eager to discuss price. The place needed a lot of work, he said, some of it expensive. After ten minutes of back and forth, they settled on $7,200, a fair deal, Lawrence felt. It was tight but they could make it work.

"What's your realtor going to say about this? Will you tell him you're selling to a black man?"

"My realtor works for me. He'll do what I tell him," Bernsten said, speaking like a chief accustomed to having orders followed.

Lawrence wasn't sure about that but his instincts told him to trust this guy. It was clear he needed to make a deal, and soon. Bernsten shook his hand, patted him on the shoulder and agreed to call as soon as he heard from the realtor. Lawrence drove away, flush with excitement. He did it.

Chapter 20

"Nigger lover." The words, ugly and mean, stared up at Lawrence. They were written in black ink on a small piece of white paper wrapped around a rock and secured with a rubber band. Not much bigger than a baseball, the rock sat in the center of the dining room table in the Williams's kitchen. Lawrence, Anna Louise and his parents looked at each other and then back at the horrid stone violating their home. Chief Bernsten stood to the rear. A minute earlier, he knocked on the door and was invited in. Without saying a word, he walked into the dining room and placed the offending object firmly on the table.

"That was thrown through my front window about two this morning," Bernsten said.

"How in the hell did the word get out?" Lawrence asked, incredulous. "It's been two days."

"The only one I told about our deal was my realtor. The asshole must have alerted someone in the neighborhood association."

Lawrence picked up the rock and turned it around in his hand like a jeweler valuing a rare stone. He was surprised by this turn of events but not shocked. Going into this search he prepared for the worst and hoped for the best.

"That's just the start," Bernsten said. "A Mr. Swenson, president of the homeowners, paid me a friendly visit this morning. He spent five minutes lecturing me on how covenants were enforceable under law and the consequences of violating them."

"What the hell can they do?" Lawrence retorted. Let 'em sue."

"They can destroy my home, that's what they can do," he shot back. "He was subtle but clear that the rock through the window was just the start if I insisted on going through with this sale. He said the home owners weren't going to stand by and watch their values go in the shitter because I sold to undesirables."

Undesirables. Lawrence heard that word before. "What are you going to do?" he asked, knowing the answer.

"I can't sell you the house, Lawrence. I'm sorry, I hate going back on a deal, but I can't babysit that house. I leave for D.C. in a few days and God knows what will happen. I told Swenson I'd leave the house on the market for now."

After Bernsten left, the family sat around the table staring at the rock, a talisman of trouble in their lives. The letdown from two days ago was heart sickening. When Lawrence told the family about his deal, Anna Louise squealed with delight. Gerald and Ida looked skeptical but congratulated him nonetheless. They drank gin martinis and talked about their plans for their new home. The boys were excited about the swing and nearby beaches. Anna Louise had yet to see the place, but it hadn't stopped her from redecorating.

Anna Louise looked at her husband. She was disappointed, but more saddened for her husband. The frustration on his face brought her nearly to tears. "You had enough yet, Lawrence?"

He looked back at her, silent.

Chapter 21

For the first time in five years, Frank could see a vibrant patch of daylight parting the clouds of hardship that fell over his family. He sat on a swing in the playground behind the Hunt Hotel where he and his family resided for the last four months. But this hotel was like no other. No valet parking, beautifully adorned lobby, or friendly staff to greet you from behind a reception desk. It was a school building at Fourteenth and Weller southeast of downtown. It was one of dozens of temporary accommodations readied for returning Japanese who lost their homes.

The Hunt, named after the Idaho city where Camp Minidoka was located, was previously the home of Nihon Gakko, the Japanese Language School. Before the war, Issei parents sent their Nisei children there to study the Japanese language and culture. Frank remembered resenting the imposition of attending two schools. When the bell rang at three at Bailey Gatzert Grammar School, the white kids were free for the afternoon. Frank and his siblings were not. They trudged the ten blocks to Nihon Gakko to learn to speak and bow and kneel and a thousand other customs that supposedly made someone Japanese.

Sakura Watanabe swung lazily next to Frank. Her family returned to Seattle shortly after the Sasaki's. The two families were among thirty living in a former school because war workers still occupied their homes. Wartime housing shortages only worsened in the year following VJ Day. Thousands of Japanese were homeless but now they hoped for brighter days.

Frank watched Sakura slowly push the swing. It was a pleasant evening following two days of rain. A warm breeze pushed up from the Sound as the setting sun cast a pink glow to the western sky. Traffic noise from Rainier Avenue hummed in the background.

Children played nosily on the slide and monkey bars. Sakura hummed a tune he didn't recognize. She was twenty years old. She wore clothing their church donated. The pleated plaid skirt, white blouse and tight-fitting blue sweater made her look sixteen. Her long, dark hair fell across her shoulders. Like most Nisei girls, she wore makeup, lipstick and eyeliner.

"Why do you put all that stuff on your face?" Frank asked.

Sakura planted her feet in the dirt to stop the swinging and looked at Frank. "What do you mean?"

"Do you wear it to look like white American girls?"

"No, I wear makeup because I like it. I think it makes me pretty. "Don't you like it?"

"I do like it but you're kidding yourself if you think it will help you get accepted by white people. You can't change the color of your skin or the shape of your eyes no matter how much you try to cover it up. We'll never be accepted as true Americans, the last four years have taught me that."

Sakura pushed off with her feet and picked up her swinging. "You sound like my father, Frank. I don't need another father to tell me how I should dress or comport myself. Father doesn't approve of me attending university either. He thinks I'll never get a job as a teacher. He says I'd be better off going to a business school, where I can learn to type and file and serve tea to some old chairman of a Japanese trading firm."

He knew she was looking forward to enrolling in the University of Washington in the fall. She wanted to major in education. "He might be right," he replied hesitantly.

"So I shouldn't try?" she responded, more sharply than she intended. "Just be the good daughter and honor Father's wishes? I want to teach, Frank. I'll be a good teacher. I taught math to the kids at Tule Lake and loved it. Teaching made camp life livable." Frank said nothing, wishing he'd not mentioned her makeup.

She resumed her swinging and Frank looked back at the last three months. He was relieved anti-Japanese sentiment and violence were waning and thankful for the unfailing support of Seattle's Christian community. People demonstrated kindness and magnanimity. Pastors throughout the city implored parishioners to put up Japanese families in their homes. They donated clothing, bedding, towels and toiletries, Attorneys offered legal services. Doctors attended the sick. Church council attorney Arthur Barnett called it old-fashioned neighborliness. Having fought a futile battle to prevent evacuation at the onset of war, Seattle's Christians embarked on a new crusade to ensure Japanese were treated fairly when they returned. It was a Christian's sacred duty. Nothing less than the soul of Seattle was at stake, Barnett said. Frank expected to get his home back eventually, but only God knew when. A hearing was scheduled for next month. Barnett was confident of a favorable ruling, but made no promises.

Meanwhile they were making due at the Hunt. Frank, his sister, Toyome, and their parents, Sanjiro and Toyo, shared a one-time classroom with three other families on the second floor. Makeshift curtains, merely blankets and drapes strung from the ceiling, offered a modicum of privacy in a living space that was twenty-five by forty feet. They lived out of suitcases and boxes. They slept on military cots, cooked in a community kitchen on the first floor and dined in an adjoining cafeteria. The only light came from windows and a kerosene lamp. A coal stove provided heat. There was a small laundry on the first floor, and men's and women's bathrooms on both floors. A thriving garden provided a steady supply of fresh vegetables. Children played monopoly and gin rummy in the cafeteria and ran about in the playground. The situation was an improvement over Minidoka, but only because they were now in the comfortable confines of a city. They were no longer surrounded by barbed wire fences and armed guards in towers. It was crowded and inconvenient to say the least, but they settled into the rhythm of a daily routine. Frank and Sanjiro spent most days at the Tokyo. They opened in May after retrieving their cookware and supplies stored at the Japanese Congregational Church throughout the war. More Christian neighborliness.

The skies grew even brighter when Frank met Sakura. Her name translated to cherry blossom, and she was all of that. The Watanabe's were interned at Tule Lake in Northern California. It housed Japanese presumed to have posed a greater risk to national security. Mr. Watanabe owned a wholesale trading business. He traveled to Japan routinely, putting a target on his back. Frank sat on the front porch eating a sandwich the afternoon the Watanabe's arrived. He saw them trudging up Waller Street from King Street Station carrying suitcases. Sakura wore a dark winter coat, carrying a suitcase in each hand. She looked frazzled and a little scared. Frank thought her lovely immediately. The Sasaki's helped the Watanabe's get settled at the Hunt and Frank wasted no time getting to know their daughter. A month later, he was thoroughly smitten and the couple was inseparable. They went on long walks, picnicked in Volunteer Park and led outings for the Hunt children to Lake Washington, Woodland Park Zoo and the downtown waterfront.

Sakura stopped swinging and looked at Frank. "What about you? Is the Tokyo your future?"

"It's all I've ever known," he said. "It was a decent business until the war. It paid for our house. We had a good life." Frank's life centered around being the dutiful son. His parents cherished their culture but understood the realities of living in America. Knowing their citizenship wouldn't count for much, they encouraged their children to embrace the customs of their birth country without losing touch with Japanese culture. Calling him by his middle name was just the beginning. The family dined on sukiyaki one night, fried chicken with mashed potatoes the next. He enjoyed drinking green tea from a *yunomi* but preferred strong coffee from a mug. He excelled at jujitsu but loved baseball. The family partied on New Year's Eve but dined quietly together eating *osechi* on *Shogatsu*, the Japanese New Year. He admired the philosophy of Shintoism but worshipped and attended Sunday school at the Congregational Church. Eventually, the Japanese American transformed into an American whose parents happened to be Japanese. He loved America, its culture, its opportunities and its people. He embraced his Americanness. But the powers of revenge, fear and hate were swift and unrelenting. The wholesale disregard for his constitutional rights hurt. But the injustices heaped upon his family were the hardest to bear. The current struggle to regain their property– all of it – stripped away the veneer of acceptance. It left him naked, void of an identity, facing an unsure future.

The status of the family business underscored the precariousness of their situation. Since it reopened last month, customers trickled in, mostly regulars from before the war. Japantown was barely crawling back to life as a handful of businesses repaired the damage from vandalism and opened their doors. The Annex Hotel, Panama Drug, Main Street Grocery and the Higo Ten Cent Store were open but slow. The only thriving enterprise was the Toyo Club and Pool Hall on Maynard Street. Frank occasionally stopped there after work for a beer and a few games of eight ball. But even as shops opened, Frank suspected Japantown would never be the same. The small town where everyone knew everyone else was blown away like leaves in the winds of war. He remembered the energy that once gushed from its depths. He missed the hustle and bustle of shoppers and merchants scurrying about, delivery trucks blocking the streets, impatient motorists honking their horns. Squalling children once played kickball in the alley. The Tokyo once buzzed during lunch, its tables full, a line forming outside. Today, he saw only empty streets and empty tables. Was the Tokyo a lost cause, a fool's errand?

Sakura rose from the swing and stepped in front of Frank, interrupting his thoughts. She smiled at him. "Where have you been, Frank? Lost you for a minute."

"Sorry, I was thinking about your question about the future of the Tokyo. Honestly, I'm not sure any more."

She reached out and grasped the ropes of his swing and leaned in close, their lips inches apart. "I don't know either," she whispered. "I know you'll do the right thing, though. You're the best thing that's happened to me since this awful mess began. I want to be with you, Frank, to help you. We can figure this out together."

Together. He loved the sound of that. TO-GETH-ER. Three common syllables adding up to uncommon hope. The clouds of doubt and worry parted even farther. A future with Sakura seemed boundless. He could handle any hardship with her at his side. She leaned in close, her lips parting to kiss him – their first kiss. Frank dreamed about that kiss but doubted it would happen. Twice he tried to summon the courage to ask for a kiss but the words stuck in his throat. She smelled of lavender, her breath warm and inviting. Their lips just touched when a loud slamming of a door shattered the moment.

"Frank! It's Father! Something's happened to Father!"

Frank looked up to see Toyome at the top of the second floor staircase waving at him to hurry. He shot out of the swing, sprinted across the playground and bounded up the back stairs two at a time, Sakura rushing to keep up. He flung open the door and entered their living space. Sanjiro was on his back, unmoving, eyes closed. Frank knelt down beside Toyome to exam his father. His face turned a pasty grayish blue, sweat rolling down both cheeks. "I think he's having a heart attack," Frank said. "There's a doctor living on the first floor, Dr. Chihara, I think. Sakura, run and see if he's here. Hurry!"

Three minutes later, a short bespectacled man wearing gray trousers and a white shirt rushed in, He carried a small black bag. He set it on the floor and knelt next to Sanjiro. He felt the carotid artery to check Sanjiro's pulse. Nothing. "Help me turn him over," he ordered. With Frank's help, he turned Sanjiro onto his stomach. Dr. Chihara then moved around to kneel in front of Sanjiro's head. He then maneuvered his arms so the hands were under his head and his elbows sticking out like chicken wings. He began to perform the latest development in artificial respiration. He placed both hands on the patient's back and pushed down and forward firmly like he was using a rolling pin. He then grabbed both upper arms and pulled them up and towards him. Press back, lift arms, over and over, ten times a minute. Frank saw a demonstration of the Holger Nielson method in Boy Scouts but never thought he'd see it in real life. It wasn't widely used, he knew. Toyome wrapped her arms around Mother. Sakura clutched Frank's arm, hand over her mouth. Everyone cried as they watched the life-saving dance unfold. Press back, lift arms. After ten repetitions, the doctor stopped to check for a pulse. Nothing. He shook his head and resumed his revival efforts. After ten more attempts, he checked for a pulse a second time. Ten terrifying seconds later, Dr. Chihara looked up at Frank. His eyes said everything.

There's no use. I've done all I can. Residents on the first floor and children playing outside heard Mother's wails.

Chapter 22

"To everything there is a season,
a time for every matter under heaven;
a time to be born,
and a time to die . . ."

Pastor Hirayama from the Congregational Church read from the third verse of Ecclesiastes, but Toyo stopped listening. She'd heard the verse before and the words hurt, a sad reminder of the awful events of the past month. There is a time to die but not a place to die. Not a proper place. Not for Japanese.

Toyo sat in a brown folding chair adjacent to her husband's open coffin. A small group of family and friends gathered for Sanjiro Sasaki's burial at the cemetery in Auburn. They huddled under a canopy offering cover from the steady rain. Frank, Toyome and Aiko stood on either side of Toyo. Aiko took the train from Indiana. Fukashi remained in Tokyo, denied leave. On the other side of the open grave stood Sakura and her parents, several other Hunt residents, and Arthur Barnett and his wife, Virginia. Lawrence and Anna Louise heard about Sanjiro's passing and asked Frank if they could attend the services. Yes, of course, he said.

The insistent patter of rain on the canopy was almost deafening. A flock of crows pecked at the grass around them. The air smelled of cut grass and turned up dirt. Everyone stood with eyes closed and heads bowed as the minister read the closing stanza of the verse.

"A time to mourn,
and a time to dance;
a time to keep,
and a time to cast away."

Yes, cast away, Frank thought. Sanjiro was cast away. It began two days after his death when Toyo, Toyome and Frank rode the bus to the Lake View Cemetery on Fifteenth Avenue at the north end of Capitol Hill. A Mr. Schmidt, whose name tag read "Grief Counselor," greeted them in the front office. He was short, thin and wearing a gray suit with a dark red tie and matching pocket square. He didn't look happy to see the trio who had entered the reception area.

"Can I help you?" he asked flatly.

Frank introduced himself and his family. He explained that they wished to purchase a burial plot for their father who died that week. They also hoped to buy a second plot for his mother who wanted to lie next to her husband when she passed.

Schmidt looked at Toyo and Toyome and then back at Frank before responding. "I'm sorry, but we can't help you."

"Why's that?" Frank asked, suspecting the answer.

"I'm not allowed to. It's against the rules."

"What rule is that?" Frank asked, forcing Schmidt to give voice to the wrong.

The words curdled out of Schmidt's mouth, sour and distasteful. "The rule that says I can't sell plots to Japanese or anyone who is not white."

There it was, a final insult to Father in a life riddled with insults. Frank's face flushed but he did his best to conceal his anger. He heard Mother whimper behind him. "We can pay," Frank explained. "We have the money."

"Look, I can't help you without losing my job, but the cemetery in Auburn might. I'll give you their number." Frank looked at Schmidt, his face expressionless. *That's the best you can do, give me a phone number? Did they teach you that in grief counseling school? You know nothing about grief. You humiliate the bereaved. You're blind to their pain.*

"Auburn? That's at least thirty miles from here. How can we visit our Father when he's in Auburn?" Frank rode the bus to Auburn for a Garfield baseball game, ninety minutes each way.

They left with a curt thank you and returned to the Hunt. The following day, Frank called the cemeteries listed in the Seattle phonebook: Evergreen Washelli in North Seattle, Crown Hill in Ballard, Calvary in Laurelhurst, Mount Pleasant on Queen Anne Hill, Forest Lawn in West Seattle and three others in the south end. The calls started out pleasant enough until they asked for Frank's name. The woman's response at Washelli mirrored all the others. "Sorry but we don't sell plots to Japanese," she said and hung up. Restrictive covenants were everywhere, even for the dead. Funeral homes in King County enforced legally binding covenants regulating plot sales. Contracts guaranteed customers would lie next to whites only. The fact Father still lay in a refrigerated box at the morgue infuriated and shamed Frank. Was there no end to offense in this country? Would fighting for dignity and respect consume his life?

It took three weeks and Arthur Barnett threatening a lawsuit before the Auburn Cemetery agreed to sell the Sasaki's two plots in their international district, a euphemism for coloreds. Segregation was alive and well even for the dead. An incident at the cemetery five years earlier explained the company's reticence to sell to Japanese. Shortly after Pearl Harbor, vandals ravaged the international section. They urinated and spat on headstones with Japanese names. They toppled them over or smashed them with a sledge hammer, chunks of cement left scattered across the graves. Frank was relieved to see the headstones were at least righted. But signs of neglect and disrepair were everywhere. Headstones were tilted this way and that, grave markers covered with grass and weeds, lawns that hadn't seen a mower in weeks. Frank shook his head as he looked around. *What was Mother thinking about this? Just one more affront perched on a pile of insults. I hope she finds some peace here.*

Toyo stood and approached the coffin to say goodbye to her Sanjiro for the final time. She was thankful that he did not know about the latest offense in a lifetime of offenses in America. He came to this country in 1906 with hopes of working the gold and silver mines in Eastern Washington and Idaho. More sojourner than immigrant, he dreamed of making it rich in America and return to Japan. He planned to build a new life in his home in Kumamoto Prefecture on the western end of Kyushu Island. But the riches failed to materialize and the dream of returning to Japan faded. He did manage to find work at a coal mine in Cle Elum when white miners went on strike. But crossing picket lines proved hazardous. Yelling "go home scabs," strikers threw eggs and insults at the Japanese, Chinese and Negroes who just wanted a steady job and a living wage. They inhaled coal dust working hundreds of feet underground for two weeks. The fear of explosion or cave-in ever present. Sanjiro was relieved when mine operators settled with their white workers.

Sanjiro came to America when anti-Asian violence was at its worst since passage of the Chinese Exclusion Act of 1882. Designed to curb violence, the act inspired violence. In 1885 and 1886, city and business leaders in Tacoma and Seattle rousted hundreds of Chinese out of their homes and businesses. They forced them to board trains or ferries, and warned the "yellow bastards" never to return. In Seattle, a riot broke out and five white men were wounded and another killed when police attempted to stop the expulsion. The exclusionists made no distinction about ethnicity. Chinese, Japanese, Korean, Filipino, East Indian, it didn't matter. All Asians were mongoloids, creatures of a lesser biological order. Simply put, they were invading a land God intended for whites.

In spring 1908, Sanjiro signed on to pick strawberries and blueberries in Issaquah. That year, the United States and Japan entered into a "Gentlemen's Agreement" to slow migration and curb anti-Japanese violence. But no one told the pickers in Issaquah. Tensions erupted when farm operators placed the Asians in the better fields because they worked faster and cheaper than whites. Sanjiro was months into the job when white pickers stabbed two Japanese during the night and left them for dead in their tents. Sanjiro didn't like the feel of the place after that, or the fact he was paid less than whites, so he quit. He threw his satchel over his shoulder and walked seventeen miles to the ferry dock in Kirkland. He paid the ten-cent fare and rode the *Fortuna* passenger ferry across Lake Washington to the docks at the foot of Madison Street in Seattle.

He found lodging in Seattle's burgeoning Japantown. He shared a room in the Tokiwa boarding house with three other men for a dollar a week. He scraped together a living doing odd jobs for the salmon canning company, George T. Myers, at the foot of Dearborn Street. He loaded cases of salmon onto trucks. He hosed and swept the cannery floor at the end of the shift. He cleaned the monstrous Iron Chink, the automated fish butchering machine named after the thousands of Chinese who had for decades gutted and cut up the salmon by hand. He was told the Chink could prepare salmon for canning fifty times faster than butchering by hand. It put hordes of Chinese out of work. But the machine still needed operators. Within a year, Sanjiro earned seventy-five cents a day running the machine and helping Myers ship out a thousand cases of canned salmon per day, six days a week.

His break came when he struck up a friendship with a cannery worker, Asahi Takenaka. He ran a restaurant in Nagasaki and asked Sanjiro to partner with him in the restaurant business. It was little more than a hut set up on Jackson Street. They prepared boiled cod, fresh crab, dried salmon, clams and mussels purchased wholesale. They made a steady but meager business selling to immigrants looking for work and a bed. Sanjiro kept his job at the cannery and helped Asahi at night. Working twelve to fourteen hours a day, the partners eventually earned enough to lease a space on Yesler Avenue with a small kitchen and a few tables. They named it The Tokyo. Asahi and Sanjiro were now permanently entrenched in the restaurant business.

Piece by piece, Sanjiro built a life in America. The country he chose was beginning to fulfill its promise of opportunity. He enjoyed steady income at the cannery and shared in the growing profits of the Tokyo. He could afford his own room at the Tokiwa, played *chō-han* and drank sake with friends at the Jinai Club on Saturday nights. He attended Sunday services at the Congregational Church and thanked God for his many blessings. But there was a crab-pot-sized hole in his life. God had yet to bless him with a wife. It was the missing piece of an otherwise fulfilling life in America. Alone in his room at night he longed for the companionship of a woman. He needed someone to talk to, to caress, to deliver him a son. On a rainy evening in April 1912, Sanjiro wrote his parents. He didn't write often but he knew they enjoyed hearing from their only son. Mother pestered him in her letters about finding a wife but he held back. His life was too unsettled, prospects uncertain. He remembered a pretty girl from his village named Toyo Nakamura, the daughter of a baker. She must be of marital age by now. Was she unmarried? Would she make a proper wife? If her parents approved, would they send a picture?

"Mother, are you all right?" It was Toyome standing behind her. "Do you need more time with Father?"

Toyo wasn't sure how long she'd been standing over Sanjiro. She looked around at the family and friends gathered to say goodbye and share in her grief. She was surprised they were still there. They looked back at her silently, rivulets of rain pouring from the canopy. It was time to go. She reached into her purse and pulled out a white envelope. Inside was a small black-and-white photograph about two-by-three inches in size. It showed the signs of having been carried around for thirty-five years. It was bent and curled around the edges. White streaks ran across the image like cracks in an old mirror. A photographer her father hired took the photo. Toyo was framed by a *shoji* screen at the Nakamura's home in the village of Izumi. She sat on a *tatami*, a traditional Japanese mat with a diamond pattern. She sat erect, *seiza* style, legs folded under her thighs and resting on her heels, hands on her lap. She remembered the kimono she wore that day. Wrapped left side over right and secured with a sash or *obi*, it was deep blue with a flower pattern. A tea set, or *kyusu*, was placed in front of her. She looked into the camera, her long, layered black hair pinned up and wrapped into a bun. Her solemn expression, she couldn't make herself smile, hid the anxiety. She did not remember the man who asked for the photo but he must have remembered her. It felt like he was in the room, standing behind the camera, judging her. She was beautiful. She was elegant. She was sixteen years old.

After receiving the photo, Sanjiro wrote back immediately that he'd soon travel to Japan to meet and marry Toyo. She was one of thousands of picture brides who came to America early in the century. Marrying an American was a chance for a girl or young woman to fulfill the traditional obligation of marriage, as well as escape poverty. But the thought of marrying a stranger and moving across an ocean terrified Toyo. She knew the journey was fraught with risk. She heard stories about picture brides in America. Most did not speak or read

English. *How will I ever learn the strange language of Americans?* At least she'd met the man she'd committed her life to before marrying him. Most brides were shocked to see their new husbands were older and poorer than they were led to believe. Others ended up in abusive marriages. Many were abandoned and ended up in bath houses. Sanjiro wasn't much to look at, but he was far from unattractive. The rundown boarding house repelled her but his room was clean and tidy. She believed God had blessed her with good fortune.

A photograph is a snapshot in time. It captures a moment but reveals little about the people in the picture or events before or after that moment. Toyo held the photo out, her hand steady. *Anyone looking at the photo of me would know nothing about my story. That I married a stranger but grew to love a man with a kind heart. That I gave him four children who made him proud. That I worked side by side with him from my first day off the boat to provide for our children.* She understood the photo told none of those stories, yet it revealed a bigger story, Sanjiro's story. Slipped into the back of his billfold, he'd carried it with him everywhere. She looked at the scrap of photographic paper smaller than a playing card one last time. Sanjiro carried it with him throughout his life, and so it must be in death. She leaned down, kissed her husband on the forehead and placed the photograph over his heart.

Chapter 23

"That's not a proper football."

"Sure it is, why do you say that?"

Footballs are round. That one looks more like a rugby ball. It's shaped like an egg. Why do you call it a football?"

"It's an American football. What can I say?"

Ellie nudged her husband and smiled to show she was teasing. They were attending a game between the University of Washington Huskies and the Oregon State College Beavers at Husky Stadium. It was Ellie's first American football game. A neighbor was watching their son, John Jr. They were seated in the cheap seats, about ten rows up from the field behind the west endzone of the horseshoe shaped stadium. Some thirty-seven thousand fans braved the October rain and wind, many huddling under umbrellas or wearing rain slickers. John and Ellie, wearing light coats and hats, had neither.

The elements did not bother John. As he watched the Huskies work their way down the field in the game's opening drive, he was enjoying life as a free man. He'd been out for about two months, released early due to good behavior and to address over-crowding at the Washington State Reformatory in Monroe. *Some reformatory, John thought. I was lucky to have survived seventeen months in that hellhole. It was a prison not a reformatory.* John read about Monroe. It opened in 1910 as a social experiment in prison reform. Since Washington became a state in 1889, all felons were incarcerated at the prison in Walla Walla regardless of their age or the seriousness of their crime. Boys as young as sixteen, guilty of nothing more serious than stealing a car or petty burglary, were thrown in with hardened criminals. *How could anyone reform in such a breeding ground of perversion and corruption?* It was a travesty. Prison reform advocates designed the Reformatory as a more humane and constructive alternative to a state prison, but learned firsthand that there was none of that. For prisoners who presented no danger to the public, the Reformatory was, in theory, a social hospital. Felons were not inmates but patients needing treatment to address a disease, a social pathology. If unaddressed, the pathology would fester and get infected. Effective treatment consisted of daily doses of instruction in arts and sciences. They learned correct morals and to respect authority. But when the cell door slammed shut behind John in Spring 1946, the vision of creating a healthy environment for reform was nowhere to be seen. He was one in a population twenty-five hundred inmates. They were nothing more than a criminal mob barely held in check by overworked, underpaid and easily corrupted guards.

To men serving lengthy or life sentences for violent crimes, John was fresh meat. Young, slight of build and attractive, with a thick crop of dark wavy hair, he stood out like a beauty queen in a junk yard. Twice he'd been cornered by inmates who wanted a piece of him. He managed to escape unscathed the first time when a guard sensing trouble intervened. The second time he was not so lucky. Three months after arriving at Monroe, he was peeling potatoes in the kitchen for that night's dinner. He walked back to the storeroom for flour when three men jumped him from behind. They pushed him inside the storeroom, slammed the door and forced John to his knees.

"Don't make a fucking sound if you want to keep your teeth, Jacobson. Be nice and this will be over real quick. You never know, you might even like it." It was the inmate known as Smitty. John saw him in the yard and spotted him staring in the chow hall. Short, stocky and thick around the shoulders, Smitty stood in front of John. Large patches of sweat stained the underarms of his blue dungaree shirt. He was unshaven and smelled of cigarette smoke. John could see yellow teeth behind his lascivious smile. John had no intention of being nice and struggled to stand, but he was powerless to resist. The second man pinned John's arms behind his back while the third wrenched his head back by his hair. He struggled harder, almost toppling the third man before Smitty punched him viciously twice in the face. John's resistance evaporated. They forced him to the floor, pulled his dungarees down around his ankles and flipped him onto his stomach.

They took turns with him, then left him on the floor of the storeroom humiliated and alone.

"Touchdown!" John and the entire stadium stood and cheered as the Husky tight end took in a short pass from the quarterback and skittered ten yards around the right side of the OSC line for the game's first TD.

"What happened?" Ellie asked. The scoring play occurred at the far end of the stadium, and all she could see was a flurry of bodies slamming into one another, which wasn't even a proper scrum as far as she could tell. This strange American game was neither football nor rugby. Leave it to Americans to tinker with the perfect game, Ellie mused. She wasn't much of a sports fan but remembered going to an Arsenal FC game with her brother, Ronnie, when she was nine. Eating chips after the game, Ronnie and his friends joked about American football.

"It isn't proper football," Ronnie claimed. "I heard someone call it hand-egg."

"Hand-egg? Why do they call it hand-egg?" Ellie asked, puzzled.

"Because the wankers use their hands more than their feet and the ball looks like a bloody egg," he quipped, drawing a laugh.

Ellie, whose plaid skirt and light jacket offered scant protection from a blustery Saturday in Seattle, was cold and wet. Rain dripped off her hat. The green army blanket John draped across their laps kept her legs warm but it, too, was damp. But her discomfort and disinterest in the game did not dampen this day out with her husband. Between his job, school and caring for John Jr. they'd enjoyed little time together since his release. He worked nights as a janitor at the County City Building downtown. He attended classes at the U in the morning and slept much of the afternoon. On weekends his brother Luke and their friends came over and they'd party well into the night. His first weeks home were reassuring. After many months of fending for herself, she relished having her husband home. The problem was the parties and the booze. At first, John's need to celebrate his freedom was understandable. But two months out and the party roared on. She'd get up on Sunday morning to feed John Jr. only to find strangers passed out on their couch or curled up on the floor. The house stank of cigarette smoke and stale beer. John would wake up surly and sullen. They quarreled often. Ellie felt caught in a swirling current pulling her ever further from her husband.

The Husky's early lead didn't last long. The OSC tied it up in the second quarter, and the game was reduced to a succession of incomplete passes, fumbles and wobbly punts. It was a rain-soaked comedy of errors. Frustrated fans began to boo the home team. Others, cold and bored with sloppy play, began streaming out of the stadium. John was enjoying his first game in years. With the score knotted at seven in the fourth quarter, he wasn't going anywhere.

"Hold on to the damn ball," he yelled after the Husky's fifth fumble of the day. Although frustrated with a close game that should have been a runaway, John kept it in perspective. Losing a football game cannot compare to losing your freedom. Fortune shined on him at the Reformatory. The attack in the storeroom, he couldn't call it what it was, rape, was the last. A week later, his fortunes turned when he met Carl Becker, a reported Communist. Facing twenty to life for murder, Becker was tall, rail thin and about fifty. He sat next to John at breakfast.

"Quite a shiner you got there, Jacobson," he said between bites of scrambled eggs. The swelling was better but both eyes were rimmed with patches of blue and yellow. Just three months into a possible twenty years sentence, depressed and scared, John wondered if he'd last another week.

What does this ass want?

"Looks like Smitty and his boys had quite a time with you," Becker said.

John looked into his coffee cup and didn't respond. He'd told no one but apparently the word spread anyway. *I can't talk about this with an another inmate. Are there no secrets in this dammed shithole? Is my humiliation the gossip of the day?*

"Look, John, can I call you John? Forget those assholes. They're not worth the scraps on my plate. Take my word for it, you'll have no more trouble with that bunch. I'm wondering if you'd be interested in helping me with a little project?

John looked up from his coffee but again said nothing. He wondered if Becker was a homosexual.

Sensing John's apprehension, Becker smiled, revealing straight white teeth, and offered his assurances. "Don't worry, John, you're not my type. I like big tits and a fat ass so there's nothing to fear from me." John looked him in the eye and seemed to relax, so Becker pressed on. "I see you reading in the library a lot. You're always carrying a book around." Becker was right, John spent as much time as possible in the library, reading anything he could find on psychology and sociology and a lot of fiction. He liked to read the Seattle newspapers.

"I also know," Becker continued, "that you got canned for picketing for the Teamsters in Seattle. I admire that. Consider me your brother in arms."

"How do you know about that?" John asked, speaking for the first time.

"I pay for information. I know a lot about what goes on around here and who walks through the front gate."

John learned later that Becker was not a typical down-on-his-luck inmate. When he arrived at Monroe, he had a five-figure bank account and spent freely for information and protection. Several of the guards were in Becker's pocket. Smitty and his gang would no longer bother John.

"What kind of project are you talking about?" John asked, not sure he wanted to know.

"I expect to get out of here in a few years, and I plan to pick up where I left off. I plan to build a presence for the CP in Washington state. Right now, I'm building a cell, uh . . . discussion group. I'd like you to join."

"I'm not a Communist," John said emphatically.

"That's okay, you don't have to be. Continue your reading. Take part in our discussions and make up your own mind. You're a smart guy, you'll figure it out. That's why I want you to join us. No strings attached." With that he handed John a small book, picked up his tray and left.

John picked up the book without looking at it and returned to his cell. His cellmate Rod, an auto mechanic doing a nickel for burglary, wasn't there. John sat on his bunk and inspected the volume in his hand. A mere thirty pages long, it was more pamphlet than book. The faded red cover was worn and ripped along the edges. The loose binding suggested it could fall apart any minute, pages slipping to the floor. The pages themselves were yellowed and slightly curled. Someone underlined entire paragraphs in pencil. He closed the book and looked again at the cover. In old English script the title read *The Manifesto of the Communist Party* by Karl Marx and Friedrich Engels.

"For Christ's sake," John yelled as the crowd's boos and groans rained down on the field. The score was knotted at seven deep into the fourth quarter. After another fruitless drive, the Huskies punted from deep in their end zone. An OSC lineman blocked the kick, scooped up the ball and ran it back for the go-ahead score.

Ellie was bored with the game she didn't understand but thankful she sat next to her husband. For nearly two years she'd been alone, dependent on John's family for support. The Jacobsons were good people but their strict Christian ways and devotion to the church overwhelmed Ellie. She remembered the first time she attended services at the Assembly of God Church in Ballard with John's family soon after arriving in America. Harold led the services and introduced his daughter-in-law to the congregation. Compared to the Anglican Church, where the Walkers were infrequent attendees, this American church was, in Ellie's, mind barmy. It was worlds apart from the sedate, ritualistic services of the Church of England. Was this how all Americans worshiped? They prayed and sang, and prayed and sang some more, each time with hands raised in unison, waving back and forth like tall grass in a brisk wind. An elderly woman in front began babbling nonsense. Ellie learned later it was called speaking in tongues in a language only God understood. A puzzled Ellie took her lead from John, who seemed disinterested and didn't join in the devotions. He'd rejected his parent's faith and quit going to church after leaving home, he said. The topic of religion seldom came up when they dated. He said he attended that day only for Ellie's benefit. After the services, Margaret introduced Ellie to other parishioners. Their restrained greetings suggested they believed the public perception about war brides. They were loose women intent on sinking their hooks into gullible American boys.

John and much of the crowd stood and headed for the exits.

"Did we lose? Is it over?" Ellie asked.

"It might as well be," John said in exasperation. "Let's go."

Chapter 24

Three weeks later, the marital whirlpool that held Ellie in its tow threatened to pull her under when John hit her. It was Sunday morning following another weekend of parties at their rented house in Union Bay Village. The village, built by the University of Washington for married vets, addressed the postwar housing shortage for students. Sterile white prefab houses with six hundred square feet of living space were originally occupied by workers at the Hanford Engineer Works and the Naval Shipyards in Bremerton. They were brought in by barge or truck and hauled to the muddy landfill north of Husky Stadium. By 1947, more than four hundred homes, including duplexes and four-plexes, covered twelve square blocks adjacent to the upscale Laurelhurst neighborhood. The Jacobson's paid $35 a month for two small bedrooms, bath, tiny kitchen and living room. The homes, crammed so close together, wives could hang their laundry on a line stretched from one house to the next.

The fight started much like most of their fights. John read while eating a simple breakfast of coffee and a slice of white bread doused with milk and sugar. John Jr., standing in his playpen with pacifier firmly in mouth, watched his mother clean. Ellie was on hands and knees trying to remove beer stains from the oval throw rug in the living room. She could hear car doors slamming and kid's playing in their neighbor's postage-stamp yard. All was quiet inside, disguising the waves of tension that wafted through the home.

"There's another cigarette burn in the carpet, John. Can't your friends smoke without practically burning the place down? That's why we have ashtrays." John looked up briefly but said nothing and returned to his reading. She stopped cleaning and looked at her husband, expecting him to respond. He sensed she was waiting for him to say something so he pushed his empty bowl next to an open bottle of milk. He put down the book and lit a Camel.

"What do you want me to say, Ellie? I didn't burn the rug."

"I don't want you to say anything. I'm just tired of cleaning up your damn mess."

"My mess? Why is it my mess? You were here too."

She was there but in body only. She didn't drink and nursed one beer before switching to coffee. She mostly sat at the kitchen table, smoking and making small talk with Angelina, a neighbor, whose daughter, Louise, was Junior's age. At one point it seemed the whole damn neighborhood was crammed into their small house. The room stank of beer and sweat. Cigarette smoke curled around the overhead lights and permeated every corner of the room. Benny Goodman played on their RCA Victor. The rapid-fire riffs of One O'clock Jump spilling onto the front porch and into the street. It was so loud Ellie feared someone would call the cops.

The excuse drummed up for this party was to sample the first batch of beer John and Luke brewed at home. They worked on it for weeks, mixing and boiling wort, hops, yeast and water, a syrupy sledge they transferred to large ceramic kegs to ferment. Two weeks later, they poured the stinking brew into brown bottles sealed with swing-top caps and let them sit for another two weeks. The whole thing made a big damn mess, Ellie thought. The kegs took up precious space in the kitchen. Bottles were stacked in the hall closet to keep them cool. John looked like a mad scientist scurrying around his lab discovering a cure for cancer. He paid more attention to his damn beer than his son, or me, Ellie thought. On Saturday they opened the first bottles and celebrated their success as home brewers. Ellie thought it tasted like sour apples. By two in the morning the crowd thinned but John, Luke and a few of the guys hung on. Ellie went to bed at eleven wondering when it would ever end.

The argument escalated throughout the morning, neither combatant giving ground. John sat at the kitchen table, his psychology text open in front of him. John Jr. sat in the high chair. Fair skinned, blue eyed and sporting a thick crop of wavy blonde hair, his Norwegian heritage was in full display. He played nervously with his Cheerios, sensing the tension between Mommy and Daddy. A barrage of complaints rolled around in Ellie's head as she banged about the house, opening and slamming cabinet doors, washing the dishes, dusting, and sweeping and mopping the floors. The more she cleaned the more pissed off she got. *I don't know how much more of this I can take. His drinking, his parties. He's never home. He works all night and in classes all day. When he is home, he's got his nose in some damn book. I waited for him all those months only to be shut out. I feel like I'm watching my husband's life through a picture window. I can see him but not reach him, not touch him.*

John remained mostly silent through all this but patience was giving way to anger. *Would she ever shut up? Did she have to bitch about every damn thing? Ellie seemed perpetually cross about one thing or another but this morning was too much. I'm trying to study, for crying out loud.*

John set down the book, removed his glasses and looked up at his wife. "Ellie! What. . . do. . . you. . .want?" he asked emphatically, punctuating each word, his temper rising.

She leaned the mop against the kitchen counter and looked at her husband. Junior stopped playing with his cereal. He looked at Mommy like he wanted to hear her answer too. "What I want is for you to listen to me," she pleaded. Junior looked back at Daddy waiting for his response, a Cheerio lodged on his lip.

"I've been listening all morning, but I'm clueless. What's this really about?"

"You're clueless alright. Do you think I'm blind? I saw you and Ginger in the hall last night. You think I don't know what's going on between you two? I see the way she looks at you."

There it was, out in the open, lying on the table like one of his books. Ginger was a friend of Luke's, single, attractive and difficult to resist.

"I don't know what you think you saw, but there's nothing going on between us," he lied.

Ignoring his protests, she stepped in closer, her face flush with anger. "Don't insult me with your lies. The whole neighborhood seems in on the joke, and I'm the last one to know? You show absolutely no interest in me but run after that hussy?" She was right about his disinterest in having sex with his wife. Weeks went by without sex. She was a passive lover, mostly going through the motions since the day they married. Their lovemaking, if you could call it that, fell into a predictable routine, more mechanical than lovable.

"I'll take it where I can get it," he said cruelly.

Ellie felt like her head was going to explode. She could feel her heart pounding through her apron. Spittle dripped down her chin as she screamed at her husband. "Get out of my house, you bastard! Get out!"

John stood and ran his fingers through his hair. He did not intend to hit her. He'd never hit a woman, but something in him snapped and he slapped her on the left side of her face. There are slaps and then there are slaps. This one was well timed and powerful. He'd put his weight into it as she leaned in. The force of the blow sent her flying into the kitchen table and on to her butt. John watched in horror as the table skittered into the high chair, knocking over the quart of milk. High chair and milk toppled in unison, hitting the floor with a sickening thud. The bottle ricocheted off the tray, clipped Junior's chin on the way down and covered him in cold milk.

The boy's wail echoed off the walls. Neighbors stopped what they were doing and looked up in alarm. Passersby halted in the streets. Neighborhood dogs barked out their warnings. The entire planet seemed to hear the boy's screams. Something ugly was happening at the Jacobson's.

"Oh my God!" Ellie screamed. John rushed to extract his son from the fallen chair. It took longer than it should have because he struggled to unbuckle the belt that held him in place. John cursed as the restraint intended to protect his son hindered his rescue. He finally managed to pull him up by his underarms. The milk covering Junior's face was mixed with tears and bubbles of snot. He choked as he strained to breathe between sobs. John inspected his head for any bleeding but saw none, thank God.

"Give him to me!" Ellie demanded and snatched him out of John's arms. She ran into the bedroom, the boy's screams trailing behind her.

An hour later, Ellie sat next to Junior's crib watching him sleep. He'd settled down after a few minutes, his cries reduced to a soft whimper before falling asleep. John left, slamming the door on his way out. She nervously chewed on her nails as she wondered what to do now. Her anger turned to resentment and contempt for the man she thought she loved. He was unrecognizable from the charming, handsome G.I. she'd met in Kensington Gardens more than two years ago. This needed to stop. She must do something. His cheating, his cruelty, his violence could not go unanswered. She wanted this son of a bitch out of her house. She sighed, appearing to make up her mind, and went to their bedroom closet. A half dozen pairs of slacks and long-sleeved shirts hung neatly from wire hangers. She pushed all the hangers together, and pulled them off the rod. She marched into the living room and out the front door. With a heave, she tossed the clothing, hangers and all, over the porch railing and onto the soggy grass of their small front yard. She then returned to the living room and began pulling books from the bookshelf they'd bought at the Salvation Army. These were John's books. The bastard was reading all the time. He especially loved his novels. *The Power and the Glory* by Graham Greene a birthday gift from Luke. Ellie gave him Hemingway's *For Whom the Bell Tolls* for Christmas. He'd talked at length about Carson McCullers's *The Heart is a Lonely Hunter*. That's my story, Ellie thought. It took three trips to empty the bookshelf and throw all of these treasures onto the pile of clothing.

Her neighbor, Angelina, saw Ellie from the kitchen window and rushed to the front porch. "Ellie, what the hell is going on?" The rain came down harder now so she went inside to put on a jacket. She returned in time to see Ellie on the porch. She carried a beer keg in each hand, struggling to manage the five-gallon ceramic containers.

"Ellie, what are you doing?" Angelina pleaded. Without saying a word, Ellie broke the seal on the kegs and began pouring the slushy brew over the books and clothes. Steam rose when it hit the drowning mess. She threw the empty kegs onto the pile and headed inside to get the remaining kegs. Angelina ran down the steps, grabbed Ellie's arm and spun her around. She saw a mix of anger, determination and sadness in her neighbor's eyes.

"Ellie, stop! What is this about? Talk to me."

"That son of a bitch cheated on me," she hissed. She pulled herself free and, without another word, yanked the thin gold band from her left hand and tossed it into the pile, its gilded shine incongruous in the soggy heap.

Ellie went inside, slamming the door behind her. Angelina looked down at the pile of John's belongings. The smell of beer offended her nostrils. She bent down, picked up the ring and returned to her house. The discarded heap of clothing, books and beer, the detritus of a failed marriage, laid there, exposed to the elements for all the world to see.

Chapter 25

John finally accepted the truth, one he'd denied since his wedding day. His marriage to Ellie was a colossal mistake. The beer saturated mess on his lawn confirmed that. He was working in the six-story County City Building on Third Avenue downtown, which housed the King County Courthouse and city administration. Tonight he was cleaning the fifth floor offices. He wore dark gray slacks and long-sleeved black shirt. The overhead lights cast the entire floor in bluish tint. He could hear the late-night traffic below on Third Avenue. He was alone with his thoughts as he worked his way from one office to the next emptying waste-paper baskets, vacuuming carpets, and mopping tiled floors.

Yes, the marriage was a mistake but not the biggest of his life. That one was in a class all by its own, for which he'd paid steeply. But that was in the past and his troubled marriage was in the now. He remembered standing next to Ellie at the altar of St. Luke's Parish in London. Serious doubts swam through his mind, threatening to spoil the day. He'd chalked it up to typical pre-marital jitters. Everyone goes through that, right? Never lacking in confidence, John believed he could make it work despite his serious misgivings.

It didn't. And it was his fault as much as hers. First cheating on his wife and then striking her were wrong. These were errors not to be repeated. He reluctantly admitted to himself the drinking and partying were getting out of hand. His studies suffered as a result. But the fact was he did not love his wife. He'd certainly been smitten by this young, beautiful, fun-loving Londoner. No doubt about that. But that lively Jilly was nowhere in sight today. The things that drew him to her were stripped away by the pressures of marriage, parenting and living alone in a foreign country. She became unpredictable, impossible to read. Loving and charming one minute, shrew-like the next. He thought he understood the risk of marrying the youngest of eleven children. She'd grown up with aging parents doting over the baby of the family. Her siblings, especially her brothers, gave in to her every demand. Let's face it, Ellie Walker was a spoiled brat accustomed to getting her way. So, yeah, she was a handful, but he began to believe something more troublesome was at work. When he rose from bed most mornings, he wondered which Ellie was waiting for him in the kitchen. Her moods were so volatile his rudimentary knowledge of psychology suggested she may suffer from mental illness, maybe schizophrenia. Given a choice, he could file for divorce and put her on the next plane to London. But he couldn't because they shared a son, John Jr., the only decent thing to come out of this marriage. So John senior was stuck. The point of no return was so far back he couldn't see it in the rearview mirror. He could not run from his responsibilities.

After finishing his duties, John rode the elevator to the second floor where a meeting of his union was underway. Building Service Employees International Local 6 represented window washers, janitors, elevator operators, parking attendants and just about anyone who worked to keep the city's buildings clean and operational. John entered the lunchroom to find five men seated at a table talking.

"Hey, Jacobson," take a seat." It was Stefano Ricci, their Local 6 rep in the County City Building. Everyone called him Stef. A big guy, muscular, who weighed two-fifty at least. A wide smile and kindly brown eyes betrayed his rough exterior. He'd been in Local 6 for a decade, as pro-labor as they came. He was well liked even for a suspected Communist. John nodded a greeting to his coworkers and sat at the end of the table.

"Negotiations with building owners are set for next week We're going to ask for a six percent raise, time and half for anything over forty hours and increased pension benefits," Ricci announced. The men nodded in agreement at the news.

"What makes you think we'll get that?" asked Mark Sanders, who John worked with a few times. "Those assholes are as tight as my pucker." The men chuckled at the sarcasm.

"Because they can afford it and we have leverage," Ricci countered. He held up a copy of *The Militant*, the radical labor newspaper out of New York. "Word out of the CIO is labor productivity, by that I mean *worker productivity,* has increased. Corporations can afford thirty percent or more." The head nodding grew more vigorous. Some wrapped knuckles on the table, others raised fists in salute.

"If they can afford thirty percent, six should be nothing," one man said.

"Here's the deal, boys. There's no free lunch," Ricci continued, pointing to the front page of *The Militant.* "Prices are going through the roof. Groceries are up thirty-four percent since the end of the war."

More nodding heads.

"It's not enough that you get screwed in the grocery store, they've also got you by the short ones at home. Your rent is headed in the wrong direction, boys. Congress is trying to raise the rent ceiling by fifteen percent or abolish controls altogether."

"Those asses can't do that!" Sanders said.

"Yes, they can," Ricci insisted loudly. "Without rent controls, millions of homeless veterans and workers in dire need of low-cost housing will be caught in the squeeze play." The men looked at each other questionably. Can you believe this? John could see Ricci gained their full attention now. Where was this going? Was he recruiting for the Party?

"We got to stand together, boys. When the shit comes down, and it almost certainly will, we must stand united. If they force our hand, we will . . ."

A thunderous slam of the cafeteria door stopped Ricci in mid-sentence. Everyone looked up to see three men storm into the room and march up to where the group was sitting. Two were dressed in business suits and ties, the third was a cop.

"What in the hell are you doing?" Ricci shouted. "This is an authorized union meeting. You have no business in here."

"This is not a union meeting. This is a meeting of the Communist Party, and I won't have it in this building." It was Lloyd Henderson, building superintendent. He was thin, bespectacled and stood about five-five. His gray wrinkled suit looked two sizes too big. He looked like a child standing next to Ricci, but he was not intimidated. He stepped in closer and looked the bigger man squarely in the eye. "You're all a bunch of damn Commies and you're all fired," he declared emphatically.

"These men are members of Local 6 of the Building Services Employees Union. They are not Communists," Ricci insisted. John noticed Ricci did not include himself in the statement. Did he inadvertently admit his membership in the CP?

The second man dressed in a suit, who John hadn't seen before, stepped behind Ricci and picked up *The Militant*. He held it up to for Henderson so see. Their exchanged looks said "what other proof do we need?"

"You can't fire us. We got a right to organize," Sanders spurted. He pushed his way to the front and confronted Henderson. The policeman stepped in and roughly pushed Sanders back with his night stick.

"Step back, boy, or you'll spend the night with the drunks and the whores," the cop promised.

John remained at the rear of the group to remain inconspicuous. With his prison record and still on parole, he couldn't afford to get arrested especially for being accused a Communist. He thought about his political discussions with Carl Becker in the Reformatory. He read the Communist Manifesto that Becker lent him. He found it enlightening but not life altering. Some of Marx's theories made sense, some didn't. John certainly accepted the reality of a perpetual conflict between the so-called Bourgeoisie and Proletariat, fancy names for the corporation and the worker. The battle between the rich and the poor, or the haves and the have nots, was an unassailable fact of life. He also believed corporations kept wages as low as possible to maximize profits. No secret there. His union activities were meant to address the inequality between working stiffs and their bosses.

He sat with Becker in the prison library. Hearing John's skepticism about Marx, he asked, "So where do you think Marx is off the mark?"

"It's his conclusion about the final outcome. I don't believe class conflict will eventually lead to some vast leveling. That everyone will share equally in the means of production and its profits like one big happy community. That all workers around the world will inevitably turn to communism."

Becker pressed further. "Why do you disagree with that?

"Because it's being tried as we speak and it's not working, Becker. As far as I can tell the Communist experiment in the Soviet Union has failed. Marx's great leveling is a myth. The only equality in the Soviet Union is everyone in the working class is equally poor. They don't control the means of production, the state does. Russia executed its Czars and replaced them with tyrants. They're dictators who control everything in a repressive state."

"If you're not a Communist then what are you?" Becker asked, unperturbed by his mentee's reasoning.

"Socialist maybe, I don't know. Not Communist. I've always considered myself a Roosevelt Democrat, a New Dealer. But I don't know anymore. You've helped me sort through that, but I've got more questions than answers."

"Let's go, Jacobson. Get your stuff and get out of here. You've been terminated," Henderson said. The other men headed for the door. The cop pressed his stick into John's back and nudged him forward. John knew it was useless to plead his case, to deny accusations regarding his political beliefs. He retrieved his jacket from the locker room, took the stairs down to street level. He exited through the service door and stepped into the night. He could see rain slicing under the streetlights. A brisk wind blew from the south. Third Avenue was nearly deserted in the pre-dawn hours. He saw no other pedestrians. He stuffed his hands into his jacket pockets, lowered his bare head to fend off the rain and briskly walked north on Third. He now feared his future was as ruined as his marriage.

Part 3 – 1948-49

Intolerance is itself a form of violence and an obstacle to the growth of a true democratic spirit.

Mahatma Gandhi

Chapter 26

Joanne's feet hurt, the black leather oxfords, seemingly a sensible choice for walking a picket line, cutting into her ankles. Her back ached even more. The sandwich board that read "Aeromechanics STRIKE" felt like dead weight on her shoulders.

"Scab! Scab! Scab!" picketers chanted through bullhorns, heckling strike breakers who managed to push through the front gate at Plant Two for the afternoon shift. Joanne didn't yell at them but believed they were nothing less than traitors to the cause.

And her head throbbed. A storm of conflicting emotions ricocheted around her skull. It started when the aeromechanics walked off the job two months earlier, The cost to her family and purse growing daily.

"No contract no work!" strikers yelled, directing their venom from strike breakers to a gaggle of suits gathered on the other side of the gate. "No contract no work!"

The picket line outside the main gate on East Marginal Way was a three-ring circus of union activity. The June sunshine and cool breeze were a welcomed relief from the persistent rain in the strike's first weeks. Dozens of picketers worked their way up and down the line. Older machinists, gray and grizzled, marched with grim determination. The younger men, with heads held high and fists pumping, strutted like peacocks, chanting enthusiastically. The women on the line looked empowered and ready for whatever came next. At the direction of union leadership, most donned skirts and high heels on "Sunday Best Day." Union leaders wanted the public to see the feminine side of working women. Joanne ignored the ban and wore pleated slacks and the stupid Oxfords.

One woman rode a tricycle up and down the line, looking decidedly unfeminine, her knees jutting out like coat hangers. A local merchant pulled up in a truck and unloaded cases of donated Coke. Earlier that day, a bakery delivered free donuts and coffee. A man standing on a flatbed truck yelled through the bullhorn, admonishing the dozen or so workers who braved crossing the line. Some made it through, others turned back out of fear or guilt. A union photographer snapped a picture of each defector to be posted on the "the dishonor wall" in the union hall. Newspaper reporters worked their way through the crowd asking questions, taking notes. A dozen uniformed police officers idled nearby, smoking and chatting, not expecting trouble. University of Washington students handed out "Work with Wallace" flyers. Former Vice President Henry Wallace, the darling of young voters, was the Socialists Party candidate in the 1948 presidential election and a fervent unionist.

Nearly eighteen thousand aeromechanics, machinists and their supervisors, the heart and soul of a company that was itself the heart and soul of Seattle, were in the third month of their strike. No settlement was in sight. Over the previous sixteen months the officers of aeromechanics District 751 bargained with Boeing negotiators for a raise of thirty-cents per hour. They demanded a more equitable system for employee promotion and retention and full recognition of their union. Negotiations were stalled on the runway. Boeing President William M. Allen played hardball. He offered a fifteen-cent raise but refused to negotiate with District 751. The strike was unauthorized and its leaders illegitimate, he claimed. Authorized or not, the work stoppage all but shut down production of Boeing's top-selling aircraft, the prized B50. It was the latest generation in long-range bombers, a major upgrade over the WW II workhorse B29.

The city's biggest company with the biggest payroll was likely to experience the biggest work stoppage, but it enjoyed plenty of company. Over the three-plus years following the war, strikes became almost a daily occurrence in and around Seattle. The front pages of the *Seattle P-I* and *Times* were replete with news about workers demanding increased pay, overtime pay, sick pay and paid vacations. Workers streaming into the city for jobs were driving up prices, especially after wartime rationing and price controls ended. Workers pounded on management's door demanding relief from the shrinking value of their paycheck amidst runaway inflation.

Joanne looked through the gate at the parking lot on the south side of Plant Two. She could see her husband's new maroon Plymouth Deluxe parked in the lot reserved for engineers. He'd given her the family Ford after being promoted to assistant chief engineer this year. Eleven hundred engineers voted not to join the strike, a severe blow to the mechanics.

You can engineer for a month of Sundays but you can't build them without mechanics, Joanne thought to herself. When she decided to honor the strike in April, and support her fellow mechanics, George shook his head and looked her in the eye, not masking his displeasure. They sat at the kitchen table after dinner, the dirty plates and glasses not yet cleared. George nursed a beer while Joanne poked at the remains of her baked potato. Danny was in his room doing homework. Natalie, now a freshman at the University of Washington, lived in a campus dorm.

"Don't give me that look, George. What do you expect me to do, force myself through the line while my friends call me a scab? You did what you had to do, how am I any different?"

"It's a lot different," he said without looking up.

"How so, why is it any different?"

"Because you can't win, that's why," he said, his voice rising, looking at her now. "You're going against the biggest employer in the city, and worse the Department of Defense. The Communists are raising hell all around the world and tensions are running high in the company. Our national security is at stake to say nothing of hundreds of millions in contracts."

Joanne stood and began clearing the table. "Those seem like pretty good reasons for them to negotiate. It's the leverage we need."

"You have no leverage," he countered, more irritated now. "Allen is not going to give in to your demands. You'll be banging your head against a brick wall. He won't move off his offer of a fifteen-cent raise, I promise you that."

Joanne looked at her husband, waited, knew there was more to come.

George drained the beer and set the bottle on the table. "I just don't think it's right. Boeing is a good company. It pays the highest wages in the industry. You're asking for too much. If this drags on for too long all you'll manage to do is lose the jobs. The company has already moved some operations to the Wichita plant. Workers there seem pretty happy with what they got. What's to prevent the company from packing up the entire assembly plant and moving to Kansas? Believe me, they'll be welcomed with open arms."

Joanne knew the risk. They'd endlessly debated the pros and cons at the union hall. But when all was said and done, members voted overwhelmingly to walk out. She couldn't, she wouldn't, go against that.

"Joanne, look it's the railroad!" It was Dorinda, the bucker. She'd stood by her side throughout the strike. Joanne looked up to see several picketers running towards the tracks that paralleled East Marginal Way and entered Plant Two from the south. It was the regularly scheduled delivery of aircraft fuel. The Milwaukee Railroad was pulling several tank cars, each holding thousands of gallons of high-octane fuel.

"There's our leverage, George. No fuel no fly," she said as she scrambled after Dorinda towards the tracks. By the time she arrived, twenty or so picketers were blocking the tracks. They waved their strike signs in protest, yelling at the train to stop. Joanne stood back from the throng but could see the train about a mile out, already slowing. Suddenly the whine of the train's whistle assaulted her ears. It was unlike any whistle she'd ever heard. Insistent, relentless, ear-piercing. It screamed at them to clear the tracks. "Get out of the way," it demanded. Soon the screech of the train's brakes joined in, a crescendo of steam and smoke and steel-against-steel rolling right at them.

Joanne looked triumphantly as the train came to a full stop about twenty-five yards in front of the picketers. The heat from the engine rolled over them like an August wind on the farm. Up close it seemed hopelessly big and ominous to Joanne. The front of the engine was rounded and black. The single headlamp at the center stared at her like a giant cyclops. She could hear it breathe. The fuel tankers looked like enormous beer barrels laid on their side, black cylindrical monsters ready to swallow them whole.

"Clear the tracks! Clear the tracks!" Joanne turned to see several police officers with batons in hand running in their direction. They held their sticks with both hands chest high and began pushing the strikers off the tracks. "Let's go! Let's go! Get off the tracks!" Most of the strikers quickly gave way but three refused to move. They sat cross legged on the tracks, locking arms. She didn't know the two men. The third was Dorinda. Back straight, head held high, the picture of determination and grit.

"Get off the tracks now or you'll be arrested!" a police officer yelled.

The threesome didn't move.

"This is your last warning. Get off the tracks now!"

The threesome didn't move.

Joanne hurried in and grabbed Dorinda by the arm. "Get up, Dorinda! You can't afford to get arrested. You've got Web to think about. Who's going to care for him if you're locked up?" Dorinda looked up at Joanne, uncertainty edged into her face.

"It's not worth the risk, get up. Please!" Joanne pleaded. The police hesitated, waiting to see how this played out. Arresting a woman, especially a colored one, created too many complications.

Dorinda looked up for a long moment, unsure what to do. She finally nodded, stood and let her friend lead her away.

The remaining men locked their arms tighter and stayed put. Two officers began swinging their batons, landing blows to the arms and shoulder. They pried the men apart, forcing them face down into the gravel between the rails. They handcuffed them behind their backs "You're under arrest for failing to obey a lawful order from the police," an officer barked.

The cop's words faded as the reality of the situation hit Joanne like a bucket of cold water. The real source of authority was now abundantly clear, and it wasn't the Union. Leverage came from armed men swinging clubs. It belonged to people who held the power to sweep in and remove any obstacle in their way. How long until they're all swept away like so much litter in the street? As the police escorted the prisoners to a waiting squad car, her belief in the righteousness of their cause began to cloud. The hope that she'd carried around like her sandwich board started to curdle and shrink inside Joanne. In its place rose an emotion with which she was all too familiar, self-doubt.

Chapter 27

“If you're a Socialist, you're a Communist. If you're a liberal, you're a Communist. If you're a Democrat, you're a Communist. If you're a labor activist, you are without question a Communist.”

John Jacobson listened to the speaker with interest. He knew all too well the propensity to slap the Communist sticker on anyone whose politics fell left of center. Rousted out of his jobs at Rainier Beer and the County-City Building John needed no more proof. A Communist is anyone who fights for a fair wage.

He'd enrolled in the class at the Pacific Northwest Labor School at the base of Queen Anne Hill. The school was a joint effort among Seattle's many labor unions to develop a new generation of leaders. His union, the Building Services Employees, helped him land a new job in the University District. Seeing his promise as a leader they invited him to enroll and paid his tuition. All the students attended the school at the behest of their unions. He was in month two of the weekly classes learning a great deal about labor organizing. They studied public speaking, economics and political science. Having been fired unfairly from two jobs for his activism, he believed he could help the movement. So did the others in the class. Joanne, an attractive middle aged woman sitting to his left, belonged to the aeromechanic's union. She currently spent her days on the picket line. Sitting to his right was Lawrence, the Negro bus driver. His union, the Street Electrical Railway and Motor Coach Employees, just settled with Seattle Transit. As far as he could tell, they were not Communists, nor were any of the other students.

“If I sound cynical, let me assure you I am profoundly serious,” the speaker continued. “George Bernard Shaw wrote that 'the power of accurate observation is commonly called cynicism by those who have not got it.'" John knew the speaker, Professor Ralph Gundlach. He taught psychology at the university. Tall, lean and in his mid-forties, he sported dark, receding hair and a broad face framed by rimless glasses. He'd taught at the university for nearly twenty years. John, majoring in psychology, took two of his classes and found the professor's passion and teaching style invigorating.

"Today, you don't have to look too hard to find people of authority who observe too little and condemn too much," Gundlach said. "The legislature in Olympia, the media, even my university, see Communists in every corner." He looked around the classroom, making eye contact with each student. "They see Red before they see reason. They fear what they don't understand, remember that. The world around them is changing, and if conservatives fear anything it's change."

The changes, of course, were the unsettling political events worldwide. The Soviet Union, America's ally in the war, was now an adversary. Under the dictatorship of Joseph Stalin, the Soviets became obsessed with security on their western borders. They rolled their tanks across Eastern Europe. Czechoslovakia, Hungary, Poland and the Baltic nations were under the thumb of Soviet control. Tensions in Germany continued to mount in the second year of the Berlin Airlift. America's humanitarian actions won the hearts of East Germans but embarrassed the Soviets. It was a topsy-turvy world where allies became enemies and enemies became allies. On the other side of the globe, Communists, led by Mao Zedong, waged a brutal revolution against the American-backed government of Chiang Kai-shek. It appeared the United States would soon "lose" China. These events only served to fuel fears Communists were hell-bent on world domination. That included dismantling capitalism and a democratic government in America. In response, the American right believed the Reds must be eradicated from every corner of the country.

Nowhere was red baiting more evident than with the Washington State Legislature's formation of the Fact-Finding Committee on Un-American Activities in 1946. Albert Canwell, a first-term Republican representative from Spokane, was chair. His committee was charged with rooting out Communists from the Washington Pension Union and various labor organizations. The WPU was one of the first old-age savings programs in the United States. Numerous reports claimed Commies now controlled the agency. During a raucous week of testimony in January at the Field Artillery Armory at the foot of Queen Anne Hill, Canwell's prosecutors grilled dozens of witnesses and suspected Communists. Each was asked the deadly question "Are you now or have you ever been a member of the Communist Party?" Protestors inside the Armory continuously disrupted the questioning, shouting "Witch hunt! Witch hunt!" The state patrol did not hesitate to show them the door. Outside, dozens of protestors paraded up and down Harrison Street carrying signs and chanting "Abolish the Canwell Committee."

The most shocking accusation during the hearings pointed directly at the University of Washington. Reports claimed without evidence that no less than one-hundred-and-fifty faculty members were Communists. That revelation led to a call for a second set of hearings in July focused solely on the presence of Communists on campus. Eleven UW professors, including Gundlach, received subpoenas to testify about their Communist ties. Most had agreed to appear, but not Gundlach.

"Professor Gundlach, if you're not a Communist why did you refuse to testify and clear your name?" John asked.

The professor looked directly at John. "First, you will be pleased to hear that I have changed my mind and agreed to testify. I will release a statement to that effect soon. My initial refusal was based on the fact the committee isn't interested in finding subversive activities. They're firing a shotgun at liberal and progressive teachers. They care little about inventiveness and new ideas. They want conformity, not creativity."

"So, you'll deny being a Communist?" Joanne asked.

"You're asking the wrong question, Mrs. Novak. At issue is whether they even have the right to ask the question. Where in the Bill of Rights or Constitution does it say that any of us can or cannot belong to any political party? We all have a constitutional right to make those choices. The question is a violation of those rights. I won't be a part of it."

"Okay but I'd think you'd want to go on the record denying it," she insisted.

"What good would that do? In today's toxic atmosphere, a Communist is someone who denies being a Communist. How do you combat that? How do you prove a negative?"

Joanne fell silent, understanding the dilemma, unsure how to respond.

"Class, let's see if we can debunk some of the myths surrounding socialism and communism. Who can tell me the difference?"

Joanne, whose political awareness blossomed throughout the Boeing strike, raised her hand. "In communism there is no such thing as private property. The state and the community share all property evenly. Under socialism individuals still own property."

"A Communist is anyone who joins the NAACP," Lawrence declared, drawing a laugh from the class. He'd joined the organization just last month. Leaders advised him of the risks of labor activism. Communists would assuredly come calling. They believed Negroes were justified in rejecting democracy. Why support a system of government that doesn't support you? They may be right about that, Lawrence thought, but he wanted no part of it. In spite of its faults he wouldn't turn his back on a country he'd fought to protect.

Other students warmed to the effort, joining the discussion.

"Communists use force against the upper and middle classes in order to redistribute the wealth."

"Socialists hold elections and use the democratic process," said a student wearing coveralls and work boots.

"Socialists reward individual effort," said another.

"Communist countries are run by dictators. Leaders in Socialist countries are elected democratically."

"Social programs like Social Security can work in a capitalist system."

"Socialism is less militaristic than communism."

"Communists are atheists."

Professor Gundlach smiled and raised his hand to end the defense of socialism, pleased with the response. They've been listening the last few weeks, he thought.

"Thank you for that. Let's hear from others now." He pointed to a man sitting in the last row of desks who had yet to speak up. He looked to be about thirty-five. He wore pleated black slacks and a short-sleeved gray shirt revealing well-defined biceps. He looked military.

"Welcome to our class, sir. didn't get your name."

The man hesitated like he needed to think about it. "Smith. Bob Smith."

Alarm bells clanged in John's head as everyone turned to look at the man in back.

"To which union do you belong, sir?" the Professor asked.

The man said nothing.

"So you're not in a union. Then your employer must be nonunion and you're here to learn about the many benefits of representation."

The man sat motionless and silent, hands clasped on the desktop, eyes boring into Gundlach.

Gundlach nodded, took off his glasses and began cleaning them with his necktie, The tension in the room palpable. John's hair tingled, his underarms damp. The professor returned the glasses to his face and stepped around the podium. He seemed to have reached a decision.

"Class, we're most fortunate tonight. We have a special guest. This man who has blessed us with his presence is not named Bob Smith, and he's certainly no hourly wage earner. He's none other than Mr. Paul Fischer, special agent in the Seattle headquarters of the Federal Bureau of Investigation."

Fischer sat straight up in his chair, looking directly at Gundlach. Everyone turned in their chair to look closer at this intruder. The only sound in the room came from John's pounding heart. Joanne wrote

Fischer's name in her notebook. She wondered whether she should tell George about this.

"I want to thank you for coming to our humble school but I'm a little disappointed by your performance, Mr. Fischer. I would have expected a more creative nom de plume than Smith. They don't teach that in Surveillance 101 at the academy?"

This was classic Gundlach, John observed. His bluntness, his confrontational, take-no-prisoners style and his progressive politics landed him crosswise with the university's administration. It jeopardized his tenure status. On top of that, he's now facing possible dismissal for his suspected affiliation with the Communist Party. John admired the prof's courage. Wondered if he'd do the same.

"More to the point," Gundlach continued, "it's a bit of an overkill don't you think? You've already installed wiretaps in my home and office. You've recruited students to spy on my classes. Seems like you'll go to any length to implicate me and my colleagues in your witch hunt. Aren't you getting what you want from those intrusions of my privacy? Are you not satisfied with violating the Fourth Amendment rights of a Constitution you claim to hold so dear?"

John heard about the student accused of spying for the FBI earlier this year. The guy jumped out of a second-floor dorm window to keep from getting his butt whipped.

Fischer heard all he needed to hear. He stood, gathered up his notebook and papers and headed for the door. Ignoring Gundlach, he turned and surveyed the students. "I don't know anything about you people. But I know a Communist Front when I see one. Your so-called labor school is nothing more than a subversive organization working for the American Communist Party. You folks don't know the ruthlessness of the people you're associating with. They want nothing less than for Stalin and his puppets to take over America." With that, he left the classroom, the door banging loudly behind him.

Chapter 28

Joanne eased her Ford into the driveway at their Capitol Hill home following the bizarre ending of class at the labor school. The incident disturbed her. Was she now a target of the FBI, a suspected subversive? That's the price for her activism, she concluded. She worried more about Professor Gundlach, clearly in the sights of authorities. A good man and effective teacher, he didn't deserve persecution. She'd attended a half dozen of his lectures. Not once did he encourage anyone to join the Communist Party. Granted he was a leftist but his lectures were balanced. He criticized the shortcomings of capitalism, but he'd been equally critical about the Communists Party. Its authoritarian policies and persecution of political dissidents were counterproductive and cruel. She chatted after class with the UW student, John, and the bus driver Lawrence, and they all agreed to help defend Professor Gundlach during the upcoming hearings. "Solidarity," they said in unison.

Joanne sensed trouble before she closed the front door. She hung her jacket on the coatrack and walked to the kitchen. A sense of dread rose in her throat. George sat at one end of the kitchen table, Natalie at the other. Her daughter often came home on weekends if for no other reason than for her Mom to do her laundry.

"Did you know about this?" George demanded immediately, holding up a single piece of paper.

"He went through my notebook!" Natalie protested. "*My* notebook! He can't do that."

"It was sticking out. It looked curious. Besides I have a right to know what my daughter is doing at a school I'm paying for," John retorted.

"You don't have a right to go through my things, Dad," she said angrily.

Joanne placed her purse on the sideboard and sat in the chair between her husband and daughter, a go-between of sorts. Dirty dishes from the chicken dinner she'd prepared before leaving for class were stacked in the sink. She considered pouring a drink but thought better of it. Best keep a clear head. She reached out to take the flyer from George but he snatched it away and began to read.

"Greetings from the American Youth for Democracy and the Communist Party." He stopped reading and gave Joanne a can-you-believe-this look. He continued reading slowly, punctuating each word. "Today's youth are faced with a grave international crisis." Another look from George. "American world domination is actively preparing for World War III against the Soviet Union! Americans who fought bravely in the war to crush Fascism are now threatened on a battlefield of a reactionary cause. Join AYD today and contribute to our struggle against the menace of a new world war." He stopped reading and flung the paper in Joanne's direction. It skittered off the table and floated to the floor.

"This is the crap she's learning in school now? Is this what I'm paying for?"

"I'm not going to join the Communist Party, Dad, okay?" Natalie insisted. "Some guy was handing them out on University Avenue. He wasn't even on campus. I just shoved it in my notebook and . . ."

"I don't want this poison in my house," George declared angrily, interrupting his daughter in mid-sentence.

Joanne watched the exchange but said nothing, and gave Natalie a look of sympathy. "Natalie, why don't you go to your room and let your Dad and me sort this out." Joanne watched Natalie head up the stairs and turned back to George.

"What's this about, George? Why get so upset about a little political propaganda handed out in the street? You know what's going on. This stuff is everywhere today even in Sunday mass." Father Everett expounded on the evils of communism just last week. Quoting from a letter from Pope Pius XII in Rome, he claimed "Communists were preying on unsuspecting Christians who were more comfortable wearing a dunce cap than a thinking cap." He called socialism and communism nothing more than a "phantom led by henchmen working to divide and confuse people with sinister propaganda." It struck Joanne as a bit overwrought.

"I think you've been listening to Father Everett too much. Don't you think Natalie is smart enough to know nonsense when she sees it, to make good decisions?"

"I'm not sure what she's capable of. I'm not sure I even know her any more, not since she went to that colored school."

Here we go again, Joanne thought, the high school argument reborn. After giving birth to Michael, Natalie didn't want to return to Holy Names. Dismissing George's protestations, she entered nearby Garfield. It isn't a "colored" school, although many of the students were either Negro or Asian. Actually, Joanne was pleased. Natalie seemed to thrive in an atmosphere less structured than a girl's Catholic school. It was rough going after giving up her baby, a now thriving two year old who called Natalie "Aunt Nattie." The family frequently visited Enumclaw on weekends to see her parents and family, especially Michael. Natalie enjoyed the time she spent with her son, but often left depressed, sometimes for a day or two. In spite of all that, she'd maintained an A average for two years and earned a scholarship from the UW. She hoped to enter the pre-med program after her freshman year. But Garfield changed Natalie. The racial mix of students and faculty exposed her to the inequities heaped on Negroes and others. She'd made friends and joined in campaigns for fair housing and equal employment opportunity. She volunteered for the Henry Wallace presidential campaign and spent Saturdays handing out "I'm wild for Wallace" buttons. To Joanne's delight and George's frustration, their daughter matured into a full-fledged liberal determined to right society's many wrongs. God bless her, Joanne thought.

"Natalie isn't your little girl anymore. She's an adult capable of making her own decisions. You need to give her space. I enjoy having her home on weekends but she'll stop coming if you keep on her like this."

Ignoring the admonition, George pointed at his wife. "This is your fault, you know."

Joanne looked at her husband, said nothing. She knew where this was going. Everything was her fault, of course, from letting Natalie get pregnant to the Communist takeover of America.

"It's not enough that while I'm working my wife is outside the company gate blocking railroads from delivering oil, or screaming "scab!" at any one who wants nothing more than to do their job." Joanne screamed at no one but workers who cross a picket line should expect a dose of public ridicule, she believed.

"If that weren't enough, you take our children to the picket line? What if a fight broke out? Radicals have been known to bomb picket lines, you know. What's the matter with you?" Joanne indeed took Natalie and Danny to the picket line last month for what the papers tabbed "Stroller Day." The labor radical Clara Fraser organized the event to show solidarity among Boeing women. It was fun and certainly not dangerous. Dozens of Moms pushing strollers and children of all ages spent the afternoon singing Joe Hill tunes and lunching on sandwiches, cookies and coke.

"Natalie told me she admired that woman, Fraser, a Red if I ever saw one. That's where she's getting these crazy ideas. I want you to keep our daughter clear of that one."

Clara Fraser, an assembly line electrician at Boeing, was a known Communist but God that woman made sense, Joanne believed. Keenly intelligent and articulate, she boldly expressed her political views. They talked for over an hour last week as they worked their way up and down the line. It was a perfect Northwest afternoon, mothers chattering away, kids running back and forth. Drivers on Marginal Way honked their horns in support. At one point, Clara stopped and turned to Joanne. "Why are you here, Joanne?" What's in it for you?"

Joanne hesitated, thinking about the question.

"You've got your nice house, lovely children and a husband with a good job. His paycheck is certainly bigger than yours. You're going to get a raise of some sort when this is over and you can go back to pounding rivets. What difference will the fifteen or twenty cents make to you? What's important here?"

Joanne thought about that question a lot. The truth was simple. It was about more than a raise, much more. It was never about the money, at least not for her. It was about dignity. It was for Dorinda and Anita and all the women forced to pinch every penny. It was for divorced women barely getting by. It was for all women fighting for independence and recognition. As much as it caused cracks in her marriage, she was in this to the end and would not desert coworkers and friends. Clara called women the most endangered species on the planet. Colored women, older women, divorced and married women. Prostitutes, domestics, all working women. They were all sisters in solidarity, Clara believed.

"And now you're going to this God damn labor school," George said, interrupting her thoughts.

"The FBI was there tonight," she said calmly, looking her husband in the eye. She decided earlier not to tell him about tonight's event to avoid another argument, but that train left the station.

George threw his hands in the air. "For God's sake, what's next?"

"They're after Professor Gundlach. He's the target. They think he's a Communist, some sort of subversive, planning to overthrow the government. I don't know. It doesn't make any sense."

"So you were there. The FBI knows who you are. That's just what we need."

"I've done nothing to draw fire from the FBI, and won't, I promise."

"You don't have to," he said emphatically. "That's the point. You get painted with that red brush there's no washing it off."

"Well that may be but nothing is going to change. I've accepted the fact you may be right about hitting that brick wall at Boeing. The trouble on the tracks was a huge wakeup call. But I'm in this to the end, George. The strike, the labor school, everything. I owe it to the girls, to myself."

George nodded, but said nothing, resigned to the fact he was married to a woman he no longer understood. He stood and headed up stairs to bed without so much as a goodnight or their routine kiss on the cheek.

As she watched him trudge slowly up the stairs, Joanne decided to have that drink after all. She pulled a glass from the cupboard, opened the refrigerator's icebox and pulled out the aluminum ice tray. It was frosted and cold, but held only one cube. George didn't bother to refill it. So much for the drink, she thought. She added the tray to the stack of dirty dishes in the sink. She sighed, put on an apron, and filled the wash basin with hot soapy water. She began washing the dishes from a dinner she'd prepared but didn't eat.

Chapter 29

"Ethiopian? Why would you think I was Ethiopian?"

"I don't know. All you people look alike to me."

Lawrence let the racial stereotyping slide for now. He wanted to understand what this man was saying. Some of his friends wore the colorful dashiki shirts to affirm their African roots. Lawrence, on the other hand, wore a dark blue suit, white shirt and a narrow red tie, hardly African attire. "Okay, but why Ethiopian?" he asked again.

"A letter from the Capitol Hill Community Club said we couldn't sell or rent to Ethiopians." The man was about fifty, short, balding and carrying thirty pounds too many. Eye glasses with heavy black frames and thick lenses hung over a bulbous nose. Lawrence thought he resembled a near-sighted Humpty Dumpty.

"Can I please see this letter?" Lawrence asked. The man nodded, closed the door and left Lawrence alone on the front porch. He was volunteering for Christian Friends for Racial Equality, one of several civic groups dedicated to combating racial discrimination and segregation in Seattle. Founded in 1942, Friends was run mostly by wealthy and middle-class white women. It attacked the practice of racial exclusion mostly through the courts.

It went against everything he believed, but Lawrence finally gave up his quest for a decent home. Anna Louise pleaded with him to stop. "How much more abuse are you gonna take, Lawrence?" she asked. Mom and Pop often joined in the chorus. He'd resisted for months, unsure what to do. For weeks he sat up late, alone, drinking cheap port, ruminating about where things turned south. He finally admitted the obvious. His dream sank to the bottom of Lake Washington. *Fuck it. You can't beat whitey at his own game. He's been screwing colored people for 200 years and getting away with it. Nothing is gonna change.* Resigned to living in the CD, he moved his family out of his parent's home and rented a two-bedroom affair on East Cherry.

A month later, Christian Friends Chairwoman Madeleine Morehouse Brake called. She heard about his troubles. Would he join Friends in their campaign to end restrictive covenants? He raised the issue with Anna Louise that night. She was against it. She knew where it was headed. She'd seen her husband hurt far too much. Lawrence listened to his wife. He understood her fears, but he couldn't say no. This could change things for the better.

With Morehouse running interference, they researched real estate records at the Seattle and King County recorder's offices. Lawrence sat next to Frank Sasaki, the Japanese fellow he'd helped at his family's restaurant in Japantown some months ago. Christian Friends recruited him to help undo the covenants at cemeteries. The office wasn't much bigger than a walk-in closet. It felt stuffy and smelled like mothballs. They sat on opposite sides of a table stacked with boxes packed with plat maps and property deeds.

"It looks like most of these covenants go back a long ways," Lawrence said, holding up a stack of deeds. "The first Seattle ones were written about the time Negroes started moving here."

Frank looked across the table and frowned. "Guess whose signature that is," he said . "That's none other than Bill Boeing." He walked to the other side of the table to exam the documents more closely. "His name is all over the place. Look at this." He lined the deeds side by side and stabbed at each one. "Richmond Beach. Richmond Heights. Innis Arden. Blue Ridge. Shoreview. These are all new developments. Whites only need apply. We can thank Seattle's favorite son for this." He plopped down in a chair and threw his hands in the air.

Keeping undesirables out of older neighborhoods like Capitol Hill required more creativity. Alarmed, homeowners took steps to keep the growing population of blacks in the CD. Hundreds of homeowners living in a 90-square-block area of Capitol Hill signed covenants in the presence of a notary. The legally binding document required current and all future owners to sell to whites only.

"I see why Friends is all over this," Lawrence said. "These covenants were good for only twenty years. They're all about to expire. Shit, we've got to get on top of this." The two men looked at one another, understanding the urgency of their mission.. A week later, Lawrence was one of several volunteers knocking on doors asking homeowners to sign a pledge not to renew the soon-to-expire covenants. Frank would focus on cemetery owners.

Lawrence looked around Federal Avenue as he waited for the homeowner to return. Maple and birch trees lined both sides of the street. The two-story houses with manicured lawns and lush shrubbery spoke of affluence. He'd already knocked on a half dozen doors, getting mostly curt refusals or vague commitments to think about it. Mr. Weinstein, a jeweler of Jewish descent, signed the petition eagerly. He said he personally experienced discrimination and wanted no part of the community club's campaign. As the sun beat on Lawrence's back he regretted wearing a suit, but he knew a colored man walking through a white neighborhood better look his best. A boy on a bicycle rode slowly north, throwing rolled-up newspapers onto front yards. A woman across the street pruned rhododendrons lining her front walk. Humpty Dumpty, whose real name was Edwin Schneider, was the registered owner of this house according to the county registrar's office.

Schneider opened the door and proffered a piece of paper with the Capitol Hill Community Club letterhead. "Look, it says right here," Schneider said, pointing to the second paragraph, "No Ethiopians."

Lawrence took the letter and began to read. The ugly words jumped off the page. "Persons not of the White race, including Ethiopians, Hebrews, Malays and persons of Asiatic extraction, shall not be permitted to occupy any portion of this lot except as a domestic servant." Lawrence surmised Ethiopians meant Negro, while Hebrews were Jews, and Asiatic extraction meant anyone from the continent of Asia. He wasn't sure what a Malay was. He'd have to look it up later. Apparently Negroes were tolerated only if they did the laundry and changed beds for their employers.

"Do you think this is right, Mr. Schneider?"

"I didn't do this. This was my parent's house. They signed it back in '27."

"I understand," Lawrence replied, "but that agreement is about to expire. The community club wants you to agree to an extension. Their plan is to continue violating people's constitutional rights. But it's your choice. They can't make you sign anything."

Schneider looked down at the "Welcome" doormat outside the front door, the irony of the message lost on him. Clearly uncomfortable with the conversation, he mumbled "I guess people are afraid their home will lose value."

Lawrence reached into his brown leather satchel and pulled out a three-paneled brochure. "Here, Mr. Schneider, read this. It explains the myths about what happens when coloreds move into a neighborhood. The fear is it will go to pot because homeowners will sell in a panic at prices below the value of their property. Pretty soon their neighbors feel like they gotta sell too, driving down prices even more."

"This house is all I have. I'm a bookkeeper making a buck ten an hour with no retirement. This house is paid for. It's my retirement."

"Read the brochure, Mr. Schneider. It shows statistics from several major American cities. There's no evidence of panic selling, white flight to the suburbs or depressed values."

Schneider held the brochure in his stubby fingers and scanned it for a minute, squinting at the small print. Sweat ran down his forehead as his eyes shifted back and forth from Lawrence to the brochure. Lawrence remained silent, sensing Schneider was at a turning point.

"Well okay. You seem like a decent guy and frankly I'm not comfortable with this whole whites-only business. Where do I sign?"

After getting Schneider's signature he continued working his way north on Federal. No one answered his knocks at the next two houses. He rang the doorbell at the third. It was another two-story, painted light green and well kept. Rose bushes lined the front yard. Two wooden armchairs and a small table took up most of the space on the front porch. An American flag hung limply from its pole. The front door was the kind with a large rectangular panel of etched glass set in a wood frame. Lawrence rang the bell a second time. He was about to give up when he heard footsteps from behind.

"What do you want, boy?"

Lawrence turned to see a man who apparently walked around from the back. He looked hard at Lawrence, unsmiling. He was tall, solidly built and about thirty. He wore gray cords and a sleeveless white undershirt. Multiple tattoos covered both arms, and he held a pump-action shotgun.

Chapter 30

Frank wondered if the droning would ever stop. Two hours into this meeting and nothing settled. He was in the offices of Christian Friends located in the Arcade Building downtown. They were meeting with cemetery operators to discuss the cemetery covenants. It started well enough but since evolved into a cacophony of whining about legal obligations, lawsuits and grave shortages. He tried not to clench his jaws, and ignored the churning in his stomach. Clouds of cigarette smoke irritated his eyes.

"You need to look at it from our customers' point of view," claimed John Cooper, attorney for the Washington Cemetery Association. The group represented the dozen or so cemeteries in and around the city. "First, as you can appreciate, we've been dealing with an acute grave shortage since the war. Second, our customers purchased gravesites under the assumption loved ones would rest in peace among their own kind. We have a legal and moral obligation to honor those wishes."

Moral obligation? Frank's jaw tightened.

Several cemetery operators including Harold Pyle of Washelli agreed to the meeting. Madeleine Morehouse Brake organized the meet. Andrew DeBow from the NAACP, and Dorothy Stimson Bullitt a philanthropist and business woman who owned KING Radio were there as well. Well known and respected, Bullitt proved to be a serious business woman and devoted advocate of oppressed peoples. Like her name suggested, Bullitt was not to be toyed with.

"We appreciate your commitment to your customers, Mr. Cooper, but we are committed to a higher cause," responded Brake. "Christian Friends just wrapped up a study revealing the sad truth about the whites-only policies of cemetery operators."

With that, she handed out copies of the study. "Nearly all cemeteries in this area refuse to sell plots to nonwhites. That makes it nearly impossible for them to bury lost family members with any sense of decorum." She held up her copy of the study. "To cite just a few recent cases, we have documented evidence that many Japanese families waited up to a month to bury family members. In another case, a colored woman was refused the purchase of a plot next to her white husband." She then pointed at Frank. "We invited Mr. Sasaki today because he can speak personally to the injustices heaped upon his family. What should have been a time of mourning for the Sasaki's was soiled by ignorance and exclusion. It was unchristian and nothing less than a wholesale disregard for the rights of others."

Frank wondered if anyone in the room could hear his stomach rumbling. *I doubt any of these so called gentlemen and Christians have any morals. They're committed only to the unmoral pursuit of making money.*

"Are you questioning my Christian values, Mrs. Brake?" Cooper asked. "I am as God-fearing as any man in this room. Our position remains unchanged. Nonwhites are claiming rights they never had. These property restrictions are no different than long-standing zoning restrictions in King County neighborhoods and all around the country. We have residential zones and we have commercial zones. Now we have white zones in cemeteries. Owners have a right to preserve the value of what's theirs, be it a home or a grave."

"Your argument is ludicrous and bordering on cruel. Property owners or cemetery owners don't have the right to deny rights to others," Brake countered.

"Are you advocating that we strive to achieve some utopian equality, Mrs. Brake?," his patience waning. "That sounds communistic to me. We live in a democracy and a capitalist economy. Discrimination is as much a part of nature as the law of gravity. Forced social equality, as you progressives seem to favor, is a form of tyranny."

Frank's teeth hurt from clenching his jaw while listening to Cooper's asinine argument. *His position was more than unchristian. It was uncivilized and unintelligent. Thank God for Christian Friends.*

He was more than grateful for the string of good deeds. They helped him renew his faith in God and America. They'd worked tirelessly on behalf of Japanese. They played hardball with the building owner who didn't want to renew the lease on their restaurant. They got a judge's order to evict the war workers squatting in the family home. After living in the Hunt Hotel for months, the family rejoiced at the news. Frank remembers Mother in tears when she saw the unkempt yard, dirty floors and messy kitchen of their home.

"I'm beginning to wonder why you agreed to this meeting if you remain steadfast in your position, Mr. Cooper," Brake said.

"The problem is that our hands are tied, Mrs. Brake. I can't knowingly violate legal agreements with our customers. Thousands of families signed contracts that forbid us to sell to coloreds. I can't change that without running the risk of dozens even hundreds of lawsuits."

"You know as well as I do, Mr. Cooper, that the Supreme Court ruled that racial restrictive covenants are no longer enforceable," countered Brake. "They violate the equal protection clause of the Fourteenth Amendment."

"I know what the liberal Roosevelt judges in Washington ruled. Now let them enforce it," Cooper responded sharply.

Frank and the entire Japanese and Negro communities initially cheered the news about the case *Shelley v Kraemer*. For once, the highest court in the land came down on the side of the righteous. Finally, families could live where they wanted or bury their dead at a cemetery of their choosing. The justices spoke and now justice would prevail, at least that's what Frank initially believed. But Arthur cautioned him not to expect immediate compliance with the court's ruling. The river of fear and prejudice ran deep in America.

"Do not expect property owners or cemetery operators to suddenly see the light and open their gates to all with a collective hallelujah," he said. "It will take months even years before we see any meaningful change." Arthur was probably right about that, Frank thought, but this meeting was an attempt to begin dredging that river.

"I think Washelli has a solution to our problem," announced Pyle abruptly. He was pushing sixty but his trim build, dark wavy hair and high cheekbones made him look closer to forty. Sitting fully upright, he folded his hands and rested them on the table. Looking around the room, waiting for everyone's attention, he spoke slowly and soothingly like guiding a grieving family through the agonizing decision of purchasing the perfect coffin for grandma. "Tomorrow, Washelli plans to issue a press release announcing the expansion of our property to include an international section reserved solely for our colored and Oriental customers." With that, he sat back triumphantly, smiling broadly at this perfect solution. What else was there to say?

The other funeral home operators nodded enthusiastically or clapped softly, affirming what was obviously a perfectly reasonable solution. Each made a mental note to take the idea back to their boards of directors. Thanks to their desire for fairness, these coloreds, these interlopers, may soon have the privilege of purchasing plots in the city's finest cemeteries without disturbing the tranquility of white plot owners. Ingenious.

A man seated at the far end of the conference table cleared his throat and stood. It was DeBow from the NAACP. If Pyle was a youngish sixty, DeBow was a grizzled forty. His dark skin was blotched with darker lines under both eyes. His ample waist and prominent chest and shoulders strained the buttons of his white shirt. Earlier he removed his suitcoat revealing sweat stains under both arms. His gravelly voice contrasted sharply with Pyle's velvety tone.

"I congratulate you, sir, on presenting what on the surface appears to offer an equitable resolution to our dilemma," DeBow said. "But before you strain the muscles in your arms patting yourself on the back may I offer an alternative point of view?" The funeral operators nodded grimly. Okay if you must, their looks said.

Making air quotes with both hands, he asked "How is this 'international section' any different from the status quo? Is it not, sir, just another form of exclusion disguised as a solution? Can it be anything other than segregation clothed in accommodation? Shall we now have whites-only sections in cemeteries like whites-only sections in our city? Where is the equity in that?" The funeral home operators shifted in their chairs, shuffled papers or stared into empty coffee cups. None offered a response.

"You're asking some very fair questions, Mr. DeBow" Dorothy Bullitt offered. She stood and waved away a cloud of cigarette smoke. "I for one consider Mr. Pyle's idea of an international section as a half step at best, one that may worsen rather than solve our problem." Her well-cut, dark blue dress, pearl necklace and perfectly quaffed short black hair radiated wealth and power. In her mid-fifties, Bullitt was the daughter of the lumber magnate C.D. Stimson who reportedly owned half the forestland in Washington. Last year she bought a small AM radio station with the call letters KEVR and immediately changed them to KING after King County, an early sign of her marketing acumen.

"I propose we adjourn for now and meet again next month. That should give everyone time to reconsider their positions. "Mr. Pyle, please make sure my news people get a copy of your press release, and we'll give it airtime. But rest assured I will devote even more time to telling a less flattering story if I don't see some movement on this. I'm sure the good people of Seattle would be shocked to learn their fellow citizens must endure the indignity and humiliation of being unable to bury their dead."

Bullitt's admonition brought an end to the discussion and everyone stood and gathered their belongings, preparing to leave, except Frank. *Don't just sit here, Sasaki. Say something. These gentlemen need to hear the truth. Make them understand your pain.*

"Excuse me," he said. When no one looked up he raised his voice. "Excuse me," he repeated more loudly. Those headed for the door stopped and turned. Others set their briefcases on the conference table and looked at Frank. Mrs. Bullitt, who was about to stand, returned to her chair. "Do you have something to add, Frank?" she asked.

Frank looked around the room seeing mostly puzzled expressions. "My father always coached me to show patience. *Shō ga nai*, he preached. It is what it is. Accept your fate. He certainly practiced what he preached. He accepted without complaint a lifetime of being treated as an outsider in this country, scorned, even feared. His only sin was working all his life to build a reputable business and raise four children. Many of his fellow immigrants gave up on America and returned to Japan, but Father stayed. Eventually he grew to love this country even though it did not love him. He taught his children to love America, too, and was proud we were American citizens."

Frank took a deep breath, stood and perched his fingertips on the table like a pianist at his keyboard. "But a lifetime of being treated like a second-class citizen did not end with his passing. I watched him take his last breath lying on the floor of a school house we were forced to live in for months because our home was occupied by strangers. I embraced my mother as the life drained from the only man she ever loved." He stopped to make eye contact with the funeral home operators. "I'm sure most of you have known the pain and grief of death. But you turn a blind eye on the grief of others." He pointed to a man standing closest to the door, owner of the Lake View Cemetery on Capitol Hill. "You, sir, refused to bury my father. You, sir, make my mother ride the bus to the Auburn Cemetery every week to visit her husband even though your cemetery is a ten-minute drive from our home. Auburn has a so-called international section, too, but I'd bet my last dollar none of you would want to be interred there."

Frank stopped speaking for a moment, trying to cap his emotions. This mountain of ignorance wasn't going to vanish with one meeting. Speaking more softly, he said "Mother has to carry her gardening sheers and trowel on the bus so she can cut back the grass and weeds around my father's headstone because no one bothers to attend to it. The rest of this so-called international section suffers from the same neglect. So don't talk to me about your moral obligation to your customers. It's laughable and insulting, and I will never forgive the hurt you caused our family." With that, he thanked Mrs. Brake for leading the meeting, picked up his notebook and walked out of the room.

Chapter 31

The man gripped the barrel of the rifle in his right hand with the butt nestled into his right hip, pointing the barrel upward at a forty-five degree angle. Lawrence recognized the weapon. It was a Remington semi-automatic shotgun, powerful and deadly. He'd seen firsthand the damage it could do from ten yards. To demonstrate the danger of the weapon to his son, his neighbor, Eddie, fired it into a watermelon perched on a log in his backyard. The boy screamed and Lawrence jumped with the ear-splitting report that resembled his carrier's ten-inch guns. The watermelon exploded into a million pieces. It sent red pulp, seeds and rind flying in every direction. It was a terrifying demonstration of what a high-velocity shell traveling at one thousand feet per second can do to a human body from close range.

"I'm going to ask you again," the man said. "Why are you on my property?"

Lawrence considered the man holding a gun on him. *This cowboy thinks he's Randolph Scott in a Zane Gray western. He's holding the weapon up at 45-degrees. He's all show and no dough. Stay calm, this isn't the first time someone's pointed a gun at you.* Lawrence was confronted by some angry Hawaiians when he accidentally ventured into the wrong neighborhood in Honolulu. But that was war and this was now. He needed to deescalate the situation.

Lawrence continued to assess the man who he now thought of as Randolph. He sported multiple tattoos on both arms. The largest was a bald eagle perched on a globe emboldened with the letters U.S.M.C. "You Jarhead, huh," Lawrence predicted.

The man grunted in affirmation.

"I was a Swabbie. Pacific. Carriers."

With that, the man seemed to relax but held the shotgun in place.

"Do you have something against Negroes," Lawrence asked.

"Not if they behave themselves," he said

Another white man who likes only good Negroes Stay in line and you'll be fine. "Look, I want no trouble and I'm happy to leave. I volunteer for a Christian group, that's all. We're talking to all the homeowners in this neighborhood. I rang your doorbell but you didn't answer."

The man looked Lawrence over, seeming just now to notice his professional appearance. "What do you want to talk to homeowners about?"

"It's about their property deeds But obviously this isn't a good time so why don't I come back later."

"No, I want to hear about the deeds."

"Okay, but first put that gun down, man. I'm unarmed and not a threat to you or anyone else in this neighborhood."

Randolph set the butt on the ground and held the end of the barrel in his right hand like a sentry at his post. Lawrence wondered if there was a shell in the chamber but he wasn't about to ask. He just wanted to get the hell out of there. *Let's give Randolph just enough information to verify my credentials.* He reached into his satchel and handed over a copy of the brochure. He began a truncated version of his pitch when he heard a car pull up in front of the house. Both men turned to see a black and white squad car brake to a halt. A second squad car pulled up seconds later. Four uniformed officers climbed out of their cars, slammed the doors and walked toward the yard.

As four cops descended upon him, Lawrence thought he was in the movie *Naked City*. He and Anna Louise saw the murder mystery just last week. *Shit, first some jarhead cowboy gets in my face, and now four of the city's so-called finest are about to ruin what had been a pretty good day.*

"Did you call the cops?" Lawrence asked Randolph.

"Wasn't me."

Lawrence looked across the street. The woman he saw pruning flowers was now watching the proceedings from behind her front gate. Must have been her, he thought.

The approaching officers hesitated when they saw the shotgun. "Drop that weapon, now!" ordered an officer wearing sergeant stripes. Randolph complied immediately, slowly lowering the shotgun to the faded lawn. The officer picked up the shotgun, opened the action and checked the chamber for shells.

"It's empty he said," handing the gun to his partner.

"What's going on here?" the Sergeant asked.

Lawrence immediately launched into his version of events. "Well, Sergeant, I rang the front doorbell and was waiting for someone to answer when Randolph here came around from the back carrying that shotgun."

The former Marine looked questionably at Lawrence.

"Why the gun?" the Sergeant asked

"We don't get a lot of coloreds around here. He looked kind of suspicious to me. Who called the cops?"

"Somebody reported seeing a colored prowler," he answered.

There's that colored thing again, Lawrence thought. Not just a prowler but a colored prowler. The adjective followed him everywhere. Colored war hero, colored bus driver, colored father. The newspapers were the worst. A colored driver caused a three-car pileup on Aurora. A colored man robbed a Piggly Wiggly. Christian Friends lobbied the papers with little success to drop the color designation when it wasn't relevant to the story. The only relevant question – and he knew the answer -- would Mrs. Busy Body have called the cops on a white man? He knew the answer to that.

"Sergeant, please let me explain. I am a volunteer for a nonprofit organization, Christian Friends for Racial Equality. Maybe you've heard of them? We're canvassing Capitol Hill neighborhoods regarding the homeowners' deeds. I've been working this block all morning until Randolph . . ."

"Why are you calling me Randolph? My name's Merlin. Merlin Shaw."

Lawrence knew that of course, his last name, anyway. The deed is registered to a Mr. Virgil Shaw. Merlin must be his son.

"Okay, we got the picture," the Sergeant said. He pointed at Lawrence. "You got what you wanted, now why don't you go home where you belong."

These cops are pressing all my buttons today, Lawrence thought. *One more person of authority telling me where I belong. I can hear Anna Louise now. "You know your stubbornness leads to nothing but trouble, Lawrence. Take a deep breath and walk away." Sorry, Anna Louise. I can't let this go.*

"Where do you think I belong, Sergeant?"

"Not here," he responded tersely.

"See that's just what Friends is trying to change. We do belong here. We have a right to be here as much as anyone else. To own a home here. To send our children to schools here," he said with growing indignation. "I've got a plan, sergeant. If you're so intent on keeping coloreds out of these neighborhoods, why don't you just build a wall around the CD so none of us can get out?"

"I'm not going to argue with you, boy. You don't have the right to be prowling around in people's yards."

Lawrence looked back at the sergeant in disbelief. Boy? *Prowling? This guy is determined to piss me off.* He stepped closer to the police sergeant. "Do I look like a boy to you? You address Randolph here as Mr. Shaw, but I'm a boy? I'm nobody's boy, especially yours."

The Sergeant was about to draw his baton when a dark Plymouth screeched to a halt in front of the Shaw home. A woman who looked to be about sixty climbed out and walked up the sidewalk. She was wearing a dark gray suit, the skirt covering her knees, the broad-shouldered jacket cut at the waist. It was Edith Steinmetz, Christian Friends cofounder and board member. A devout Christian and fervent civil rights advocate, she built a reputation as a Baptist missionary in the Philippines. She taught the principles of democracy to Filipinos based on the Bible and the Constitution. Lawrence knew her to be all business but kind. As he watched her trudge towards the house he saw that a small crowd gathered on the sidewalk.

"What's the problem here, Sergeant?" Steinmetz asked.

"Who are you?" he responded. "This is police business."

"I'm a member of the board for Christian Friends for Racial Equality." She handed him a business card. "Mr. Williams is one of our most devoted volunteers. He's here on our behalf."

"Leave the guy alone! He's only doing his job," a woman yelled from the street. It was Mrs. Gundy, who eagerly signed the petition minutes ago.

"He has every right to be here," yelled a woman pushing a stroller.

A man walking a Scottish Terrier chimed in. "Do your job and go after criminals. Quit harassing innocent people," he shouted. Everyone in the crowd nodded in agreement. The dog barked in affirmation.

Joanne Novak, who lived on the other side of Federal Avenue, stepped outside to pick up the her paper and saw the commotion at the Shaw house. Two police cars, red lights blinking, spelled trouble. *Has Virgil had another heart attack*? She dropped the paper, walked briskly across the street and pushed through the growing crowd. She saw four officers, and elderly white woman, Merlin and a colored man gathered in the front yard. She immediately recognized Lawrence Williams from the Labor School. He'd told her about the canvassing project.

The sergeant saw a woman walking up the driveway. She wore green knee-length shorts and a white blouse. Her dark hair was tied up in a bun. "Ma'am, everything is okay here. You need to go back to the street." The woman appeared to have not heard his instructions and kept walking toward them.

"Officer, I know this man. We attend the same school. I also know Merlin." She then saw the shotgun lying on the yard and sensed immediately what must have happened. Merlin was a hot head since high school and even after he left the Marines. Lawrence made eye contact with Joanne and mouthed "Thank you."

The Sergeant contemplated his next move. He examined Steinmetz's business card as if it held the code to unlocking the box in which he now found himself. He'd been on the force for almost twenty years. He'd dealt with every conceivable circumstance, faced off against the city's lowest and never backed down. But he was also a pragmatist and knew when he held a losing hand. First this Jewess and now a nosey neighbor. He looked at the two women confronting him. It was time to let this go.

"Okay, Mrs. Steinmetz. You and your *devoted* volunteer can go. Maybe the next time you canvas a neighborhood, you should give us a heads up so incidences like this don't happen."

Joanne followed Steinmetz and Lawrence out of the yard. She looked at her friend appraisingly. He lives with constant disapproval, she thought. Well, I know what's that like. "Lawrence, why don't you come over. We can have some ice tea and I'll sign your papers."

Chapter 32

Albert Canwell saw the world in red and white and today he saw only red. The man currently giving testimony confirmed his worst fears. Communists were everywhere, subversive and insidious.

"The first objective of the Communist Party in the United States is to undermine the loyalty of American youth," the man declared from the witness chair. "They get them to question American traditions and our form of government. It's the first stage of a long-term plan to destroy American democracy. It's nothing less than an immoral, intellectual Pearl Harbor."

"Lying Fascist!" yelled a young man standing in the aisle near the rear of the auditorium.

Canwell pounded his gavel three times, the thump of the mallet echoing loudly through the crowded auditorium. "Silence! I will have no protests in these hearings." He swept the mallet across the room like a pointer, warning the entire audience. "Any further outbursts and I will order the police to remove the offenders from these proceedings, forcibly if necessary."

This was the second set of hearings of the Un-American Activities Committee, or Canwell Committee. They were meant to ferret out Communists in both state government and colleges and universities. The first hearings led to the termination of the president of the Washington Pension Fund. This round targeted radicals at the University of Washington. Canwell was about forty years old, with hazel eyes and straight black hair parted on the left. He sported a soft Hollywood look. But his attire – gray pinstriped, double-breasted suit, dark tie and matching pocket square – was all politician. He sat in the center of long table on the stage overlooking the auditorium. With six committee members flanking him right and left, Chairman Canwell was very much in charge. He was both judge and jury.

The week-long hearings took place at the Seattle Field Armory, built in 1939 for the Army's 149th Artillery Command and National Guard. The basement included a shooting range and storage area for army tanks. But the main entrance on Harrison Street, full of streamlined curves and rounded corners, belied the military origins. Visitors entered through an art-deco style portico. Two huge ornamental concrete eagles framed the rounded corners of the opening. Inside, more than two hundred spectators crammed into the second floor auditorium. Witnesses subpoenaed to testify, University of Washington administrators and faculty, and a gaggle of news reporters scribbling in notebooks sat near the front. Uniformed Seattle police officers stood ready to pounce on the next protester. A large contingent of high school and college students elbowed their way into the auditorium to defend their university and teachers. Spectators filled every chair, jammed both aisles and overflowed into the lobby. Another hundred spectators gathered in a smaller room on the first floor listening to the testimony through a sound system installed for the hearings. The entire armory buzzed with murmurs of protest, objection and outrage. Another five hundred protestors blocked Harrison Street. They paraded back and forth, carrying picket signs and chanting "Abolish Canwell!" Everyone inside and outside the Armory were there to hear one thing. Could it possibly be true that the UW, the pride and joy of the city, was a breeding ground for communism? According to the papers, hundreds of professors were poisoning students with subversive propaganda, a disturbing revelation to say the least.

Canwell put down his gavel, sat back in his chair and scanned the crowd below him. Disturbances from the Commie lovers notwithstanding, he was pleased with the direction of the hearings. A first-term Representative from Spokane, he'd gotten elected as part of a Republican sweep of the state's off-year elections in 1946. He'd campaigned on the promise to ferret out the alarming number of Communists. They took root in state government, labor organizations and institutions of higher learning in Washington. He knew a Commie when he saw one. He spent much of his career spying on suspected subversives. He worked for the FBI. He took photos and planted bugs while working as a news reporter and later a police photographer.

He'd concluded years ago that Communists placed absolutely no value on human life except their own. Ruthless and determined, they'd kill anyone who disagreed with them. If you bought their propaganda, they'd exploit your services and say anything to achieve their ends. The individual meant absolutely nothing. It was all about the party. Actually, in Canwell's opinion, it wasn't a party at all but a fanatical religious organization. He made no distinctions between Nazism and communism. Between leftism and socialism. Democrats. liberals, progressives, they were all the same. As far as he was concerned, you could stuff all the misfits in a bag, shake it thoroughly, and you couldn't tell one from the other.

Now he held the power to put the lowlifes in their place and out of business. Reports varied as to how many were employed at the university, one hundred, two hundred, even five hundred. He didn't know and refused to play the numbers game. That was akin to counting the trees and not seeing the forest. Outside of New York, the Pacific Northwest and its defense industries were ground zero for a Communist takeover of the United States. It was axiomatic that any military operation would begin in Alaska. From there it worked its way south. One Communist or one thousand, he didn't give a shit. He was going to root them out come hell or high water.

Today's hearings delving into subversive activities at the university was round two of his battle against the Red Menace. In January he'd scored a major victory taking on the Washington Pension Union. It wasn't helping old folks save for retirement. It was nothing more than a Communist front preying on the elderly. The fact that WPU was the first government-funded pension program in the United States didn't matter. He'd put them out of business, especially its Commie leader William Pennock. He'd also exposed several suspected Communists in the state house and senate. They were everywhere for God's sake. He wasn't going to stop investigating until every damn one of them was run out of town on a rail.

Canwell looked down at today's star witness, J.B. Matthews. He was former director of research for the House Un-American Activities Committee, or Dies Committee, in Washington. D.C. Its goal was to expose an alarming growth of a Communist presence in government and labor. Matthews made a name for himself with his testimony and then leveraged his notoriety to build a career as a professional witness. He'd flown into Seattle the previous day to share his expertise with the Canwell Committee.

"Dr. Mathews, are the UW professors openly recruiting students to join the party?" asked Canwell after order returned to the hearing.

"No, there's nothing open about it. They're very skillful with their deception," Matthews responded. In his mid-fifties, his neatly trimmed gray hair, rimless glasses perched on a large nose and finely cut gray suit underscored his credibility. This was a man of authority, credible and convincing. "These professors have mastered Marxism and Leninism," he continued. "They can skillfully inject their philosophy into their teaching with little risk of exposure."

The murmuring grew louder.

Mathews picked up a document and held it high for everyone to see. "I have in my hand an official pamphlet of the Communist Party," he announced. "It's titled the Road to Mass Organization of Proletarian Children. It lists multiple objectives for brainwashing our young ones." The audience turned quiet, eager to catch every astounding word from this man.

John Jacobson was outraged. He was pinched in the middle of a herd of fellow students in short-sleeved shirts and girls wearing sweaters and skirts. They crowded the right and left aisles and overflowed into the stairway. The students struggled to suppress their annoyance. Did this know-it-all think they were simpletons incapable of knowing shit from Shinola?

John planned to take Ellie and John Jr. to Woodland Park today. Ellie enjoyed sunning near the rose bushes while Junior rode the ponies. But he was glad he didn't because this guy was unbelievable. John just finished his sophomore year at UW. He'd taken courses from three of the professors named as suspected Communists. He'd heard rumors about their leftist leanings. Not once did they offer up anything questionable. Sure, they'd discussed Leninism and Marxism in the political science and psychology classes. They compared those forms of government to democracy and capitalism. He'd read the

Communist Manifesto while in the reformatory. Its failings were clear to him. He needed no convincing on the superiority of capitalism and a republican form of government.

Matthews began reading. "A special struggle should be waged at the family home by the children to win over the adults. The goal is to convince parents to reject backward ideas like religion, petty customs and traditions." Matthews set down the pamphlet and looked across the auditorium. Everyone was looking up at him. The hall grew quiet for the first time that day. He hesitated long enough for the words to sink in. "In case you're unaware, Communists are atheists, and the newly converted are expected to give up bourgeois holidays like Christmas."

The audience erupted in catcalls and boos. Christmas!

"Order, order!" Canwell shouted, pounding his gavel. "If you want to remain in this hearing room, I insist you show some decorum."

"This sounds fantastic to some Americans but there it is in black and white." Mathews waved the pamphlet around. "It starts with ten- or twelve-year-old children and continues right through university. Many colleges today, knowingly or unknowingly, have become Communist front organizations."

"Please help educate us on Communist front organizations, Dr. Matthews," Canwell requested.

"Front organizations are a half-way station between the status quo and the Communist Revolution. They are a tool of the Communist Party for seizing power. There are hundreds of them across America. I can name multiple ones right here in Seattle." He rattled off a list. "The Washington Pension Union, Students for Wallace, the Northwest Labor School, the repertory theater. There are more, believe me."

John's annoyance rumbled around in his stomach, bubbling to the surface, ready to erupt into full-fledged anger. Students standing near him stirred and grumbled.

"The U.S. Communist Party is going about it in the reverse order," Matthews continued. "They are working to convert college students today so they can raise their children to be Communists tomorrow. It won't happen right away or even in a few years. It may take decades but the evidence is clear." He stopped to gather his thoughts and looked out at the audience. "My research shows that professors who associate with front organizations on or off campus are inching our country towards the unthinkable. They want nothing less than toppling our democracy and turning America into a Communist state."

The room exploded in a roar of disbelief and indignation. Spectators stood and booed. Others screamed obscenities.

"Stop the bastards now!" a woman yelled.

"Hang the Commies!"

"Protect our children!"

"Fascists!" screamed John and several other students.

Seattle Police and Washington State Patrolmen rushed in the direction of the rowdy students. John was the first of several pushed towards the exits. Before he could react, two burly patrolmen grabbed him by each arm and dragged him towards the stairs leading to the first floor. His feet barely touched the ground as they marched him down the stairs and flung him unceremoniously through the open front doors. John lurched forward trying to regain his balance but tripped and tumbled down the concrete stairs onto the sidewalk.

The scene outside the Armory was no less chaotic than inside. Joanne and Natalie were among hundreds protesting the hearings. The last thing Joanne needed was to walk yet another picket line. The aeromechanics strike was in its fourth month and going nowhere. She's been on her feet at Plant Two five days a week. You'd think she'd give her tired feet a break and curl up on the couch with a good mystery. But she couldn't because Natalie asked her to join in protesting the Canwell Hearings. Two of her professors were under attack. The Canwell Committee accused them of furtively indoctrinating students with Communist propaganda. One was Dr. Gundlach, who Joanne knew from the Labor School. The presence of an FBI agent in class, a stark reminder of the harsh spotlight pointing at UW faculty.

She stepped out of the line for a quick break and took in the scene around her. Protesters streamed in all morning, more than five-hundred, she estimated. Most came to oppose Canwell, others in support. Cops were everywhere. At one point picketers stopped walking. They turned to an elderly man hoisting a large American flag, and sang the national anthem. She couldn't help but feel pride as she watched Natalie lead the line of picketers chanting "Abolish Canwell!" Children, mostly under ten brought up the rear. Four carried a placard, each quoting one of President Roosevelt's four freedoms. She remembered feeling hopeful when she listened to his fireside chats at her parent's home. Freedom of religion, freedom of speech, freedom from want and freedom from fear. They were unforgettable. Joanne, who took her son Danny to the picket line for stroller day at Boeing, knew children brought out the press. Danny wanted to come today but George objected strongly. She'd try to bring him tomorrow. There was an important lesson here.

So Joanne walked the line for the sake of Natalie, for Dr. Gundlach and for the greater cause of free speech. But something else motivated her, something she only recently understood. She'd grown up on a farm, attended mass with her parents every Sunday. She earned straight A's in high school and married a straight-laced football player with a degree in engineering. Together they were raising two beautiful, well-adjusted children. It was perfect. Until the war came. Until God handed her a rivet gun and the power to think about herself and for herself. Now she was almost unrecognizable from that small town Catholic girl. In her place marched a labor activist. In the minds of some, the wholesome farm girl transformed into a Socialist, even a Communist. She was a target of the FBI. But Canwellites, as they were now called, weren't just targeting pension funds and universities. They were ideologues, armed to the teeth with a political shotgun and aiming both barrels right at labor unions. In their minds, unions were Communist fronts, dedicated to controlling the means of production for the state. So yeah, her feet hurt and her activism opened a fissure in her marriage. It maybe even wrecked it, but there was no backing down, not now.

"Let me go! Get your hands off of me, you dirty cops!"

Joanne looked up to see police drag a man through the Armory's front entrance and push him past the double doors. She watched in disbelief as he tripped, rolled down the stairs and landed with a thump on the sidewalk. She couldn't see who it was but he looked familiar. She ran over as the man rolled onto his back and groaned. It was the veteran from the Labor School, John Jacobson.

"What happened, John? Are you okay? Why'd they throw you out?"

John looked up at the attractive woman kneeling over him. "I don't know, maybe it was something I said."

Chapter 33

Canwell looked down at the witness with an expression of incredulity. "You must be sworn in, Dr. Gundlach. We will take no unsworn testimony in these hearings."

"I want it understood that I protest to being sworn in."

"You can protest all you want, sir, but you will swear in."

Gundlach reluctantly raised his right hand and promised to a God in which he didn't believe to tell the truth. This was day four of the hearings investigating a Communist presence at the University. The startling revelations and ruckus from the previous day was fresh in everyone's mind. Gundlach was the last of a long line of professors and staff to testify. All cooperated to some degree, either admitting or denying having joined the party. Some willingly gave up names of other party members they'd known or worked with. Gundlach proved the most recalcitrant witness. He initially refused to even appear. He believed it amounted to recognizing the legality of an unconstitutional committee. Later, he reversed his position, concluding he could better expose this political charade with his testimony.

William Houston, chief investigator for the committee, stood and approached the witness stand. Between the hearings last January and this week's hearings he'd questioned dozens of witnesses and expected full if reluctant cooperation. He wasn't going to get it from Gundlach.

"Dr. Gundlach, do you believe in God?"

Before Gundlach could respond, his attorney, Clifford O'Brien, jumped to his feet. "Mr. Chairman, that's an outrageous question. The foundation of our constitutional government is the protection of our freedom of . . ."

Canwell employed his gavel yet again. "I will have no speeches from attorneys. We discussed this. The rules are simple. You can advise your client to answer yes or no to our questions, but that's it. No speech making." O'Brien sat down, chagrinned. The role of defense attorneys remained a point of contention from day one. The hands of defense council were tied. They were prohibited from making objections or cross examining hostile witness. It was all very one sided. A medieval star chamber, O'Brien thought.

The committee chairman acquiesced. "Questioning the witness's religious views is inappropriate, Mr. Houston, please move on."

Houston nodded contritely. "Very well, Mr. Chairman," he said, turning his attention to the witness. "Dr. Gundlach, I will ask you if you are now or ever have been a member of the Communist Party?"

Finally, Gundlach thought, the question everyone was waiting to hear. He knew it was coming of course, but the violation of his rights to privacy and free speech shocked him nonetheless.

"Mr. Houston, no Legislative Committee has the right to ask about one's personal beliefs or associations."

Without removing his eyes from the witness, Houston said, "Mr. Chairman, I ask that the witness be required to answer the question 'yes' or 'no.' He's totally unresponsive to the question."

Canwell looked down at Gundlach, a thoroughgoing Communist if he'd ever seen one. Having never attended college, academics and so-called intellectuals intimidated Canwell early in the investigation. He loathed elitists with their caps and gowns and doctorate degrees. But the deeper he dug, the more confident he became. Visiting the campus with other committee members, peeking into classes and interviewing administrators was a revelation. He realized the whole lot of them weren't intellectual heavyweights at all. Just a bunch of weaklings following orders from Moscow. He'd never seen such a disgusting collection of sheep-killing dogs.

Houston took a deep breath, trying not to reveal his annoyance. "Dr. Gundlach, I ask you again, are you now or have you ever been a member of the Communist Party?"

Gundlach smirked. "That's a loaded question, like asking when did you stop beating your wife."

The audience erupted in laughter. Joanne, who stepped away from the picket line to listen to the testimony through the speaker on the first floor, chuckled. Typical Gundlach, she thought, cut right to the quick.

Canwell suppressed a smile and looked at his witness indulgingly. "The question is entirely proper, sir. You will respond now or be dismissed and put up on charges of contempt of congress. For the third and final time, are you now or have you ever been a member of the Communist Party?"

"I will rely on my right to remain silent."

Danny looked cute gagged, Joanne thought when she returned to the picket line. The children walking the line today all wore handkerchiefs tied over their mouths to protest the committee's violation of free speech rights. She'd brought Danny without telling George. It was bound to upset him but so be it. Participating in a peaceful demonstration over constitutional rights was a fitting civics lesson for a boy. She and George argued again last night. They seemed to argue about everything lately. They were in bed following an awkward evening. Joanne tried to make small talk over dinner but George mostly grunted, uninterested in conversation.

"Don't lecture me about people's rights," George said. "You seem more interested in those Commie professor's rights than my rights."

She sat up and turned to her husband. "Who says they're Commies? What about your rights?"

"Parents have rights too. I have the right to make sure my children aren't subjected to subversive teaching, and dangerous ways of thinking."

"I've asked you this before. Don't you think Natalie is smart enough to know the difference between subversion and honest education? Doesn't it matter that neither Natalie nor any other students have complained about seditious teaching?"

"These kids wouldn't know sedition if it slapped them in the face. They think this Communist thing is exciting, a big adventure. But I'm warning you, it could lead to trouble. For all I know she could take the bait hook line and sinker. She'll get involved in sabotage or treason and end up standing in front of a firing squad."

She didn't know how to respond to that ridiculous notion. There was no changing his mind. She turned out the light and turned her back to her husband. Sleep proved elusive.

"Ban Canwell not free speech!" The picketers were in fine form today, loud and clear, she thought. "Ban Canwell not free speech!"

A car roaring up Harrison drowned out the chanting. It lurched to a halt in front of the picketers. Its squealing tires left black skid marks on the street. To Joanne's horror, she watched as George climbed out of his maroon Plymouth. He rushed towards the picketers without bothering to turn off the motor or close the driver's door. He grabbed Danny by the arm and pulled him roughly towards his car.

Joanne rushed towards them, with Natalie on her heals. She managed to block the open door ahead of George. "What are you doing! she screamed. "You're hurting my boy!"

He looked down at a dismayed Danny and yanked the handkerchief from his mouth. "He's my boy too and I don't want him around these damned Pinkos! I've made that very clear."

"Nothing you say is clear to me, George. What do you think is going to happen here? There is nothing to be afraid of. No one is going to hurt Danny."

George looked at his wife and sighed. "Whatever you say, Comrade." Without another word, he pushed Joanne out of the way and hustled Danny into the car. He climbed in behind him and slammed the door. Joanne and Natalie watched in shock as George sped away, tires squealing. Once again Joanne wondered what havoc she'd wrought.

"Let's go, I'll drive you to campus," she told Natalie, shaken, voice cracking. As they walked the two blocks towards her car, Joanne was preoccupied over what just happened. She didn't notice a man wearing blue dungarees and a sleeveless white T-shirt following from a block away.

Chapter 34

Joanne lay in bed after another night of too much tension and too little talk. She didn't want to go home after dropping Natalie off at the dorm. She drove to Volunteer Park and parked the car. The ten-story water tower loomed in the evening light. She climbed the 177 steps to the observation platform atop the water tower. Joanne often found sanctuary sitting above the city and gazing at the panoramic view. It was a warm summer evening. She loved the twilight period between dusk and dark. A light breeze blew in from the north. To the southeast she could see Mount Rainier radiating a muted pink. To the west, the Olympics looked majestic even though July stole much of its snow. To the north she could see scores of pleasure boats, sailboats and yachts working their way from Lake Union, through the Montlake Cut and into Lake Washington. But the beautiful scene on a perfect summer evening could not hide the ugliness of that afternoon.

Her husband's outrage and anger startled her. Recent arguments about the kids, her job, her activism were frequent but controlled. He'd be upset, even to the point of genuine anger. But it was a controlled anger. Their bouts had rules, boundaries. They fought inside the ropes of the marital boxing ring. They were upsetting but not unsettling. Feverish but not frightful. But today, for the first time in their twenty-year marriage, George frightened her. His reckless driving up a crowded street was bad enough. She was shocked when he grabbed Danny, practically dislocating his shoulder. He'd screamed at her in front of the crowd, roughly pushing her out of his way. The entire incident left her stunned, paralyzed. She prided herself on being a problem solver. She approached issues, especially the family kind, with pragmatism and common sense. But it was hard to make sense of any of this. There was no easy fix, no magic wand to transform her husband into something he wasn't, or her for that matter. She descended the stairs, climbed into her car and drove to the park's exit. Moments later a dark Ford sedan pulled in behind her.

She'd gotten home to see George slumped on the couch, drink in hand. He'd said very little all evening, ignoring the leftover beef stew she'd heated. He fell asleep on the couch after finishing what by her count was his third Jim Beam and water. Neither could summon the energy to argue. She headed upstairs to check on Danny and found him awake. He was sitting up in bed and listening to his Philco Radio they'd bought him for Christmas. He enjoyed listening to the popular half-hour adventure shows like the Green Hornet.

"How are you doing, sport? Can I come in?" Without waiting for a response she sat on the edge of the bed and took his hand. He was wearing red pajamas. "Tough day, huh."

Danny looked at his Mom and nodded but didn't speak. She surveyed his room, neat as usual but cluttered with boy things. A Seattle Rainier's team poster hung on one wall. A U.S. Navy pennant, a gift from George, hung on the other. Plastic models of warplanes, battleships and hotrods littered the top of his desk and chest of drawers. A thick stack of baseball trading cards perched on his lap.

Danny turned off the Philco and looked at his Mom. "Why is Dad so angry?"

Good question, probably the hardest one, she thought. Your Dad's angry because he hates change. He hates losing control of his family. And he's caught up in the same irrational paranoia that has gripped much of this city. But I can't, wouldn't share any of that with my son. Not to a twelve-year-old boy.

"Because he loves all of us – you, your sister and me. He's worried we'll get hurt."

"But nobody was hurting us. I was having fun. Are Communists bad?"

This boy knows how to cut to the chase. It's a reasonable conclusion if you read the papers, listen to the Canwell crackpots. Politicians like Scoop Jackson make it worse. They believed communism was the worst of things. It must be eradicated from

American soil. They wanted nothing less than it wiped off the planet. No wonder my boy is confused.

"Being a Communist doesn't make you bad. There may be Communists who are bad. But you'll find bad people in our government too. People, your father included, hate Communists for their beliefs. Communists want a system of government very different from ours."

"Are you a Communist?"

"No, I'm not a Communist, but I do think they have some good ideas which can work in our government."

"Like what?"

"Like helping people who can't help themselves. Not everybody is as lucky as our family. They don't have all the things we take for granted. They're unable to find good jobs. They can't feed their families or send their children to nice schools. I think our government should help the less fortunate. Some say that's a form of communism but I don't believe that. People we elect to office should help those needing help. It's nothing more than Americans helping Americans." He nodded slightly, his dark eyes revealing agreement. She said she loved him, kissed his forehead, left his room and quietly closed the door behind her.

The chat with Danny soothed them both. Finding the words to mollify George would not come so easily. She turned out the bedside lamp, rolled onto her left side and closed her eyes. She was on the edge of sleep when she heard shattering glass, followed by a deafening explosion. She shot out of the bedroom and headed towards the stairs in her nightgown and bare feet. Smoke billowed up from the first floor. The whoosh of flames coming from the living room. She scampered down the stairs, heat wafting over her. Glass everywhere. Sharp pain in her feet. Blinding smoke. Coffee table overturned, broken. No sign of George.

"Mommy! What's happening!" Danny at the top of the stairs.

"Stop. Don't come down here! Stay put!"

Flames coming from the front window. Drapes on fire, flames licking their way up the wall. More smoke, heat. Night air flowing through shattered window feeding the flames. *Where's George? Do something, Novak!*

She ran towards the flames, braving the heat. She grabbed the drapes from near the top. She yanked them forcefully to the floor, first the left one then the right. The rods fell with them, whacking her on the head. Pillows on couch. Grab them. Smother the flames. Press hard. Bury them. More pain. Darkness. Smoke.

She saw a ghostly, haunting figure approach. "It's not my fault! It's not my fault," George cried. On his knees. Standing, stumbling towards her. Face and arms a bloody spectral.

"Where's Angelos? Where's Rossi, the others? We need to run! Condition red!"

Joanne was confused. What was this? Did he cause this fire? Who's Angelos?

"They're all dead because I ignored condition red."

It suddenly came to her. *He's talking about the bombing of the airfield. He thinks he's in the Solomon's.*

"George, it's me!" Her voice urgent, desperate. "It's alright. It's me, your wife. You're at home. We're safe."

He fell to his knees, both hands raised over his head, clasped in prayer. "God, forgive me, please. I didn't want anyone to die."

She rushed to him, knelt down and wrapped her arms around her husband to smother the hurt and terror.

Two hours later she sat in the waiting room at Harborview Hospital. She wore a robe over her nightgown. Nurses bandaged the bottoms of both feet and treated first-degree burns on her arms and hands. Danny sat next to her, unhurt. Police and rescue crews arrived within five minutes of her call, sirens and flashing red lights piercing the night air. Firemen dragged the still smoldering drapes onto the front yard and drenched them with their hoses. Police checked the entire house and yard. Whoever threw the bomb didn't wait around to watch the damage unfold.

George was in the surgical recovery room after having been treated for cuts on his face and multiple second-degree burns. They also repaired his ruptured spleen. Apparently the force of the blast threw him off the couch and onto the coffee table. If that wasn't enough, Doctor Andrews said George suffered a serious concussion. He should stay in the hospital for at least two days or longer. It depended on how quickly he recovered and his spleen healed. She questioned him about George's strange behavior in the middle of an emergency.

"He was speaking nonsense about killing people and begging forgiveness."

The doctor thought briefly before responding. "Did he see battle in the war? Was he responsible for other men?"

"He was a major in the SeaBees, in the Solomon Islands. Built airstrips I think. He's always been vague about it. Never wanting to talk."

Andrews, who saw his share of action aboard the hospital ship *USS Comfort*, nodded in acknowledgment. "I think the explosion triggered a memory of some traumatic event. Has this happened before?"

"Not that I know of, but he did suffer from battle fatigue for months after coming home. Our doctor said it was common and he would eventually recover. It's been three years."

"There's no timetable for these kind of spells. They can be triggered by anything and come and go at any time. My best advice is to be patient. I'm afraid options for professional help are limited, onerous, and none I'd recommend. If it happens again there are veteran groups who meet to share like experiences. He may be more willing to open up to fellow vets. It could be therapeutic. I'll give you the group's name and number."

She thanked the doctor and returned to her seat next to Danny. She leaned her head against the wall and closed her eyes. What a night.

"Mrs. Novak, can I speak with you for a moment?"

She looked up to see Detective Karlsson walking towards her. He arrived on the scene shortly after the uniformed officers and followed them to the hospital. He was about six-feet tall, muscular and dressed in a dark suit. The jacket's shiny elbows and frayed cuff suggested heavy wear.

Joanne, wearing a green robe over her nightgown, looked up at the approaching detective. "What the hell happened?" she blurted "Was that a bomb?"

"That, Mrs. Novak, was what is known as a Molotov cocktail. It's sometimes called a bottle bomb or a poor man's grenade. Nothing more than a whiskey bottle filled with gasoline and a wick inserted through the top. When it explodes, it sprays burning gas and glass everywhere. I hope your husband is okay."

Danny looked up. He'd seen Molotov cocktails in the war movies. Usually French resistance fighters tossed them at Nazis.

Joanne struggled to make sense of it all. *Who would want to hurt her or her family? It was related to that Communist hating bastard, Canwell, she was sure. George was right all along. She'd acted recklessly taking the kids there, God damn it.*

"I've been involved in protests outside the Canwell hearings at the Field Armory all week. I must be a threat if anti-Communists are throwing bombs through my front window."

"No Ma'am. This doesn't appear related to Canwell. Yours wasn't the only home bombed this week. Homes in Renton and West Seattle were also attacked."

"What then? she asked, puzzled.

"Ma'am, the targets weren't protesting hearings. The other victims were all aeromechanics. This has gotta be related to the Boeing strike."

Chapter 35

Ellie Jacobson vividly remembered the last time she was this terrified. It was in London in 1940 during the Battle of Britain. German dive bombers swept across the city's skyline unloading their deadly cargo. The blare of air-raid sirens shattering the nighttime quiet. Mum hustling her out of bed at two in the morning. A mad dash to the underground. Huddled there until they heard the all-clear siren.

But terror comes in all colors. Today's was a much darker shade of horror. During the blitz she was dressed in pajamas, covered with a blanket, cuddled up on a bench, her head rested on Mum's lap. Tonight she was alone, nearly naked. The table on which she was lying, cold and hard. Her arms were strapped securely, her legs spread and feet placed in stirrups. She stared up at the florescent ceiling lights waiting for the doctor. For the thousandth time she questioned why she agreed to an abortion. She knew why of course. It was because John insisted and she lacked the strength to say no. It started when she told him that she'd missed her period for two months. She was pretty sure she was pregnant. His reply, emphatic and resolute, frightened her.

"Get rid of it," he'd said.

They argued then, sitting at the kitchen table in their Union Bay Village home. Junior played quietly in the living room. Using his fingers, John ticked off all the reasons why they shouldn't have a second child. They were barely getting by as it was. John Jr. needed their full attention. John was working and going to school full time. They didn't have insurance. Where would the money for the doctor and hospital come from?

"But I can manage," she countered. "I've done good with Junior, I can be a good mother to two. I want a little girl." But his point-by-point argument against keeping the baby slowly wore her down.

Doubt eventually overtook hope. The fear of losing a husband buried her desire for winning a daughter.

"Get an abortion, Ellie," he said.

"How am I going to do that? Aren't. . . aren't. . . they illegal?" She couldn't bring herself to say the word. Ending a life seemed wrong. It shouldn't be easy. Canceling a life with no more thought than canceling a hair appointment appalled her.

"Go see Doctor Stevens. They sometimes make exceptions. If they don't we'll find another way."

Doctor Stevens was more sympathetic but no more helpful. She sat on the exam table in his office. He was about sixty with a healthy crop of wavy gray hair. He attended to Ellie when Junior was born. He was kind and considerate. She liked him. He explained that abortions were illegal since the territorial days. Enforcement waned during the Depression, when tens of thousands of women lived in abject poverty. They couldn't care for the children they already had. After the war and a return to a healthy economy, the religious conservative right changed its tune. It pressured state governments to crack down on illicit abortionists. Police aggressively swept in and shut down abortion mills. They targeted legal and illegal providers.

Stevens picked up a book from his desk and read part of the statute prohibiting abortions. It was illegal to "employ any instrument with the intent to destroy a child unless it was necessary to preserve the life of the mother."

"You're healthy, Mrs. Jacobson. I see no clinical reason to abort this pregnancy. Even if you were at risk, it would be difficult. I'd have to clear it with the hospital's board and that takes time you don't have. You're nearing the end of your first trimester. It's already borderline too late. I'm sorry but you'll have to take this baby to term. The bright side is that the child appears to be doing well. You'll have a healthy son or daughter in your life."

A week later John came home with news. He'd found someone who would perform what he called an off-the-books abortion. Two nights later, they checked into a motel room on Aurora Avenue North and waited. She sat on the edge of the bed, John in an armchair,

Junior on his lap. She could smell stale cigarette smoke and Clorox. The smoke from John's cigarette nauseated her.

"Are they going to do it here? she asked, her nervousness growing.

"No, someone will pick us up and drive us to the place."

"The place? What do you mean, the place?"

They heard a loud knock before he could answer. John opened the door and let in a man who was about thirty. He was dressed in black slacks and long-sleeved black shirt. He said his name was Barry. He worked for Doctor Henry. His all-black attire reminded Ellie of the character in the radio show *The Shadow.* Each episode ended with the line "Who knows what evil lurks in the hearts of men." Ellie wondered what evil lurked in this man.

"Are you ready to go, Mrs. Jacobson?" Barry asked.

She nodded, picked up her purse and followed John towards the door.

"I'm sorry, Mr. Jacobson, you'll have to wait here. We'll drive her back when the procedure is over and we know she's stable. About two hours."

She looked at John, her nervousness morphing into fear.

John took Ellie in his arms and kissed her reassuringly on the lips. "It'll be all right, honey. I'll be here when you get back."

Barry opened the passenger door of a red, souped-up Chevy and eased Ellie into the front seat. He climbed into the driver's side. Before starting the engine he pulled something from a small box on the front seat.

"Put this on," Barry ordered. It was a black mask, the kind that covered the top half of the face. She did as she was told, and Barry started the car. They drove for only about twenty minutes but Ellie was lost. Totally in the dark, the car's engine and her thumping heart offered the only contact with reality. *Why am I doing this? I don't like being alone like this. To be in a car with a stranger. I want my Mum. I miss her. She'd make everything alright.* She recalled her enchanting few months with John in London after the war. *I'd dreamed of so much. Of family and home and a great life in America. Where is all that? What went wrong?*

The pungent smell of Barry's English Leather snapped her back to the present. She didn't see anything until they got out of the car, entered a building. Barry said she could remove the mask. Her surroundings were familiar yet strange. This wasn't a clinic or a doctor's office. She was in what looked like someone's living room. A leather couch, matching armchair and a throw rug were arranged in front of a brick fireplace. It looked like a home but yet it wasn't homey. She saw no pictures. There were no wall hangings, knickknacks or doilies. None of the odds and ends that clutter living rooms everywhere.

A young woman in a white nurse's uniform entered from the hall. "Good evening, Mrs. Jacobson. I'm Nurse Maggie. Please come this way."

She followed the woman down the hall, her uniform mildly reassuring. They entered the second room on the right. If the front room looked livable, this space was all clinical – a bedroom converted into a surgery. Some little boy or girl once played with their toys here, Ellie thought. It was brightly lit, painted white and altogether antiseptic. She could smell soap and cleaning fluid. A narrow padded table covered with a white sheet and pillow sat in the center of the room. Several stainless steel instruments were lined up on a smaller round table.

"Did you bring the payment, Mrs. Jacobson?"

Ellie reached into her purse and handed the nurse seven twenties and a ten. A hundred and fifty dollars to end a life. Nurse Maggie folded the bills in half and stuffed them in the waist pocket of her uniform. The ever-present doubt took over again. *Was she really a nurse or just dressed like one? Is she going to run off with Barry and our money?*

Nurse Maggie handed Ellie a light blue surgical gown. "You can change behind that screen over there," she said. Ellie came out wearing a skimpy gown that tied in the back. Her bare bottom was cold.

"Here, take these," the woman said, handing her two small white pills. "It's valium. It will help with the pain."

So there she was, arms strapped at her waist. legs in stirrups and hopelessly exposed. *Will I ever see my son or husband again?*

A man walked up to the table and placed his hand on Ellie's knee. "Hi, Mrs. Jacobson. So sorry to keep you waiting. I'm Doctor Henry." *Was he a real doctor?* He was about fifty, short, thick around the waist. He wore a white cotton hospital gown. Ellie could smell peppermint on his breath.

"I apologize for the cloak and dagger but we can't be too careful these days," Dr. Henry said. "As you've probably deduced by now, the authorities take a dim view on these things. It's unfortunate but they think they know what's best for women. They make the rules."

"What's going to happen now?" Ellie asked, voice cracking.

"You're going to have a D&C. It's a very common procedure. It will take only about twenty minutes. We'll keep you around for another hour to make sure everything is okay and then Barry will take you back to the hotel."

Dr. Henry's real name was Schumacher. He was indeed an MD, except for the fact he lost his license. He'd been arrested for performing illegal abortions in Minneapolis-St. Paul. He was tried for manslaughter after one of his patients bled to death. To the dismay of the prosecutor, the jury acquitted Schumacher. None of his former patients agreed to testify against him. Disgraced and out of business, he moved to Seattle and opened a clinic in a house he owned on Tenth Avenue on Queen Anne Hill. He was one of hundreds of physicians, midwives and outright quacks operating outside the law in Washington and Oregon. Vulnerable women as young as fifteen and as old as forty traveled from all over the Pacific Northwest to terminate a pregnancy in Seattle or Portland. As illegal abortions go, Henry's clinic was relatively safe. But facilities like his were open mostly to middle or upper class white women. Poor women and women of color self-induced. Many were left to the mercy of back alley abortionists. Safe or not, Henry's surgery suffered from notable limitations. While he kept it relatively clean, it was hardly a textbook example of sterilization. More telling was the lack of anesthesia. There were no antibiotics or follow-up care. If something went wrong, such as hemorrhaging, a frequent occurrence, the patient was on her own. If she managed to make it to the hospital, she risked exposing herself and the abortionist.

"Do I get something more for pain? They gave me morphine when I had my son."

"I'm afraid the valium will have to do. Anything stronger is almost impossible to get. Are you ready to get started?" Henry asked. Ellie closed her eyes and nodded.

When Ellie was six or seven years old, she often sat on the fire escape of the family's ninth floor flat in White Chapel. She enjoyed listening to Ronnie's stories about the exploits of British royalty during medieval times. Especially gruesome were tales of torture. He described in horrifying detail how inquisitors extracted information from enemies during interrogations. Being tortured in the Tower of London couldn't be any more torturous than what she was now experiencing. It was a sharp, stabbing, overwhelming pain that worked its way up her insides and exploded throughout her lower body. She cried out, writhed on the table and pulled violently against her restraints.

"Hold on, Mrs. Jacobson!" Henry demanded. "You need to keep still!"

It was impossible to remain motionless, the pain intolerable. She'd never experienced anything close to this, even in childbirth. That pain, the discomfort of childbirth, at least offered up hope. It led to joy, a new life. It gave her Junior. This pain promised nothing but guilt, regret, emptiness. She clenched her teeth, desperately trying not to move. She felt a strange scraping that went on for ten maybe fifteen seconds and then it was over.

"There. That should do it." Henry said. He sounded self-satisfied, almost proud of his *fait accompli.*

Ellie wept. The pain circled through her like dishwater down a drain.

Chapter 36

Joanne hoisted her "Aeromechanics on Strike" sign over her shoulder and took her place on the picket line at Plant Two for the first time in two weeks. To say her heart wasn't into it would be an understatement. She was discouraged, disappointed and teed off. The guilt that weighed her down felt like a blanket of wet snow. Worse, she felt vulnerable, exposed. The bombing was too much to bear. That bottle of exploding gas shattered more than her front window. It destroyed any sense of security and safety in her life. She took all that for granted because it was never tested. She feared nothing. The world in which she lived was safe. Her home was safe and her children were safe. But that was blown to smithereens like the glass scattered across her living room carpet.

George was released from Harborview after two nights. She'd stayed home to nurse him back to health. She changed the dressings on his burns. She cooked him breakfast and dinner. The injuries and concussion didn't suppress his appetite, nor his displeasure with his wife. The fact the attack appeared unrelated to the hearings mollified him somewhat. Yet he remained distant and detached. Someone bombed the home of a Boeing family. This seemed to bother him more than the bombs that rained down in the Pacific. That was war. This was personal. When she continued to press him, George finally opened up about what was gnawing at him for three years. It was the one upside to this calamity.

They were home alone in their bedroom. Danny, all boy. found the commotion and police attention exciting. He was staying with Connie until the house was put back in order. The new front window was installed the following day. They had yet to replace the carpet or paint the living room. The stench of smoke and gasoline found a permanent home in the wallpaper. Police were investigating but didn't offer much hope about finding suspects.

George was sitting up in bed. She was perched on the edge. The afternoon sunlight streamed through the open bedroom window. She told him what he'd said and done right after the explosion. "It was like you weren't even there, George. Like you were back in the war. What was all that about? Who's Angelos? You've had nightmares like that before. You call out names in your sleep."

George looked at Joanne, uncertain, disconcerted.

"If you don't trust me, find someone you can. Dr. Andrews mentioned groups where veterans get together and talk about the war. He said it helps to get it out in the open, deal with it."

He fiddled with the remains of his bologna sandwich, lining up pieces of crust on the plate like planes on an airstrip. He eventually looked directly at his wife, his eyes reflecting pools of regret.

"I made a mistake," he confessed at last. "It was a big mistake. Because of me, six men are dead. They'll never have what I have. They didn't come home to their families or get married or have children. The children they had will grow up without a dad."

She took the plate from his lap, placed it on the night stand and handed him his glass of water. "It was war, George. Why are you to blame?"

He sipped the water and handed her the glass. "It was my stubbornness, that's why. We were working on an airfield in the Solomon's. Japs bombing every day. We'd no sooner make repairs and their dive bombers would sweep in and take it all out again. We'd get warnings when they were approaching. Code yellow is a warning. Code red signals they're close. That usually means we have five, maybe ten minutes, sometimes longer. So we kept working. Before we knew it, the alarm sounded and they were right on top of us."

"So this Angelos was killed?"

"No, he lost an arm, but lived. I don't know what happened to him. He was shipped out to Hawaii for rehab. But I think about the other guys all the time. They're inside my head. I see them lying on the strip. Their dead eyes stare back at me." He stammered out their names. "Rossi. Wojcik. Walters. O'Leary. Anderson. Smyth. I was their captain. They trusted me and paid for it with their lives." He took a deep breath and looked out the window, silent for a long moment. "I wrote letters to the families, you know. Told them how brave their men were. How they died honorably fighting for a country they loved. But the letters were a lie."

She looked at him questionably. "A lie?"

"It was a lie of omission. I didn't say how they died or why they died. That they were dead because of me."

Screeching feedback from a loudspeaker brought Joanne back to the present and interrupted her thoughts. The team leader, Peter Berg, stood on the flatbed truck, microphone in hand.

"Listen up, aeromechanics. You need to know, we are winning this strike. Boeing is on its last legs." Berg declared. The picketers stopped walking and turned their attention to the speaker. "Boeing is a sinking ship. I can see rats jumping off before the water rises. They're going down!" The crowd responded with nodding heads, pumped fists and shouts of "solidarity!"

The roar of aircraft engines drowned out Berg's next words. Joanne looked towards the airstrip to see a B50 Superfortress preparing to take off to the south. A major improvement over the WW II workhorse B29, the long-range B50 bomber was faster and easier to fly. It was Boeing's pride and joy. This wasn't the first one to roll out but the first since the strike. Joanne watched as one hundred and seventy thousand pounds of aluminum, metal and fuel inched forward. Its four Pratt & Whitney engines screamed for release, its propellers rotating in a dizzying whirl. It accelerated down the runway as first the nose, then the entire aircraft fought and conquered gravity. It climbed slowly, gaining speed. With undeniable power, it climbed high in the sky, a trail of exhaust in its wake. A large crowd of Boeing supervisors, employees, reporters and photographers gathered on the tarmac applauded and cheered. The strikers watched, stunned. Their silence said "how could they do that without us?" Joanne wondered who pounded the rivets.

"What you just saw is proof of Boeing's failure," Berg shouted, sensing the angst in the crowd. "Tomorrow the front pages of the papers will tell lies about Boeing's great achievement. How they defied all odds and launched the most advanced bomber in history. They'll boast how they did it without the help of fifteen thousand aeromechanics. What they won't tell you is the truth. That plane was just two weeks from completion before the strike began." He paused to get the crowd's attention. "But it took them four months to get it off the ground."

The quiet and dispirited crowd turned its attention back to their leader.

The strikers shouted a mix of applause, jeers and boos. "Boeing claims the B50 will be the backbone of our nation's new air power program. The question is how are men without a backbone going to build them?" The line drew a big laugh.

"Let me repeat! What you just witnessed was a demonstration of Boeing ineptness. It was not a success. We will win this strike!"

"No contract no work!" the crowd responded in unison, regaining some of its enthusiasm. "No contract no work!

Joanne felt like she'd heard all this before. There's no question the strike severely hampered production. The first planes to roll out were nearing completion when the aeromechanics walked out in April. Many ended up back in the plant for rework. But things changed over the last few weeks. Joanne stood transfixed as she watched more workers crossing the line than picketing the line. According to the papers, more than half of the fifteen thousand striking aeromechanics were back on the job. A month ago union members voted overwhelmingly to stay out. Since the first day of the strike they heaped verbal abuse on anyone who entered Plant Two. They were scabs, outcasts and traitors hurting their brothers and sisters. They were refused service in taverns and restaurants. Merchants refused to cash their paychecks. They were vilified in public when billboards claiming "Boeing needs workers," were vandalized to read "Boeing needs scabs."

"Hi Joanne."

She turned to see Dorinda approaching. Joanne looked over her friend and coworker. She wore Frye work boots, blue coveralls and a light blue checkered long-sleeved shirt. She held a lunch box in one hand and a hardhat in the other.

"Interesting dress for a picket line," Joanne commented.

Dorinda didn't respond but looked at Joanne, tears welling up.

Dorinda was a top-notch bucker, and until she got promoted to riveting, they were one of the best teams in Plant Two. But she was more than a co-worker. She became a close friend. They bonded, first at work and then on the picket line. She admired Dorinda's grit and commitment to the cause. She'd been tireless on the line even risking arrest. Her stunt on the railroad tracks, a fool hearty but gallant effort in solidarity. Now, after one hundred and twenty days without steady income, Dorinda was running out of options and money. There was no end in sight to the strike. Dorinda was throwing in the towel. *Can I blame her? The situation of a single mom with a nine-year-old boy is a world apart from mine. How can I think less of my friend or anyone who prioritized their children over the cause? How long would I stick it out under those circumstances?*

"I can't go on like this anymore, Joanne. I got Web to think about. My landlord won't defer the rent any longer. I can't pay it with my strike pay and picking strawberries."

The union paid striking members ten dollars a week. But that fund was running dangerously thin. Some landlords reluctantly agreed to defer rent for a month or two. That well was running dry too. Many businesses around the city offered part-time jobs to strikers. They made ends meet with ten, fifteen hours a week. They got by working at auto repair shops, small manufacturers and retail stores. It helped but the wages were well below Boeing's. By and large these were acts of neighborliness and solidarity. Workers helping other workers in need. Truck farmers in the Kent Valley were perpetually short of workers. They even paid pickers the three dollar round trip train fare on top of one dollar per flat of berries.

Joanne cried too. She put down her picket sign and wrapped her arms around Dorinda. "You do what you gotta do, honey," she said. "I understand. You'll get no objection from me. I love you."

Shouting coming from the direction of the gate ended their moment. Both women looked up to see everyone running in that direction.

"Goddamn scab! Pound his ass!" someone yelled. Joanne and Dorinda ran to see what was happening. Three men were fighting. Joanne recognized them. Two were picketing that morning. The third was apparently on his way to work. He was getting the worst of it. He took a vicious shot to the head and went down. The attackers moved in, kicking him repeatedly in the back and ribs.

Joanne ran over to Berg. "Stop this before someone gets seriously hurt!" she pleaded.

"I wouldn't stop this even if I could," he yelled back. "This is war, Novak. People get hurt in war. This will send a message about what happens to scabs."

"I'll stop it then, damn it" she yelled and ran towards the melee.

With Dorinda at her heals, she elbowed her way through the crowd. Before she could break through, three police officers rushed from inside the gate and broke up the fight. The two aggressors backed away. The third man struggled to stand. He rolled onto his hands and knees, blood running down his left cheek. When no one came to his aid, Dorinda stepped in and kneeled next to him.

"It's best you stay down, soldier. We'll get you some help."

He looked at Dorinda, groggily. "I'm all right," he moaned. "Just give me a hand." With Dorinda holding him by one elbow and Joanne by the other he struggled to his feet. Joanne remembered his last name. It was Collins, a shop welder. They chatted on the picket line.

"Where's my lunchbox?"

Joanne spotted it near the gate and walked over to pick it up. It was metal gray, the kind with the hooded lid held closed by two clasps. Someone crushed it nearly in half. A peanut butter and jam sandwich and a red apple were smashed and uneatable, The mess, though not of her making, was one more stain on the table of her life.

Chapter 37

As much as he tried, John couldn't erase the image of the blood. He sat in a metal chair beside Ellie's bed in Seattle General Hospital at Fifth and Marion downtown. Junior slept on his lap. Only once before had he seen so much blood. It was during the godawful Battle of the Bulge in Belgium in the last year of the war. But blood in war is expected, almost routine. This was not it. It was shocking. Two nights following the abortion, John was dozing on the couch when he heard Ellie scream from the bedroom. He rushed in to find her sitting up in bed, blankets thrown back. Blood, red and black and clotted, pooled in the middle of the bed. Ellie looked up, panicked.

"What's happening?" she pleaded. Her skin turned a chalky gray, her lips blue. She was sweating profusely, her breathing shallow and ragged. Before John could respond, she lost consciousness and collapsed back on the bed. It looked like she was still hemorrhaging but he didn't know how to stop it. Doctor Henry said he inserted a gauze plug to prevent bleeding but he didn't see it. He felt her forehead. She was burning up. He could call an ambulance but God only knew how long that would take. His best option was to drive her to the nearest hospital. He scooped up his wife in both arms, carried her out to the Chevy sedan, her weight strangely light. He laid her on the backseat. He then returned to the house and lifted Junior out of his crib. Hustled back to the car and laid him on the front seat. Next came a mad dash in the middle of the night. *What the fuck have you done, Jacobson? Can't you get anything right? Mom was right. The wages of sin is death. You didn't' want the responsibility of one child let alone two. You pushed your wife into an abortion she didn't want. You left her in the hands of a quack. Now she might die. God help us both.* Fifteen frantic minutes later he pulled into the emergency entrance at Seattle General. The light traffic likely saved Ellie's life. Junior slept the whole way.

Ellie slept following surgery to repair whatever in God's name was damaged. She was lying on her back, snoring softly. An IV bag hung on a metal stand near the head of the bed. He could see the clear liquid streaming slowly down the tube and into her right arm. A woman in the bed closest to the door was reading a Bible. John could hear the morning traffic on Fifth Avenue through the open window. Junior woke up and started playing with the car keys. John wanted a smoke.

A moment later, a nurse wearing a white uniform, stockings and cap pushed through the door, followed closely by Doctor Stevens. She checked Ellie's vitals while he read her chart. He didn't speak for almost two minutes.

"Give me one good reason why I shouldn't call the police, John," Stevens said without looking up. John's pulse quickened and he could feel cool drops of sweat on his forehead. Words failed him. "Do you know how close you came to losing your wife? Ellie nearly bled to death. She has a serious infection. I don't know who performed the abortion but he damaged the wall of her uterus. Quacks like that have no business holding a scalpel."

Stevens was angry. He knew that Jacobson pushed Ellie into ending her pregnancy. His patient was seriously ill and a healthy baby is dead. In thirty-plus years practicing obstetrics, he'd attended to dozens of Ellie Jacobsons. He knew how tricky a D&C could be. One of his colleagues compared it to scraping the inside of a wet paper bag without cutting through the paper while blind folded. He'd witnessed every conceivable mishap following untold number of botched or self-induced abortions. There was no end to the hazards women would endure to take back control of their bodies. To avoid performing a D&C under surreptitious circumstances, illegal abortionists often induced a miscarriage. It forced the patient to go to a hospital where an abortion would be performed. The most common method was to insert a foreign object like a catheter with a balloon at one end through the cervix. The abortionist would then fill it with saline, putting pressure on the cervix. This caused it to dilate and expel the fetus. This method was unreliable and risky. It often lead to hemorrhages and embolisms.

The self-inducers were the most problematic. More often than not the goal was to cause hemorrhaging. This literally forced the hospital to perform the abortion. Stevens suspected that every year thousands of desperate women around the country tried to self-induce. Usually this involved using a variety of suppositories, tinctures and herbs. Just last year, he'd treated a woman so desperate to abort she got her hands on a catheter. She inserted it into her cervix and poured in turpentine. It literally cooked the inside of her uterus, requiring him to remove it. Potassium permanganate tablets, sold over the counter to treat fungal infections and dermatitis, were used to induce bleeding. Unfortunately it also eviscerated the vaginal lining. But without question, the most stupefying method was inserting a wire coat hanger or other metal object to scrape the inside of the uterus. One woman checked in to Seattle General with the straightened hanger sticking out of her vagina. She wouldn't have to worry about ever again getting pregnant. Fortunately Ellie would not meet the same fate. She would recover fully and likely have more children. If she died, he'd have no choice but to notify authorities. Jacobson would have likely been charged with manslaughter or murder.

After Dr. Stevens left, John sat in the bedside chair, bouncing Junior on his knee. Thank God the doctor decided not to bring in the cops. Already a convicted felon, John would have faced a decade in prison or more if Ellie died.

John looked at his son, whose blonde hair, blue eyes came from his side of the family. "Looks like we dodged a bullet, sport. Mommy's going to be okay and Daddy won't have to go to jail."

"Mommy sleeping," Junior said, pointing at the bed. "Is she sick, Daddy?"

Not for the first time was John impressed with the awareness and vocabulary of a boy not yet three years old. He was chatty, always asking questions, especially when John read to him. Junior loved books. He left them scattered throughout his bedroom and invariably carried one around the house like a blanket. He even rifled through John's bookshelves. He came home from work to find his novels strewn across the living room, Junior pretending to read. A happy boy with a sweet disposition, he was the healthy byproduct of an unhealthy marriage. John loved his son unconditionally. That surprised him because he didn't want this child either. He considered himself to be a good dad but he now realized love alone is insufficient. It offers the sunlight needed for life but not the rich soil and water and nurturing essential for healthy growth. Junior deserved more of all of that.

If John was lacking as a father, he was a complete failure as a husband. He sat Junior on the chair and stood over Ellie. Even with her sickly pallor and frizzled hair, John saw the natural beauty he'd married four years earlier. She was a knockout, one of the best looking women in London. Thoroughly smitten and consumed by her vitality and loveliness, John proposed marriage a month after meeting her. But it was like the gin martinis he loved Saturday night and cursed Sunday morning. He entered into a wartime marriage reduced to a marriage at war. He remembered standing at the altar in full dress uniform. Warning bells rang in his head, muffling the bells of Saint Luke's Parish. The marriage proved a colossal mistake. Now Ellie was paying a steep price for that mistake. She'd given up everything for a life with him. He'd given back nothing. His recklessness and infidelities shamed him. Now he's almost killed her. Ellie crossed an ocean for love and gotten only an ocean of grief.

"What are we going to do, Ellie Jacobson?" he whispered to his sleeping wife. He held her hand, the palm cold and sweaty. He brushed the hair away from her face. "We need to fix this for all our sakes. Our son needs us. I need to keep the promise I made to you four years ago." Squeezing her hand, he kissed Ellie gently on the forehead. "I don't know how, but I'm going to do better, I promise." With that, he picked up Junior, sat down and contemplated a future full of responsibilities but empty of love.

Chapter 38

One hundred and forty four days of lost wages.

One hundred and forty four days pounding the pavement.

One hundred and forty four days of trying to slay a dragon with a butter knife.

And what do they have to show for it? Nothing. Boeing won. The aeromechanics were returning to work. Joanne was now crammed shoulder to shoulder with thousands of others waiting in line at the main gate of Plant Two. She was reapplying for a job that was hers one hundred and forty four days ago.

The vote to return to work occurred over two nights. Five thousand strikers were crammed into the Civic Auditorium at Fourth and Mercer north of the city. On the table was Boeing's offer of a fifteen-cents-per-hour raise. It was the same damn fifteen cents the company offered prior to the strike. Vote "yes" to return to work, vote "no" to continue the strike. On the first night the "no's" appeared to hold sway. Members were appalled by the insulting offer. They cringed at giving in to greedy capitalists. Questions and protests pinballed around the auditorium. Why hadn't the company moved off its position? Where was the compromise? Why wouldn't they bargain in good faith? Harold Gibson, president of District 751, could hardly get a word in. He tried in vain to explain why it was in the best interest of the members to vote yes.

"I'm concerned about the future of this union," Gibson shouted over catcalls and boos. "We have lost our leverage. Nearly half of our members have gone back to work in defiance of our position."

More booing.

"Each of you knows what this strike has cost you personally. It cost the union plenty too. Our expenditures exceed $2 million. We have no way to replace it. We're running out of funds."

"Don't talk to me about costs, I'm about to lose my house if I don't get a paycheck soon," yelled a man obviously eager to vote yes.

"The survival of our union is at stake," Gibson warned. He was referring to the aeromechanics' years-long rivalry with the Teamsters Union. Its notorious president, Dave Beck, was a force to be dealt with. The unrivaled boss of labor in Washington State and the Pacific Northwest played hardball. He wanted nothing less than extending his power nationwide.

"Beck and the Teamsters are cherry picking our members," Gibson charged. "They want total control of all machinists and metal workers in the city. They want our union put out of business. He's gotten Boeing's attention. He's on the side of management not the worker. He's convinced them that all of you will get back in line and stay in line under his control."

"Traitor!" someone yelled amid a chorus of boos.

"Hang the son of a bitch!"

"Yes, he's a traitor, but he has the full support of the powerful Teamsters Union. We're a small local. We're in the ring with a heavyweight fighter. We can't out slug them but we can out smart them. If we go back to work now, we can reorganize. We can focus on managing this outside threat. We've lost this battle but we can still win the war."

The jeering and complaints ebbed as members line up to drop their ballot in the box. Joanne slowly worked her way forward, ballot in hand. She was about twenty feet from the front of the line when an argument erupted near the ballot box. Voting stopped and Joanne heard murmurs of cheating and ballot stuffing. Thirty minutes later, Gibson returned to the podium and turned on the microphone.

"I've received credible reports of some members putting more than one ballot into the box. Ballot stuffing is unacceptable, people. We need an honest vote. We must have full confidence in the outcome of this election. Therefore, I have no choice but to terminate the vote for tonight."

Two days later, the vote went more smoothly. Men and women tired of the whole affair, and who just wanted to get on with their lives, lined up quietly to cast their ballots. The outcome was as predictable as it was convincing. "The vote is in," announced Gibson standing at the podium with the tally sheet in hand. Yes 4,247 votes, no 385." The crowd applauded politely but there was no joy in Mechanicsville.

The next day, as Joanne worked her way towards the front gate, she thought about the reasoning behind her yes vote. She'd been unsure initially. She abhorred the idea of walking away from something she'd been passionate about. But costs were adding up for her and others. Many of her friends were unable to pay the rent or their heating and electric bills. Others were skimping on groceries. Gina Hartwell, a fellow riveter she often chatted with during lunch breaks, came to her in tears. She couldn't afford to buy new school clothes for her two children. "I've always taken pride in dressing my children for school," she said, wiping her eyes with the back of her hand.

The costs to Joanne were not measured in dollars and cents but in the currency of family peace. Her activism and persistence, and the subsequent bombing of their home, stressed her marriage to the breaking point. No more shouting matches, just silent tension. George didn't gloat after the vote to return to work. He didn't have to. He reminded her more than once he'd been right all along. "Your militant unionists jeopardized our national security," he said. "Just be glad it's over and you still have a job."

The crowd at the main gate matched the hectic war years There must be five, six thousand here today, Joanne thought. To manage the massive task of rehiring up to eight thousand workers, Boeing staggered the process. Workers were instructed to return only after receiving a telegram giving a start date. Two thousand telegrams were sent out the first day, but nearly five thousand showed up any way. To keep order, the crowd was divided into two groups separated by ropes. On one side were those simply going to work. That included the scabs who crossed the picket line weeks or months ago. On the other side were the returning strikers. Only some held telegrams in hand. Joanne received no telegram but she came down just to get it done. Newspaper reporters hovered like flies. More than a hundred uniformed police offers stood nearby to ward off trouble.

There wasn't any rough stuff like last month but tensions ran high. Returning aeromechanics booed and jeered the strike breakers. "Here comes those muleskinners, warehousemen and stable boys," yelled one man waving his telegram.

"Scabs till the end," yelled another.

Two women left their place in line and ducked under the ropes to confront the non-strikers. They pulled on the neckties of two men entering the gate. "We lost this strike because of you, traitor," one woman yelled.

Dueling loudspeakers added to the discord. "Stay in line for processing! Do not leave your line," commanded a Boeing manager.

"Return for work every morning until you're rehired," shouted a union officer through his bullhorn.

A group of strikers broke into song with the 1920's hit "Who's Sorry Now."

"Who's sorry now? Who's sorry now? Whose heart is achin' for breakin' each vow?"

Moments later, the serenading strikers switched to a Louis Armstrong tune. *I'll be glad when you're dead, you rascal, you! You know you done me wrong, you rascal you. I'll be glad when you're dead, you rascal you."*

Joanne finally reached the front of the line. "Do you have your telegram?" asked a man in a light blue collared shirt and dark jacket.

"No, haven't got it yet," Joanne answered.

"Name?"

"Novak, Joanne Novak."

The man looked at his clipboard and back at Joanne. He checked it a second time as if he wasn't sure what he'd just read.

"You need to wait over there, Mrs. Novak," he said, pointing to a table outside the main cafeteria.

Sitting on a bench at a table near the cafeteria entrance, she wondered why she wasn't inside being processed. The discordant noises of industry assaulted her from all directions. She could hear the rumble of fuel trucks on the tarmac, aircraft on the runway, the staccato of rivet guns inside the plant. She missed all those sounds It began to sprinkle. She wished she'd brought an umbrella or at least a proper jacket. A steady stream of returning strikers entered the cafeteria without looking at her.

Thirty minutes later, a man wearing a raincoat over a gray pinstriped suit sat down on the opposite bench and placed a folder on the table. Joanne recognized him from her first day at Boeing four years earlier. His last name was Chadwick from the Personnel Department.

"Good morning, Mrs. Novak. Thank you for waiting."

"What's this about?" she asked impatiently. "Why am I out here and not in there?" she asked, pointing inside.

"That's what I want to talk to you about. There's a problem. There's no way to sugar coat this so I'll come right out with it. You will not be returning to work at Boeing. You've been officially terminated."

The cacophony of noises around the airfield faded as her head buzzed in confusion. Did she hear that right? Terminated? How could that be?

"Terminated? Why?" she finally managed to ask, her voice cracking.

"Your subversive activities, Mrs. Novak. Subversives are not welcome in the Boeing family."

Chapter 39

Natalie Novak left her dorm room in Hansee Hall at the north end of the University of Washington Campus, headed for Parrington Hall. She could see her breath as she trudged through the remains of yesterday's snowfall. Her father's peacoat and ear warmers warded off the cold but it bit into her nose and cheeks. A gaggle of Canada geese pecked through patches of uncovered lawn. She could hear the sing-song chanting at Parrington Hall from two hundred yards away.

"Freedom, freedom, academic freedom!"

"I can't hear you. Louder!"

"Freedom, freedom, academic freedom!" the crowd responded with greater decibel power.

Several hundred students braved the cold to protest the hearings underway inside Parrington. UW Regents were hearing testimony from professors accused of being Communists. For the last six months administrators and the faculty senate dug into the charges made at the Canwell hearings during five tumultuous days last summer. The regents were expected to vote today on whether and how many of the professors should be disciplined.

Natalie worked her way toward the front of the crowd of protesters carrying signs. "Freedom," said one. "Seek the truth," read another. A third was directed at UW President Raymond Allen, who'd led the investigation. "Fire Allen, not faculty," it demanded. The man addressing the crowd from the front steps of Parrington Hall was Brock Adams, student body president. Natalie recognized him from his frequent photos in *The Daily*.

"As students we are taught to seek the truth wherever it shall lead. But today, *behind closed doors*, the administration and regents plan to bury the truth." The crowd quieted, wanting to hear more.

"Behind closed doors, they are trampling on academic freedom. They don't want intellectual honesty. They're not interested in exploring controversial or progressive points of view. They want academic robots who challenge nothing, who stay in the narrow lane laid out before them." Adams hesitated and surveyed the crowd.

"Behind closed doors," he repeated, "they hear only what they want to hear. To them, the truth is only that which comports with their points of view. There are no open minds in there. Only small minds. Minds already made up and ready to cast their version of justice. We demand justice and fairness!" he yelled.

Natalie inched closer to the steps, captivated by the power of Adams's delivery. She remembered Professor Gundlach, one of the profs on trial. He made the same points in class before being suspended. In a second-floor classroom in this very building, Parrington Hall, Gundlach argued that the blanket charge against supposed Communists amounts to irrational and paranoid thinking. As only Gundlach could, he used the phenomenon of a controversial radio program to make his point. On Halloween eve in 1938, the actor Orson Welles and his *Mercury Theatre on the Air* performed a radio adaptation of H.G. Wells's *The War of the Worlds*. It was staged as a series of fake news bulletins describing a Martian invasion in New Jersey. It was meant to be a hoax but unfortunately millions of listeners believed it. Calls flooded into police stations, newspaper offices and radio studios. They actually believed little green men were descending upon the Garden State. Gundlach gave examples of how people in their panic interpreted everything they saw as evidence of the invasion.

"One woman turned the dial to another station and heard the hymn *How Great Thou Art*. 'Ah, they're praying for help,' she claimed."

"Another looked out her window to see only deserted streets. 'Oh my God, everybody's gone!'"

"Yet another saw a faint greenish glow in the sky. 'They're here!' he cried. Everything they saw, no matter how innocent or innocuous, confirmed their worst fears. America was being invaded by aliens."

She remembered Gundlach hesitating and making eye contact with his students. "Misinterpreting facts to fit a predetermined point of view is exactly what my colleagues and I are facing now. This administration and the regents carry farcical opinions about alleged Communists. They believe Communists keep their party affiliation a secret so denials serve only to confirm their worst fears. When a suspected Communist advocates for a democratic government, he's simply trying to conceal his totalitarian motives. He urges peace because he wants to defeat us in war. Hysteria has set in, class. There's no changing the narrow minds of the power elite. It's not little green men coming to get them but red ones determined to take over the world."

The crowd below grew more restive as Adams hammered away at the administration. "They have found no evidence of wrongdoing. The grounds for dismissal listed in the administrative code include incompetency, neglect of duty or immorality. They found none of that. Instead they turned to spurious accusations about Communist Party membership."

Natalie knew that to be true at least in Gundlach's classes. He'd never crossed the line, not once. Sure he was a radical and an anti-authoritarian, but his lectures were balanced and honest. Even if they weren't, so what? Too many people believe, her father included, that young people were naïve, that they allow themselves to be led around by the nose by devious subversives. The fact is no one bothered to ask the students what they thought or what was going on in the classroom. They assume the young are either easily duped or eager radicals, and she was neither.

"The fact is, their actions will serve only to harm the university," Adams said, suddenly making eye contact with Natalie. "Firing professors for their political views sends the wrong message," he said without breaking eye contact. "What top-notch prof will want to come here only to be gagged by an over-zealous administration? President Allen claims he is acting in the best interests of the University but in reality he will have branded us with the mark of intolerance."

Is Adams looking at me or is that my imagination? Natalie asked herself. *No, he's definitely looking at me.*

President Raymond Allen could hear Adams addressing the protestors from the third-floor window of Parrington Hall. The hearings were in recess. *Adams is an impressive young man and will certainly go places. What's more, the boy is right. This is a done deal. The hearings are a formality. The accused are all but gone. You blame me for this fiasco, but I have no other choice. I couldn't stop this even if I wanted to, and I don't want to. I am stuck dead center between the proverbial rock and hard place. The regents want heads to roll and heads are definitely going to roll.*

Allen foresaw this day coming two years earlier when Congress formed the Canwell Committee. The university was a suspected safe harbor for Communists since the Depression. Congress gave Canwell the power to flush them out. Of the forty faculty members Canwell subpoenaed, eleven eventually testified and six were now facing disciplinary action.

"Dr. Allen, we're about to get started," a staff member announced.

"Very well, I'll be right in," he said, giving the demonstrators below one last look before turning towards the hearing room.

The atmosphere inside was no less tense than outside. At least thirty middle-aged white men wearing suits and ties filled the spacious lecture hall. Dr. Allen and seven of the regents – the judge and jury – sat at a long table in the front. The six defendants and their attorneys lined one wall, university staff and deans the other. Allen surveyed the men whose fate was in his hands. Harold Eby and Garland Ethel taught English. They, along with anthropology professor Melville Jacobs, cooperated with the Canwell Committee. They admitted to party membership but claimed to have left for philosophical reasons. Ralph Gundlach, who taught psychology, Herbert Phillips, philosophy, and Joseph Butterworth, Old English, refused to cooperate. Gundlach, especially, made a spectacle at the hearings, refusing to testify and claiming First Amendment rights. *He was entitled to do that, of course, but he lied to me. He is not fit to teach,* Allen concluded.

Allen remembered the meeting with Gundlach like it was yesterday. They sat in Allen's office in the Administration Building prior to the July hearings. Allen wanted to get everything out in the open to avoid any embarrassing revelations. The exchange, testy from the start, only got worse. "Are you denying your communist ties, Ralph?" Allen asked.

"I'll tell you what I plan to tell that charlatan, Canwell," Gundlach responded. "First, what right do you have to ask the question? My political views are personal and not open to public debate."

"I have the right as the president of this university," Allen said testily. "The reputation of this institution is at stake. Parents want to know, regents want to know, hell, I want to know whether our students are being exposed to a political dogma dedicated to overthrowing the United States government."

"So you want me to deny being a Communist. What's that going to solve? Who will believe me, you? The point is no one can prove that I'm a Communist and I cannot prove that I am not."

Allen was certain the man sitting on the other side of his desk was lying. He was evasive and devious. He may not officially be a Commie or even carry a party card, but that's likely by design, Allen suspected. Gundlach was among a select group of devotees directed to not officially join in order to better serve the party. An inconspicuous Communist is a more useful Communist, he believed.

"What proof do you have, Ray? Have you talked with my students? My classes are popular. There's usually a waiting list. Are you suggesting they come to hear the party line so they can brainwash their parents like blooming revolutionaries? And what about my colleagues? Butterworth teaches Old English, for God's sake. You'll have to look pretty deep to find seditious passages in Chaucer."

"We have reason to suspect the worst, from you especially. Your radicalism has been noticed. You were asked some time ago to show restraint in the classroom. Nevertheless, you've handed out left-wing brochures from that damn labor school and circulated materials in class about anti-Semitism."

"For God's sake, Allen, when was that a crime," Gundlach retorted, getting angry now. "Anti-Semitism is alive and well in this country. It turned a blind eye to the slaughter of six million. I will not let that go."

"You will let it go if you want to teach at this university. If students want to learn about the Holocaust let them take a history class. Your political opinions do not belong in a psychology class, just as Communists do not belong in this university."

Two hours later, the protest lost its steam as students began to file away in search of warmer confines and hot coffee. Others hung around in hopes of getting news about a verdict. Natalie grew inpatient and walked south through Central Plaza, busy with students scurrying to and from class. She almost went into Suzzallo Library to study for her anatomy exam but instead walked to Drumheller Fountain and plopped down on a bench. It was one of those crisp winter afternoons with not a cloud in the sky. Ducks splashed about in the fountain. A young couple seated on the other side was kissing, their bodies welded together for warmth. Natalie looked across Rainier Vista. The manicured promenade offered an unencumbered view of Mount Rainier. There were no clouds to cover it, no haze to obscure it. It was in perfect focus, sharp, clear and majestic.

Natalie wished her life was as clear as the view. There was clarity once, three years and a lifetime ago. Clarity came from knowing nothing and wanting nothing beyond good grades and cute boys. She accepted without question the simplicity that came with school uniforms, strict nuns and the unrelenting discipline of a girl's Catholic school. But one crazy spring afternoon she drank beer, fell for the seductive lines of a good looking sailor. Before she knew what was happening she found herself panties down in the back seat of an old Chevy. It changed everything. The backdrop of an orderly life crashed down around her. In its place was a world replete with guilt, loss and uncertainty. She gave birth to a son who three years later calls her Aunt Nattie. Would the boy ever learn the truth that his cousin Nattie was really his Mommy?

Eventually she realized the seemingly tragic event blossomed into a blessing of sorts. It opened a door from one life to another. Mom's friend, Clara Fraser, helped her see the upside. Clara was fired from Boeing for being a Communist. Natalie sat with her and her Mom drinking coffee at the kitchen table. Natalie was in one of her down moods, lamenting the sharp turn her life. Mom sat with them but said little. Dad, who didn't think much of Clara's radical politics and feminist views, was thankfully at work. Natalie never heard of feminists.

"You learned a lesson at eighteen that your Mom didn't learn until she was forty," Clara claimed.

"What lesson?" she asked.

"That there's more to life than raising a family," she answered. "What would your life look like had it not been turned upside down? You would likely have gone to college and married a nice boy with prospects. You would have skipped merrily down a road of domesticity and dependence. You would have entered a life where your husband's needs came first and yours didn't count. A life of slave labor where your only compensation was measured by his satisfaction."

Natalie looked at Clara. She was attractive but not feminine, handsome but not pretty. She wore gray pedal pushers and a tight-fitting black sweater. Her dark curly hair was cut short. She wore simple hoop earrings but no makeup. "You're making marriage sound awful. Mom's life, our life, isn't awful."

"No it isn't, and marriage doesn't have to be awful. I hope to marry when I find the right man, but I'll do so on my own terms. I will know what I want, and my future husband will accept that. What I'm saying is, before you marry, experiment with life. Explore the possibilities and decide what's important. If you do marry, make sure he accepts you as you are and supports your choices."

Over the next few months, Clara's message slowly sank in. She left Holy Names and enrolled in Garfield, a decision that caused more than a little acrimony at home. The public high school could not have been more different from the private one. Holy Names was a bastion of middle class whiteness. It was full of good girls from good families with good income. It emoted an all-American sameness that was invisible from the inside but glaringly obvious from the outside. Garfield was the Noah's Ark of high schools. On any given day, you could see two of every kind of student imaginable. They spilled in and out of the red-brick building like jelly beans from a bag. Black, brown, yellow and white, it didn't matter. They were color blind, a menagerie of young people who accepted race differences and rejected race conflict.

At Garfield she learned more than the Three Rs. It gave her a window through which she saw hardship, prejudice, injustice and, above all, resilience. Her friends thrived in the wake of segregation, internment and hate. They taught her empathy. It gave her purpose. It fostered the will to resist the unforgiving weight of intolerance. She could now see beyond the narrow boundaries of her own life. She hoped to be a doctor, a healer, a surgeon, maybe. But you can't excise hate with a scalpel like a cancerous tumor. There's no cure for intolerance. It's impossible to reason with the unreasonable. Her Mom learned that the hard way at Boeing. There's no room for the nonconforming. The spectacle at Parrington this morning was evidence of that.

"Hi Natalie. Sorry to disturb you. You looked deep in thought. "

Natalie looked up. It was Brock Adams. How did he know my name? "That's okay, I needed to get away from the commotion,"

Adams looked at Natalie, attracted by her brown eyes and thick dark hair protruding from her woolen cap. "What did you think of my speech?"

"It was wonderful. You should go into politics."

"I already have but thank you," he said, smiling, stepping closer.

Brock was a senior so he must be about twenty-three, she estimated. He was good looking in a bookish sort of way. His receding hairline made his forehead look too big. His blue eyes were too close to his nose. But the eyes were alert and friendly. His winning smile revealed straight white teeth. Why is he bothering to talk with a lowly freshman? His closeness made her nervous yet a touch excited.

"What happened in there?" she asked, stepping back.

"It turned out much like we expected, not good. Eby, Ethel and Jacobs were placed on two-year's probation and agreed to sign a loyalty oath. A loyalty oath for American citizens, for heaven's sake. Phillips, Butterworth and Gundlach were fired. They're out."

"What's going to happen to them?"

"If you're placed on probation, your career is all but over in this place. You keep your job but you're *persona non grata*. The three others will likely never teach again. What university is going to hire a suspected Commie."

Chapter 40

"Where we going, Daddy. What's the surprise?"

Lawrence looked in his rearview mirror at his youngest son, Elijah. He sat next to his brother, Gerry, in the back seat of the family Chevy. The boys seemed to grow an inch a day. Gerry, nearly fifteen, was going to be tall and lanky like his Dad. Elijah, three years younger, benefitted from his Mom's refined good looks and copper skin.

"I'd like to know, too, Lawrence," Anna Louise chimed in, more than a little bemused.

"It wouldn't be much of a surprise if I told you now, would it? Everyone hold onto their britches and you'll know soon enough." With that, he put the Chevy in gear and headed east on Madison.

This was no ordinary surprise. Lawrence bought a house. Not just any house. It was the one on which he made an offer two years earlier. The deal fell through thanks to a rock-throwing racist and a handful of homeowners dead set against fair housing. About a month ago, Lawrence was working the Madison Park neighborhood asking homeowners not to renew the soon-to-expire real estate covenants. On a damp Saturday morning in April, Lawrence saw that the house at Thirtieth and Republican was back on the market. He called the attorney Arthur Barnett. He offered to call the owner, Chief Bernsten in Washington DC, who had stopped renting the place. When the last tenants moved out, he listed the house with a realtor but so far no takers. He was fed up with the whole mess and wanted to get rid of it. He'd gladly sell to Lawrence and tell his former neighbors to go to hell.

With the help of the banker at Washington Mutual, the FHA expedited the loan approval. He'd signed the papers a month ago without telling Anna Louise or his parents and immediately started the rehab work. He wondered who was living there because its condition worsened since Lawrence first toured it. He started with the cedar shake roof. He replaced damaged shingles, treated the moss and cleaned the gutters. They'd need a new roof soon but that could wait. From the roof, he could see Lake Washington dotted with pleasure boats. The water sparkled from the late morning sun.

"How much you charge for roof cleaning? Mine needs some work too," came a voice from the street.

Lawrence looked down and saw a man standing on the sidewalk looking up at him. He held a German shepherd on a leash. Lawrence sighed in exasperation. Another white guy who thinks coloreds are at their beck and call. They're allowed in the presence of the privileged only when they work for the privileged. "I don't work here. I'm moving here. I own this house," Lawrence said, and returned to scooping pine needles and leaves from the gutter and plopping them in a tin bucket.

The man and the shepherd looked up at Lawrence for a long moment. "So it was you who bought the Bernsten place? Just like Bernsten to stick it to his neighbors. You've bought a house full of trouble, I hope you know that."

Lawrence stopped and looked down at the stranger. "Who's going to give me trouble, you?"

"I can certainly make it happen."

Lawrence decided he couldn't shut down this asshole from his roof, so he climbed down the ladder and onto the front yard.

"You need a new script, pal," Lawrence said as he approached the man and his dog. The man wore gray slacks and a brown cardigan sweater over a white collared shirt. He looked to be on the back side of seventy. A brown fedora covered most of his gray hair.

Lawrence pulled a rag from his back pocket and began cleaning his hands as he stepped forward. The shepherd growled menacingly. "You see, mister, I've seen this movie before," Lawrence said, with one eye on the dog. "Next you're going to tell me how unhappy we'll be here. That we need to be with our own kind. That we'll have trouble getting city services hooked up. Our electricity won't be turned on, or our garbage collected. Cars will block our driveway. Our kids will get roughed up walking to school. Do I got all that right?"

The man remained silent. The dog showed his teeth.

In reality, Lawrence knew better. This man was still living in 1930. While working for Christian Friends, Lawrence spoke with many of the Madison Park homeowners. He found them mostly friendly and willing to sign the pledge. One woman was so anxious she practically grabbed the clipboard from his hand. Another volunteered to help him door knock. Lawrence must have missed this shithead in front of him.

"This is a nice neighborhood, peaceful, crime free. We want to keep it that way," the man said.

"Oh, I understand perfectly. You're worried that when coloreds move here your neighbors will sell in a panic and drive down prices. Madison Park will become a ghetto. In no time, knife-yielding coloreds will prowl the neighborhood in their Cadillacs. They'll sell drugs to sixth graders and pimp out white girls. What a shame that would be." With that, Lawrence pulled out his small pocketknife, opened it and began cleaning his nails.

The shepherd barked twice and lunged at Lawrence.

"Sit, Frankie!" the man ordered, tugging on the leash. The dog complied but continued to strain the leash.

Lawrence jumped at the lunge but didn't back away. "What you don't seem to realize, mister, is that I'm doing you and our neighbors a favor. By the time I'm through, this dump is going to match any house on this street. If you don't believe me, I'm happy to show you my place in the CD." The man didn't respond, the idea repulsive.

"No? Okay then, I would be very appreciative if you and Frankie here would just head on down the street so I can get back to work on *my* house." With that, Lawrence returned to the yard, climbed the ladder and continued with the gutter cleaning.

That was the end of trouble. Over the next few weeks, with help of fellow bus drivers and volunteers from Christian Friends, they transformed the house. What was once a rundown rental now compared favorably with any in the neighborhood. They painted the exterior dark gray with white trim. The two columns framing the front porch and the double garage doors were painted a matching white. They repaired and painted the ancient picket fence. On the interior, they scrubbed and dusted every corner. They installed a new sink to replace the old-fashioned standalone one. They painted the kitchen and the three bedrooms and bath upstairs. Sakura Sasaki, Frank's bride, hung fruit-patterned curtains in the kitchen, planted pink rhododendrons in the front yard and added multiple other feminine touches.

Lawrence and Frank were now close friends, in spite of their racial differences. The covenants brought them together in a shared purpose. Coloreds and Japanese were crammed together in the same twenty-square-blocks for decades but seldom mixed. Lawrence thought that was unfortunate because he liked the Sasaki's. They were honest, straightforward people he could trust, allies in the same struggle for fairness. He and Anna Louise attended the Sasaki wedding in March at the Japanese Congregational Church. Sakura looked stunning in her white, full-length gown. White and Japanese guests mixed freely at the reception. The Williams's were the only Blacks there. Sakura and Anna Louise quickly bonded and had since become friends.

Frank and Sakura were installing new curtain rods in the kitchen. He reflected on the changes in his family and his life over the last two years. He was happy Lawrence finally gotten his house. But meaningful inroads with cemetery owners proved slow if nonexistent. Washelli offered to sell the Sasaki's plots in their so-called international section but Mother would have none of it. "*Sore wa jigokuda*," she'd snapped (to hell with that). Father was at peace and would not be disturbed. She would lie next to him when her time came. His sister, Toyome, drove Mother to the plot in Auburn every couple of weeks. She would sit at the gravesite and talk to her husband. Toyome trimmed the grass around the headstone and replaced the flowers in the porcelain vase.

"I want a house of our own too," Sakura said suddenly. Frank was standing on a chair installing the hardware for the rods, Sakura handing him whatever he needed. She put down the curtain rod she'd been holding and looked up at Frank. "I love Mother and Toyome but I want to hang curtains in my kitchen. I want to plant flowers in my front yard."

Frank understood. He wanted a house too, but they couldn't afford it. Not yet, too much change since Father's passing. Business improved at the Tokyo but not to prewar levels. It probably never would. Japantown was a shadow of itself. Frank and Sakura both attended the University of Washington. Frank majored in business and Sakura in education. He continued to help out at the Tokyo on weekends. He planned to leverage his business degree to acquire more properties and grow the restaurant business. He sensed changes in the business that promised to draw in a larger, more profitable clientele – white diners.

Frank stepped down from the chair, faced his wife and put his hands on her shoulders. For the thousandth time, he admired her youthful looks and delicate features. "The house will come, Sakura, I promise. I have great hopes for us, for our business. We're going to own more restaurants. Not in Japantown but downtown, uptown and even across town. I've seen more and more white customers coming to Japantown for lunch at the Tokyo and other Japanese and Chinese places. Whites don't like Asians but they sure like Asian food. We're going to serve them all they can eat."

. . .

Anna Louise sat in the passenger seat beside her husband. She wondered what Lawrence was up to. This was not like him. He wasn't the surprise kind of man. Straight forward, tell it like it is, no secrets, that was Lawrence. His behavior today was puzzling.

"What is this? What's going on?" she blurted, as Lawrence turned onto Thirtieth and pulled into the driveway of a gray two-story house.

Without responding, Lawrence got out, walked around to the passenger side and opened the door for his wife. The boys climbed out the back and followed their parents onto the front yard. A group of about twenty people were waiting for the Williams family. One held a sign that read "Welcome to Madison Park." Christian Friends board members Edith Steinmetz and Madeleine Morehouse Brake, as well as Arthur Barnett, were there. So was the business woman Dorothy Stimson Bullitt. Frank and Sakura, and Lawrence's friends from work stood near the back. Several Madison Park residents were also there to welcome their new neighbors. It started raining lightly and a stiff breeze blew up from Lake Washington but the weather wasn't going to spoil this day.

Edith Steinmetz stepped forward and held out her hand to Lawrence. "I want to offer my congratulations on buying your first home, Lawrence. But that word is totally insufficient. What you've done here is momentous. Racial hate and ignorance have cast a dark cloud over this city for too long. Your determination and hard work will not just benefit your family but many others who seek racial equality and fair housing. It shouldn't be this hard to buy a home, but you have made it easier for others."

The anticipation and excitement building in Lawrence for a month was now bottled up in his throat. He could barely get the words out. "Thank you, Mrs. Steinmetz, it's been quite a journey," he responded, surprised by the welcoming committee. He wanted to say more, to thank Christian Friends and everyone else but words failed him. He reached into his front pocket, pulled out a key and held it in front of Anna Louise. "Happy anniversary, honey," he said and handed it to her.

Anna Louise was beyond speechless. She was astonished. Could this be true? Her husband bought a house? Their seventeenth anniversary came and went but who cares. The tears came now, rolling slowly down her cheeks. How did he do this? She was shocked but not surprised. Lawrence never quit anything. When he goes after something he doesn't let go until it's firmly in his grasp. She'd often called him stubborn but his determination and doggedness paid off more often than not. She ached for him when the house deal fell through. She would never forget the pain and anguish on his face. God, she loved this man.

A blonde woman stepped close to Anna Louise. "Welcome to Madison Park, Mrs. Williams. I'm Jeanie Foster your neighbor." She was holding what looked like a freshly baked pie. She was about thirty-five and cute, her thick hair made up into the popular victory roll. She pointed to a two-story cottage directly across the street. "I live right there," she said. "My husband sits on the homeowners board. If you have any trouble at all, you come see me. We're good people here and don't favor any of that covenant nonsense." She held out the pie. "I baked it just this morning. It's apple. I hope you and your boys enjoy it."

Anna Louise managed to stammer a thank you. "You baked me a pie," she said. It wasn't a question but a statement of fact. It was a kind gesture to a victim of too much unkindness.

"That's what neighbors do," Mrs. Williams.

"Are we going to live here, Daddy?" Elijah asked, unbelieving.

"Yes we are. Let's check it out." He took Anna Louise's hand and walked up steps lined with potted white petunias. The boys trailed behind, the small crowd watching in silence. The front door was painted red. Lawrence spent hours sanding, priming and applying two coats. A large green wreath hung just below the window. Lawrence took the key from Anna Louise's shaking hand. He unlocked the door, opened it, and ushered his family into their new home.

Chapter 41

Joanne removed her coat, threw it on the empty table and set to work sorting and cataloging copies of *The Dispatcher*, the longshoremen's union newspaper. The audacity and brazenness of the news coverage of the ninety-five day waterfront strike amused her. It contrasted sharply with the staid, pro-business coverage of the Seattle dailies. In large, all-caps type across the top of the various front pages, the headlines made no effort at objectivity.

"FINAL OFFER FULL OF JOKERS," read one headline.

"WATERFRONT BRICKS HOT," read another.

"SHIPOWNERS PUSH PHONY PROPAGANDA"

And finally, "UNIONS HIT JACKPOT IN VICTORIES."

"What do you want to do with all this stuff?"

It was Curt Jaworski, a retired ship worker who immigrated from Poland during the depression. He was helping Joanne organize the records for the International Longshoremen and Warehousemen's Union Local 19. They were working on the second floor of an office building at Second and Yesler, extra workspace leased during the strike. The ILWU pulled off something the aeromechanics could not – a win.

Joanne accepted a job with Local 19 shortly after getting fired from Boeing for her alleged subversive activities. But her former employer wasn't content to just fire her. They ensured she was locked out of the metal-workers trade permanently. "Don't hire Joanne Novak. She's a subversive," they said. "She was a decent riveter but do you really want to deal with another trouble maker? Don't you have enough problems with your unions?" Joanne applied for one job after another only to be turned away. "The job has been filled," claimed one hiring manager, even though the ad appeared in that day's paper. "I'm sorry, you're over qualified," claimed another.

The personnel officer at Pacific Car and Foundry, which manufactured trucks and tanks for the war, was honest at least. "We don't hire terrorists," he said flatly. She looked at the man on the other side of the desk. His name was McClain. He wore a cheap dark suit and a stained green tie. He looked at Joanne, waiting for her response. Joanne was saddled with multiple labels since walking the picket lines at Plant Two. Subversive, Commie, leftist and even radical top the list. George warned her about that. She would be smeared with indelible red ink, permanently staining her reputation and barred from well-paying jobs. George was right, God damn him, but terrorist?

"How am I a terrorist?" she asked incredulously.

"Labor activists are nothing more than terrorists," McLean responded unapologetically.

That ended hopes of finding work matching her skills. She was blacklisted, blackballed, and banned. Call it whatever you want. She was a pariah. Hire Novak and she'll infect other workers with the red virus.

That did not end her working life thanks to her friend, Clara Fraser. The labor activist called with an invitation. She asked Joanne to attend a rally of shipyard workers who walked off the job the previous week. Ports from Anchorage to San Diego were shut down. Thriving ports reduced to waterfront ghost towns laden with ships waiting to be loaded or unloaded. Twenty thousand dock workers stood idle including eight thousand on Puget Sound. The union president, Harry Bridges, was going to speak. "You don't want to miss hearing this man," she told Joanne.

The Civic Auditorium was packed with longshoremen, warehousemen, firemen, oilers, watertenders, radiomen, and cooks and stewards. Just about anyone in Seattle who kept the shipping industry afloat gathered to hear their leader. Sitting near the last row of the auditorium, Joanne was transfixed. The adulation for the man on the stage was eye opening, his message compelling. "Labor cannot stand still. It must not retreat. It must go on, or go under," he claimed. "We're stronger together," he promised. The crowd couldn't get enough, applauding with almost every line. "This is your union," he declared, pointing his gnarly finger at the audience. "We are a rank and file democracy. Power comes from the bottom up." They ate it up.

When Bridges finished, he was immediately surrounded. Dozens of waterfront workers wanted to congratulate him, shake his hand or just be in the presence of greatness. Clara took Joanne's hand and led her out of the auditorium and to an office behind the stage.

"Where are we going?" Joanne asked, puzzled

"I want you to meet him. He wants to meet you."

Joanne couldn't imagine why the infamous Harry Bridges would want to meet an unemployed, better yet, an unemployable, aeromechanic, but she went along. Twenty minutes later, the door to the office opened and Bridges strolled in like this was just the next in a long day of meetings. Joanne stood but he immediately waved her to sit.

"Thanks for agreeing to meet with me, Mrs. Novak," he said.

What? Joanne didn't recall agreeing to anything. She looked at Clara questionably wondering what in the hell was going on. Clara just smirked. Joanne knew of Bridges, of course. Anyone in labor read about his triumph in the 1934 waterfront strike. It turned into a deadly eighty-three-day affair in which police shot and killed six longshoremen, including two in Seattle. Bridges won major concessions from ship owners. His leadership and bargaining skills got him elected union president. The popular refrain on the waterfront was Bridges transformed longshoremen from "wharf rats" to "lords of the docks." Soon, this iconoclastic misfit held a place at the table with the big boys. It was a come-from-nowhere story the media couldn't resist. In 1938, *Time Magazine* put him on their cover. Joanne remembered it only because it was so unusual. From Joanne's perspective, labor leaders were usually photographed in suit and tie. They wore fedoras or smoked a giant cigar. Not Bridges. On the magazine's cover, Bridges wore a sleeveless white undershirt. It was soiled and wrinkled. His bare arms and face darkened from years on the docks. He was bent over a bathroom sink, washing his hands while smiling back at the camera. Good old Harry, just another working stiff cleaning up after a hard day longshoring, ready to share a pint with the fellas.

Joanne knew his notoriety came at a cost not dissimilar to hers. With the help of the press, ship owners labeled the Australian immigrant as a Commie. He was an alien and agitator. He cuddled up to the Soviets in his lust for power. He was tried for being an agitator and Communist and acquitted. Over the next several years, he faced deportation multiple times. He lost a case in 1941 but the U.S. Supreme Court overturned the conviction. All attempts to rid America of this troublemaker failed spectacularly. In 1945, Bridges, who loved and admired his adopted country, finally won citizenship. A shipbuilder who fought Bridges in court for a decade finally saw the light. "If we deport Harry Bridges he'll organize the whole British Empire against us. Better to keep him close where we can keep an eye on him," he told reporters.

"Clara speaks highly about you, Mrs. Novak. Says you have guts."

She did? I do? What's this about? Joanne said nothing

"You know what's going on here Joanne," he said, switching to her first name. "This will likely be a bloody long strike. I'm going to be hopping from one port to another up and down the coast. I need someone in Seattle to help keep me organized and informed about events here. I need an assistant. I'd be honored if you'd come to work for us. The pay is garbo but the work is invigorating. It's for a just cause."

Assuming garbo meant garbage, she evaluated Bridges closely. He was an Aussie but she heard only a touch of that cockney, working-class accent. Tall and slim, he sat relaxed in a folding chair. He crossed one leg over the other, smoking a cigarette. He radiated confidence. No tee-shirt today. He wore a gray, pin-striped suit, white shirt and maroon tie. But the business attire could not conceal Harry the working man. This man believed in the righteousness of his cause. He valued worker solidarity. He promised to run the union like a constitutional democracy. Power lied not with management but with the rank and file. The aeromechanics, Joanne realized, failed to show that kind of internal strength and vision. In fact, the humiliation of the defeat in the Boeing strike nearly soured her on unions altogether. It taught her that power lies not with the worker or the union. Capital, corporations, government held the cards. She was sick of losing. But it wasn't just the strike and getting canned. The shameful red-baiting of the Canwell Committee was a blight on the university and the entire state. Three university professors, decent men punished for their unconventional beliefs, lost their jobs. The labor school, where she learned economics, labor history and organizational skills was shuttered like a condemned building. Another loss in a stack of losses.

"Harry, you need to get out here," demanded a man who burst through the office door. He wore coveralls and a checkered flannel shirt. "There's a disturbance in the hall. Some boys are going after each other. You better come out," he said hurriedly.

Bridges stood. "I'll be right out," he promised, and turned back to Joanne. He maintained his relaxed, self-assured posture. He'd seen hundreds of such disturbances and would deal with it in good time.

"Will you think about my offer?" he asked

"I don't like losing," she said curtly.

Bridges stuck a fresh cigarette in his mouth, using the nearly finished one to light it. "We don't lose, darling," he declared. "I know what happened with the aeromechanics. Your leadership let you down. You can't run a union from the top. It has to start from the bottom. It's like democracy. Power comes from the people. In a union, power comes from the worker. We're stronger together."

She looked back at Bridges, unsure how to respond. "I'm not a longshoreman, know nothing about the waterfront."

"You don't need to. You're an organizer, a tiger, someone who will help me get things done and support the boys."

Joanne promised to think about it, but it didn't take much thought at all. Bridges made her feel important and valued, attributes missing in her life in recent months. He exuded power and she wanted to be close to it. She wanted to learn from it. George objected of course.

"You're really going to work for that Commie?" he asked, incredulously.

The next three months was a whirlwind of meetings, picket lines and organizing. It was a far cry from the Boeing disaster. She had been on the outside looking in. This time she was on the inside looking out. She didn't carry picket signs, she printed them. She didn't walk the lines, she organized them. She handled Bridges' correspondence, scheduled and attended his meetings. She arranged media interviews in advance of his arrival in Seattle. In a matter of months, she grew into a labor organizer in the truest sense of the word. She found a calling. It wasn't building airplanes, but helping workers build a better life.

Bridges' panache impressed her at every turn. He could burrow into an issue, putting the other side off guard. During one negotiation meeting, a ship owner opened with a warning. "I don't know what you want, Bridges, but I promise you the answer will be no."

"I don't know what we want either," Bridges countered, "but I can promise we won't take no for an answer."

At stake was retaining concessions earned in the 1934 strike. Retaining the hiring hall topped the list. In winning the strike, unions gained control of hiring for the first time. The union, not the ship owner, decided who worked any given shift. Workers were selected based on need, ability, seniority and an equitable rotation. Prior to 1934, ship owners held sway over hiring. During the height of the Depression, when unemployment reached fifty percent in some industries, there were far more workers than jobs. In shipping, men were hired at the "Shape-up" or in the "Fink Hall." These euphemisms dehumanized and demeaned workers. At the beginning of each shift, dozens of men gathered at the shipyard gate. They shouldered and pushed each other. They jockeyed for position, desperate to be seen and selected. "See me," their desperate faces said. "Give me a little work, please, to buy milk. I'll bust my ass for you." Some would get chosen, most would not. The system was replete with corruption, kickbacks and bribes. Men out of work for a week were passed over for those who could buy their way in. Today, ship owners "final offer" demanded the end of the hiring hall. Never again, Bridges pledged, would the union return to the old way.

Owners also wanted union leaders to sign a noncommunist pledge. For a decade, the specter of communism hung over Bridges like a rain cloud, trailing him everywhere. He made his position clear when surrounded by a crowd of reporters outside union hall on a blustery October afternoon. A *Seattle P-I* reporter asked Bridges about the ship owners' demands.

"We will sign no such pledge," Bridges promised.

"But it's in their final offer," the reporter responded while scribbling on his notepad.

"The only final offer is the one we accept," he said.

"Are you a Communist, Harry?"

"Look, lad, have I worked with Communists and hired them? Sure, they're good workers. Do I favor Socialist ideas like social security and a national healthcare system? Absolutely. But I am not a Communist. I have not and will not join the Communist party. So you know where you can stick your bloody questions about communism."

"You were kind of hard on that reporter," Joanne said as they climbed into the backseat of the waiting car.

"Newspapers are on the side of the greedy at the expense of the needy. Don't forget that," he responded.

Chapter 42

Thirty seconds is the time it takes for our eyes to blink a few times, to wash our hands or brush our teeth, for the traffic light to turn green. These moments come and go throughout the day, unnoticed and forgotten.

In an earthquake, thirty seconds is half a lifetime. On April 13, 1949, at 11:55 am, time slowed to a crawl in Seattle and much of the Pacific Northwest. The ground gave way to powerful tectonic forces deep inside the earth. Seattleites experienced thirty seconds of terror they would never forget.

The city is built directly above a series of overlapping plates. These rigid slabs of earth extend from the Olympic Mountains to the foothills of the Cascades. The science behind earthquakes is simple, really. Dirt and water and pressure and time, all seeking equilibrium. The plates, perpetually jockeying for space, push against their neighbors, while fighting the unrelenting force of underground rivers and lakes. A nudge here, a thrust there. One plate pushed up, another down. It never stops. Earthquakes occur in Seattle almost every day, nearly all mild and unnoticed. Until they're not. Eventually the underground shoving match gets out of hand. Explodes to the surface. The earth shudders, cracking open the ground. The hard reality is that the endless conveniences of a major city require stable ground to remain upright. Call it a thirty-second lesson in geology. Welcome to the Subterranean Wrestling Championships, ladies and gentlemen, it's time to shake, rattle and roll.

At 11:55 am, a sixth grader at Lowell Elementary in Tacoma exited through the school's front doors. He was about to start his shift as a crossing guard. He'd taken just a few steps when the building's facade collapsed. It buried him in a ton of brick. The first of eight to die in the next thirty seconds.

At 11:55 am, a seventy-one year-old woman sought salvation in the Duwamish River. Panicked, she ran out of her home on Fifty-Second Avenue South and jumped into the polluted river. A neighbor came to her rescue and drove her to Harborview Hospital. Later, engineers calculated the quake permanently narrowed the river six inches near Spokane Street.

At 11:55 am, at the Blue Mouse Theater in Tacoma, movie goers were enjoying their popcorn and soft drinks while watching the 1935 film, "The Last Days of Pompeii. " It's a drama about an eruption of Mount Vesuvius in 79 AD that destroyed the city and killed all its people. When the theater seats began to vibrate, patrons squealed in delight at the special effects. The squeals soon morphed into shrieks when the shaking intensified. The screen went dark and the theater operator ordered everyone to walk, not run, to the exits.

Just west of the theater, a twenty-three-ton metal saddle that supported the suspension cables on the Tacoma Narrow's Bridge dislodged from its cradle. It dropped to the deck, injuring two workers. The vibration was almost as terrifying as the falling bridge parts. Both workers witnessed the 1940 collapse of the first bridge, known unlovingly as Gallopin' Gertie. Was Puget Sound about to swallow whole its second span in nine years?

At 11:55 am, Seattle's thirty-eight-story Smith Tower swayed like a drunken sailor. It struggled valiantly to remain at attention. Men at desks, women at typewriters, janitors sweeping floors stopped work. They rushed to the elevators only to find them shut down. They made their way to the stairs and clamored down to Second Avenue.

At 11:55 am a young Salvation Army volunteer was handing out pamphlets at Second and Yesler in Seattle. This is a lonely job. Pedestrians rushing in a midday rush ignored the proffered literature. Until the earth moved. Hundreds of people dashed out of shops, offices and restaurants. Many grabbed the pamphlets as they scurried by. In the next thirty seconds, the volunteer calmly offered salvation to more people than she did all morning. Whatever it takes for people to see the light, she thought.

When the shaking stopped, ten thousand chimneys and two thousand brick walls in Western Washington collapsed or were heavily damaged. The concrete path circling Green Lake split open like a deep gash under a boxer's eye. Three Seattle schools were so heavily damaged they were later condemned. The three bridges crossing the Duwamish were jammed shut, stopping water traffic. KJR Radio's 570-foot tower buckled near the top. It resembled a giraffe bending to eat its favorite succulent. Geysers from broken waterlines flooded streets, leaky gas lines threatened to start fires. Thousands of books toppled from shelves of the Seattle Public Library.

By far, the quake wreaked its greatest havoc in Pioneer Square. The city's oldest buildings were erected on backfill from the 1889 Seattle Fire. These multi-story structures were built before widespread use of steel, or rebar, to reinforce concrete foundations and masonry walls. Floors, roofs and internal walls were made of wood. The foundation supported the first floor, which held up the second and so on. All good enough. But while these aging sentinels of an emerging city stood straight and tall, they don't dance well. Lateral or sideways movement can be fatal. Think of a building made of Tinker Toys.

The Hotel Seattle, home to the Busy Bee Café at Second and Yesler, proved the point. When the shaking started, the café owner blocked the doors to keep panicking patrons from rushing outside. He likely saved their lives. Seconds later, the building's decorative cornice crashed to the sidewalk, crushing several cars parked on Second Avenue. Fortunately they were unoccupied.

Chapter 43

Joanne lay unconscious on the second floor of the Commerce Building. Nearly all occupants escaped except her and Jaworski. When she regained consciousness, she wasn't sure where she was. It took a minute, then the light went on. She knew exactly where she was. She was on her back in an office building whose ceiling collapsed on top of her. As her head cleared, she tried to sit. Mistake. Waves of pain rolled over her like the surf at high tide. Something was holding her down. Worse, something was terribly wrong with her right leg. She lifted her head and tried to see through the fog of plaster dust. A huge wood beam was pinning her down. She couldn't move her legs. The realization that she was trapped sent her body involuntarily into panic mode. Clenched fists, rapid breaths, heart thumping loudly. The signs of near panic. "Get ahold of yourself, Novak. Do not panic," she said, her voice cracked and wispy. Turning the panic meter down a couple of notches, she remembered she wasn't alone.

"Jaworski? she yelled" Silence.

"Jaworski!" she repeated more loudly. More silence.

Suddenly, a new fear struck like a smack upside the head. My kids! Where are my kids? There'd been an earthquake, a big one, she was sure of it. Think! Where are they? Eventually she remembered. Danny was with his Boy Scout troop touring the capitol building in Olympia. Could the quake have hit that far away? Natalie was likely in class at the UW, more worrisome so close to the city. Where was George? She didn't think he was at Plant Two today. He'd said something about business in Alki. She tried one more time to summon Jaworski while pushing down the panic. Nothing from the kindly Polack. All she heard was a cacophony of creaking lumber and shifting plaster coming from above. We're not quite done with you, it said.

. . .

Danny and twenty of his fellow scouts in Troop 109, all in uniform, were in the cupola near the top of the massive legislative building in Olympia. Danny thought the cupola was a sight to behold. How could anything this big be so beautiful? He'd visited Plant Two on Boeing's Bring Your Kids to Work Day. The plant was much bigger than this but a thousand-foot runway short of beautiful. Danny looked below and admired the massive Tiffany glass chandelier hanging from the cupola. Weighing in at ten thousand pounds, it hung at the end of a one-hundred-and-fifty foot chain, suspended fifty feet above the floor. Danny thought it looked bigger than his bedroom.

"At 287 feet, the dome, which is made totally of stone, is the fifth tallest dome in the world," claimed Mr. Gustafsson, their troop leader. "It weighs more than thirty million pounds, and is totally self-supporting. Each stone supports the other, each fits snugly to the next, holding the entire structure up." He swept his arm around the dome with a sense of pride, like he'd personally fitted every last rock.

"Mr. Gustafsson?" Danny asked. "If all the stones are self-supporting like you said, what would happen if one came out? Would the whole thing crash?"

Gustafsson smiled at Danny patronizingly. "In theory, yes, Danny. But it would take a lot more than one for the building to lose its integrity. But you don't need to worry about that, it will never happen."

But it almost did. The quake's epicenter, or as Danny would have called it, ground zero, was just a short drive up Highway 99 towards Tacoma. The unseen waves of tectonic energy slammed into the capitol. The cupola lurched violently. Stones were wrenched from their lodging and crumbled to the floor. It knocked over Mr. Gustafsson and some of the scouts. Danny grabbed a doorknob and managed to remain upright. He wasn't sure how long the shaking lasted. With his acuity in math he tried to keep track but lost count while dodging shattered rock skittering around his feet. He looked down and saw the massive chandelier swinging back and forth. A monstrous metronome keeping time to an unearthly concerto.

As the quake's energy moved north to claim its next victims. Mr. Gustafsson scrambled to his feet and headed for the exit. He instructed his scouts to line up and hold hands. He then led them down a circular iron stairway that wound down to the next level. Cracked plaster and crushed rock tumbled at their heels. They arrived at a landing above the main floor and could see the capitol grounds outside. A large crowd gathered a safe distance from the building. Broken columns and white rock littered the grounds. Danny looked back at the chandelier. It was still keeping time to the music and wouldn't come to rest for days.

. . .

Natalie sat in the back of the first floor auditorium in Denny Hall attending a lecture on "Naturalism in Russian Theater." But her mind was on drama of another sort. Last night she and her Dad argued for the umpteenth time. This one was over her activism. The latest round was about her vocal opposition to the anti-communist witch hunt. George branded it as Communist. What was communistic about standing up for your professors or fighting poverty and racism? She loved her Dad. He'd called her Kitten when she was little. She looked up to him. She swelled with pride and relief when he returned home. But their relationship soured ever since, and worsened when she'd enrolled at UW. He exploded when learning she'd signed and circulated a petition objecting to the dismissal of the three profs. She stood her ground, though, believing it was the right thing. The abuse of faculty rights was an abuse of student rights. What is a university for if not the free exchange of ideas?

"Look what happened to your mother for her foolishness," he said, referring to her dismissal from Boeing and ending the argument.

Natalie sat up in her chair and tried to focus on Professor Glenn Hughes, head of the drama department. He'd been teaching drama and writing and producing plays at UW for decades. Today he was expounding on a Chekhov theme that carried through many of his plays, the idleness and wasting away of Russian royalty.

"The Cherry Orchard is a case in point, ladies and gentlemen. The orchard itself and its destruction is a metaphor for the decay of the Czar's family and . . ." The sentence, like thousands that day, was interrupted at midpoint. Never finished. The professor stopped speaking and surveyed the two hundred or so faces staring back at him. The entire auditorium wobbled and hummed like a clothes washer in the spin cycle. He knew Denny Hall was built with brick and stone in 1895. It was the oldest permanent building on campus. Professor Hughes wasn't sure how much spin cycle the old girl could take.

With the urbanity of a seasoned actor gifted at understatement, Hughes picked up his papers and stepped down from the podium. "I don't care for this at all, ladies and gentlemen," he said calmly. "I suggest we leave at once. Walk but do not run to the exit." Natalie was the first out the door.

. . .

George sat at a stoplight on southbound Admiral Way when his car began to shimmy. At first he thought it must be a problem with the suspension. Then he looked out the windshield. The power poles were bouncing around like balloons on a string. The light turned green, but George kept his foot on the brake, mesmerized by the scene. Drivers behind him joined in a chorus of honking horns, then quickly stopped. For the next thirty seconds, he watched an earthquake through his windshield like taking in a short at the drive-in.

. . .

The floor and the wall facing Yesler Way began to crumble. The brick and mortar moaned in protest as gravity did what gravity does. The gaping hole in the ceiling resembled a whale about to swallow Joanne whole. She managed to keep it together for the last hour (Was it that long?) but her nerves were ready to turn and run. The pain, unfortunately, wasn't going anywhere. It left her nauseous and soaked in sweat. She could smell urine and mildew. She longed for water to rinse the dust out of her parched mouth and throat. She had to pee. When the dust began to clear, she got a closer look at her right leg. What she initially thought was a hunk of plaster was actually bone. Bone! Another shot of nausea. From her first-aid class at Boeing, she knew it must be a compound fracture of the tibia. Or was it the fibula? She always mixed them up. She gave up calling for Jaworski. He was clearly seriously hurt or worse.

Why wasn't anyone looking for them or answering her cries for help? She yelled until her voice cracked and throat ached. She threw a brick at the window but it landed a pitiful ten feet short. The pain from the throwing motion nauseated her. For the first time in her life, Joanne was alone in every sense of the word. No one was going to help. She would have to rescue herself, but first free herself. She examined the object pinning both legs. From what she could see, it looked like a heavy floor beam. It must be eighteen inches wide, she surmised. She closed her eyes and clenched her teeth to fight back the pain and attempted to sit up to get a better look. It took three tries before she could sit upright enough to get her hands between her legs. From there she extended her arms under the beam, palms up and bending low enough to buy some leverage. Using strength that came from nowhere, she lifted the beam and rotated it forward. It moved one agonizing inch at a time. With adrenaline rushing through her, creating a strength she would later be at loss to explain, Joanne shoved the beam forward. She lost her hold on the beam and it landed on her feet. It ripped skin and broke God knows how many bones. She fell back, screaming from indescribable pain. "God Damn it!"

When she regained some semblance of control she realized she did it. Her legs were free. Damaged but free. "Thank you, God," she said aloud. But the elation was short lived. She could feel warm blood trickling down her leg. The beam must have slowed the bleeding because blood was flowing freely now. She pulled the scarf from her head and untied the knot. It was red, dotted with white stars. She'd taken to wearing scarves at Boeing to keep hair off her face. It was now more fashion statement than safety precaution. but it may now save her leg or even her life. She wrapped and cinched it firmly above the knee. The make-shift tourniquet would have to do. She rolled onto her stomach and looked around. She knew better than trying to stand. She'd have to drag herself. With her right leg flopping painfully along, she scooted around until she faced the eastside windows. The door to the hallway and stairs was closer, but she'd never make it down. Best to get to the windows about fifty feet away. Try to summon help. She mouthed a brief prayer, crossed herself and raised up on her elbows. Pushing with her left leg and pulling with her arms, she inched her way forward, leaving a bloody trail in her wake.

. . .

It took George an hour to negotiate the fifteen-minute drive from Alki to downtown. A water main burst on Admiral Way. It shut down one lane of the only entrance onto the West Spokane Street Bridge. The delay was killing him. A sense that something dreadful had happened to Joanne wouldn't go away. He worried about Natalie and Danny, too, but they were farther away and out of reach for now. *I have to get to Joanne. She needs rescue. If I can do that, I'll say I'm sorry for everything. I'm sorry for how I've walled you off. The way I've treated the kids. I know I haven't been the man you married. But I love you. I'll change. I've been an absentee husband. I come home every night but my mind is somewhere else. It's in the Solomon's, or work. Don't blame the war. You can't pin everything on the war. Take responsibility. Focus on what your family needs and less on what you've lost. Get it together, Novak.*

Once he finally crossed the bridge, he made good progress on northbound Fourth Avenue until he reached the southern edge of Chinatown. A fallen powerline blocked the street, traffic backed up for blocks. Shit. He parked on the shoulder, climbed out of the car and slammed the door. He ran north, propelled by the growing sense his wife was in trouble. When he reached Second and Yesler, the gnawing fear erupted into a five-alarm fire. Pioneer Square looked like Tokyo in 1945. Streets and sidewalks were littered with fallen brick and mortar, some of it piled a foot deep. Parked cars resembled crushed cookies. Power poles were all a kilter, the lines looping close to the streets. Shattered glass was strewn everywhere. Scores of people gawking at the wreckage blocked the streets. He fought through the crowds, stumbling twice while trying to avoid the rubble. He arrived sweating and breathless at Joanne's building. He remembered it because he drove her to work a few weeks ago. The front of the four-story brick building on Second Avenue was in shambles. The shaking chewed big bites out of the front. Bricks and shattered glass were visible in all directions. City workers in helmets and uniformed police were busy roping off the street in front of the entrance when George arrived. He shouldered through the gawkers and headed towards the steps leading to the front door, when he felt someone grab his arm from behind.

"Hold it, sir. This building is closed. It's not safe," It was a uniformed police officer.

"My wife is in there! She must be hurt."

"No sir, that building was cleared thirty minutes ago. It's in danger of collapsing. There's no one in there."

"I'm certain she's there," he said, fighting the panic in his voice. The name tag said he was Officer James Hampton. "Look, Officer Hampton, she works for the longshoremen's union. She told me this morning she'd be here today to clear the place out and lock up."

A man dressed in slacks and blue checkered shirt walked up. "Sir, I manage this building. The union people moved out over a week ago. The second floor is vacant."

George shook his head in disbelief and pushed past the men. He ran up the steps but stopped when he heard glass shattering and the thud of a brick hitting the sidewalk. It bounced to a stop at the cop's feet like a hand grenade ready to explode. George didn't hesitate. He flung open the door, took the stairs two at a time and pushed through the door to the second floor hallway. The elevator doors were to his right. There were doors at each end of the hall. He ran to his right towards Second Avenue. He flung the door open and froze. An avalanche of destruction faced him. Beams, tile flooring, asbestos, office chairs and tables, filing cabinets strewn across the floor. Everything drenched in an inch of water from a broken pipe. He could smell mildew and rot. He could hear street noise from Second Avenue. The body of a man he didn't recognize was face down, unmoving. He moved on and yelled for his wife. That's when he saw her. She was sitting up facing the window with a brick in her right hand.

"Joanne, stop! I'm here! He ran up to her, knelt, took the brick from her hand. He eased her down on her back. She felt cold to the touch, her face pale and yellowish, eyes blurred and watery. She appeared to recognize him, her eyes gaining focus.

"You came," she said, sounding surprised.

. . .

Three days later, Joanne sat up in bed at her Capitol Hill home. Four pillows propped her up. She tried to ignore throbbing pain in her leg and focus on *The Times*'s coverage of the quake. George was dozing in the armchair next to her. She could hear the kids talking downstairs. George drove her home yesterday afternoon following three days at Harborview Hospital. Doctors set her right leg and wrapped her in a cast that ran from ankle to mid-thigh. It must weigh fifty pounds, she guessed. They bandaged her tattered feet. No broken bones, thank you. She was given blood and treated for a concussion. She'd nearly bled to death and was lucky to be alive, according to the doctors.

The afternoon sun streamed through the window, wispy white clouds giving way to blue sky. The family attended Easter Services at St. Joseph's that morning, in spite of George's protestations. He disapproved for obvious reasons, but she'd insisted. She hadn't missed an Easter mass in forty years and wouldn't miss this one. She'd hobbled from the car to the church on crutches. George and Danny flanked her like security guards. Natalie carried her purse. They sat in the back near the door. At the end of a long service, the congregation stood and begin to file up for communion. She tried to stand but George held her down. She didn't argue, and spared herself the pain of shuffling to the altar and back. While painful, the service brought peace and a ray of hope. Father Sullivan preached that Easter, above all, was about hope. He read from Romans 15:13. She could only remember part of it, but it stuck. *"May the God of hope fill you with all joy and peace . . ."*

Joy may be a stretch but Joanne was filled with hope and felt at peace. Her shattered tibia aside, the Novak family survived the biggest quake in Seattle's history. She remembered the quakes in 1939 and 1946. They were minor tremors compared to this one. Nevertheless, her family was safe and the house undamaged. Unfortunately the news about the Jaworski family wasn't good.

Falling debris from the third floor landed on his head. He was pronounced dead at the scene. She'd only worked with him for a few weeks but she'd miss him. He left behind a daughter and grandson. Joanne pledged to visit as soon as she could.

She scooted a little higher in her bed, drank water from the plastic glass on the bedside table and returned to her reading. The quake left a trail of destruction throughout the Northwest, including British Columbia and Montana. The intensity level varied based on the distance from the epicenter. Puget Sound region endured the worst of it. Seismologists used the Mercalli Intensity Level Scale to quantify earthquakes. In Seattle it was an VIII on a scale of XII. A Level-I quake could be barely felt. A XII caused near total destruction of buildings and bridges. Joanne could now speak with authority on the destructive power of an VIII.

The damage to the Capitol Building disturbed her the most. If the quake had lasted another few seconds, according to *The Times*, the rotunda would have likely collapsed and buried everyone inside. God was watching over Scout Troop 109. Natalie, too, was lucky because the UW campus suffered relatively minor damage. Joanne was the unlucky one mainly because of an oversight on her part. The union moved out of the building the previous week but she failed to notify building management they were returning Wednesday to remove a few last boxes.

Harry Bridges called and wished her well. Said he needed her back and looked forward to her return. But Joanne wasn't so sure. *How much more pain was my determination to work going to cause this family? Our home was bombed, my husband injured. It damaged him mentally and physically. Worse, my absence from home drove a wedge between me and my husband. The tension troubled the kids, no doubt. Look what you've done to your marriage, your home life? The quake wasn't my fault, but I put myself in harm's way. I was at work and not at home.* The guilt that plagued Joanne four years ago tumbled back into her life like the debris that nearly buried her at Second at Yesler. She gave in to it. It consumed her. *You don't need this Novak. Best to push all that aside. Save your marriage. Work can wait.*

"You okay?"

It was George, awake from his nap. She looked at her husband, the lines of fatigue and worry under his eyes. He still wore the dark blue suit he'd worn to mass, the red-striped tie pulled lose. She loved her husband of twenty years, but the long silences and building resentment ate away at that love. The bright colors of their marriage faded. The edges were chipped and worn like an old dinner plate washed too many times. But God bless him. He saved her life. It still amazed her that he knew where she was and needed rescuing. Since then, he was constantly at her side. He attended to her every need. He said he loved her more times than she'd heard in years. Nearly losing someone you love rejuvenated that love, gave it new life.

The bedroom door swung open and Natalie and Danny walked in with an early supper. Danny held a pitcher of iced tea and Natalie carried a tray laden with Joanne's favorite meal, pork and dumplings. The fact it was leftovers from last Sunday didn't matter. Natalie set the tray on Joanne's lap. Danny poured iced tea into a glass and placed it on the nightstand.

Joanne thanked them, picked up the fork then stopped. The three of them were standing over, her grinning broadly. Their expressions of worry from the last three days evaporated.

"This is perfect, guys, but I can't eat with the three of you gawking at me. You look like the cats who ate the canary. What's going on?"

The trio exchanged glances coming to some silent agreement she wasn't privy to. George sat on the edge of the bed and smiled. "We almost lost you. It scared me. It scared all of us. Thank God you're going to be okay. We only want what's best for you."

Joanne set down the fork and looked at her husband. *Here we go again. Round 12 in the marital bout.* "You think you know what's best for me?" she asked, an edge to her voice.

He moved in closer, ran his fingers through her hair and smiled. "I think so. I can't believe I'm saying this, but your family wants what you want. We think you should keep your job. It's important work. You're needed there. It's where you belong."

Author's Note

When I was in the fourth grade, we lived in High Point, a housing project in West Seattle. It was built for defense workers in 1942, and later for returning G.I.s We lived in a two-story, side-by-side duplex that came with two bedrooms, low rent and a tiny yard. In the parlance of the twenty-first century, High Point was as diverse and inclusive as a neighborhood could be. White and Black families shared duplexes, schools, parks and grocery stores. I remember asking my grandmother about our "colored" neighbors. I wanted to know more about them. Where did they come from?

"From the South, Skipper," she said, using a nickname that few ten-year-old boys would embrace.

"Why did they leave the South? Why come here?"

"Because Seattle is good to its Negroes," she said. "It's much better here than in the South."

I didn't press Grandma further, but her opinion was entrenched in the Seattle and Pacific Northwest cultures dating back to its early history. It was a lie or at least wrong. It's what the University of Washington Historian James Gregory calls "the myth of Seattle nice." According to this myth, Seattle and much of the Pacific Northwest has throughout its relatively brief history welcomed people of color or at least accepted them. They were far more open minded than Southerners.

But like much of history, the story isn't written in black and white, but in shades of gray that defy definition. Granted, there were no "whites only" signs on restaurant windows or whites only drinking fountains. Jim Crow was alive and well in the Pacific Northwest, but hiding in the shadows. George Washington Bush, a free black farmer living in Missouri, a slave state, learned this lesson a century earlier. In 1844, he and four white families headed west to Oregon Country, a land they heard was more accepting of Blacks. But instead of tolerance, they were met with an exclusionary law written into the Oregon Territorial Constitution. It made it illegal for them to settle there permanently. The Bush party moved north to the future Washington State. At the time it was unorganized territory and beyond the reach of Oregon's laws. The Bush's farmed and built the area's first gristmill and sawmill. They opened their home to assist travelers settling on Puget Sound. They became an integral part of the community, liked and respected by neighbors. But unlike those neighbors, the Bush's couldn't lay claim to the land on which they'd built a life. When the United States took possession of Oregon Territory under a treaty with England in 1846, Oregon's exclusion laws were back in play. The Bush family was again under the thumb of Jim Crow Northwest.

The creation of the Washington Territory in 1853, separating it from Oregon, opened new doors. At the urging of friends and neighbors, the first territorial legislature in 1854 voted unanimously to confirm Bush ownership of the land. In a time when the nation was still debating the "positive good" of slavery and millions of Americans lived in bondage, white residents and a white-controlled government in Washington offered justice to one of their own.

Perhaps that act of kindness gave birth to the myth, but in Seattle at least, it wasn't relevant because the population was about one percent black prior to WW II. Nearly one hundred percent lived in the Central District. Whites and blacks found an equilibrium and coexisted in relative peace for nearly a century. You live there and we'll live here, and we'll get along just fine. And it was fine until the Naval and Air Forces of Japan attacked the United States at Pearl Harbor on Dec. 7, 1941.

Suddenly the Pacific Northwest found itself in the center of the action. The Federal Government took notice of its Northwest hinterland. Federal dollars started to flow, and where cash flows, workers follow. Climbing out of the pits of the Great Depression, they trudged west for war jobs. They came by the tens of thousands from the Atlantic east, the deep south and the middle west. They built planes, ships and tanks. They bussed north from Central America,

Mexico and the American Southwest to address a labor shortage caused by the war and the internment of 110,000 Japanese. Housewives, mothers, daughters, sisters quit monotonous jobs in restaurants, offices and stores for meaningful work in factories. Blacks, too, elbowed their way into this work party. It was the ultimate collective effort. People of all races, of all social classes joined hands. They came from lands far and near to help destroy an enemy and return peace to America. The city by the Sound swelled with pride for having helped build President Roosevelt's Arsenal for Democracy. War workers in Washington built 8,200 bombers, 103 warships, 926 tanks and 1,300 rescue vehicles. But there's more. Seattle didn't just build the B29 that delivered the knock-out blow on Nagasaki and changed the world. Seattle's neighbor at Hanford, just one hundred seventy miles down the road, created the secret sauce, plutonium, for the bomb that ended the war that changed the world.

On August 15, 1945, the world rejoiced when Japan surrendered unconditionally, ending the war and six years of death, heartache and fear. In Seattle, there was no stopping a city wild with joy on Victory over Japan (VJ) Day. They partied hard for three days, but when it was over a sense of unease emerged like a morning fog rolling in from Elliott Bay. One in three people celebrating VJ Day were recent arrivals. They didn't know the other Seattle, the Seattle before it won a world war, before it mattered. White Seattle wasn't sure, actually it was pretty sure, it didn't like this new Seattle. There was color on every street corner, black and brown, that hadn't been there before. Too many women were wearing slacks and carrying lunch pails instead of wearing aprons and pushing strollers. Mothers let their children flounder in federal child care centers or became Latchkey Kids. Workers everywhere joined unions, demanding higher wages, pensions and control of the workplace. No, this was not good. City leaders and residents wanted back the old Seattle. They missed the one with clear-cut rules and order, when everyone knew where they belonged.

But who belonged in Seattle? And to whom does Seattle belong? The answers were far from clear. GIs returned home victorious. They wanted to make families, go to university on the new GI Bill. They were going to make their mark in a peaceful America. But too much was different. Servicemen returned to wives and girlfriends changed by war. African Americans came home to find nothing changed. On their lapels, many wore what one newspaper tabbed a "Double V." It stood for victory over fascism abroad and victory over racism at home. Unfortunately, the Negro learned prejudice and discrimination are stubborn things. Japanese immigrants and citizens were stripped of home and business three months after Pearl Harbor. Four years later they wanted their property back. Sorry, but fear and loathing run deep. Go somewhere else, they were told.

Two out of three women in war jobs were cast aside by 1946. Thanks very much for your contributions, ladies, but the boys are ready to assume their rightful place on the shop floor. Most working women returned to the domestic, some willingly, some not. But you can easily scratch a woman's name from the rolls. It's harder to erase the taste of freedom and independence that came with earning your own paycheck. Eventually she will be heard.

The surprise was how quickly America returned to a war footing. By early 1946, things were anything but quiet on the Eastern Front. Warning bells clanged in the Capital when the Union of Soviet Socialist Republics, America's ally in WW II, revealed its hand. It was obsessed with border security, and armed with a military might funded in large part by the United States. It quickly moved in to dominate its bordering countries and subjugate the free people of Eastern Europe as well as East Germany. A renewed USSR, armed with an iron fist wrapped in an Iron Curtain, challenged the Free World, leading to a new kind of war, a Cold War.

So once again, the country turned to its hinterland. The postwar recession was blessedly short, and untold riches lay ahead. The question was to whom do those riches belong? Everyone wanted a piece of the action, especially workers. Led by Socialist-leaning unions, they risked bringing the whole kit and caboodle crashing down. But there would be none of that. Unions were troublemakers, Communists disguised as common laborers. They must be snuffed out, not just contained.

I chose to write about the "myth of Seattle nice" through the lives of four families. They are fictional characters or composites of real people whose stories are based on fact. The fictional Joanne Novak represents the social pressures placed on women who chose to work in their husband's absence, and who fought for their jobs upon their return. Lawrence Williams and Frank Sasaki are composites of actual people and real events. John Jacobson and his wife Ellie are semi-biographical, based in part on my parents.

Most of the secondary characters are real people beginning with Arthur Barnett and the Council of Churches. So too are Christian Friends board members Edith Steinmetz, Madeleine Morehouse Brake and Dorothy Stimson Bullitt. Christian Friends and the Seattle Council of Churches were among multiple organizations dedicated to standing up for those denied fairness and equality. More than a century after a few white folks came to the aid of their colored neighbors near Olympia, a large contingent of Seattleites stood up for their fellow citizens.

Justice was delayed, however, when it came to housing. The Supreme Court's decision in *Shelly v. Kraemer* in 1948 was both landmark and off the mark. The court decision did not prohibit racial restrictive covenants only declared them unenforceable. Largely ignored by the real estate industry and cemetery owners, fair housing was an unattainable goal in America until passage of the Fair Housing Act in 1968. Until then, only the most determined homebuyers, like the fictional Lawrence Williams, succeeded in buying homes outside the Central District. The Seattle City Council passed a fair housing ordinance in 1968 but only after voters roundly defeated a ballot measure four years earlier.

The internment of Japanese remains a black mark on American history. After the war, rather than returning to the city that rejected them, many of Seattle's Japanese resumed their lives in the Midwest or East. Those who did return, like the fictional Sasaki family, eventually regained possession of their homes and rejuvenated their businesses. Camp Minidoka in Idaho, which housed up to thirteen thousand Japanese, is now a National Historic Site. The barbed wire fences and wooden barracks are long gone but the memory of the injustices were preserved. In 1988, Congress passed the Civil

Liberties Act. It acknowledged the injustice of internment and shelled out $20,000 to more than 82,000 victims still alive in 1988.

The University of Washington sought similar redemption in 1994 when it publicly apologized for the dismissal of Professors Gundlach, Phillips and Butterworth. UW President William Gerberding stated "clearly and unequivocally" that the college was in the wrong. "This was a dark day in our history, and we must make sure that it doesn't happen again," he said. Such a reversal in ethical standards did not come quickly, however. In the 1950s notable academics like Kenneth Burke and physicist J. Robert Oppenheimer were denied professorships at the UW due to alleged Communist ties. Not to be outdone, the Washington Legislature instituted a loyalty oath for all public employees in 1951.The University's reputation suffered as leading academics looked askance at an institution that would so easily cut loose tenured faculty in violation of its own policies. Just as damning was the precedent set. The dismissals made it "all too easy for other academic institutions to turn against political undesirables," according to Historian Ellen Schrecker. Throughout the 1950s, multiple state universities demanded loyalty pledges from faculty.

The blight on the university pales in comparison to that of the fired professors. In 1949 Ralph Gundlach, who steadfastly refused to cooperate with the committee, was fined $250 and spent thirty days in jail. Blackballed in academia, he practiced clinical psychology until he retired. He never forgave the University, and died in London in 1978. Herbert Phillips failed to find fulltime employment in education. He worked as a laborer in San Francisco and died in 1978. Joseph Butterworth soon learned there wasn't much demand for professors of Old English, especially one holding Communist sympathies. Unable to hold a job, he eventually went on public assistance. He spent much of his final years drinking beer at the Blue Moon Tavern in the University District. A sad and lonely figure, he died in 1970.

The three professors placed on probation in 1949 kept their heads down and lips sealed about anything unconventional for the remainder of their careers. Melville Jacobs died of cancer in 1971, Eby in 1994, and Ethel in 1980. Ethel's life ended tragically when he shot his wife, his wife's sister and her husband before turning the gun on himself.

There were no apologies coming from Albert Canwell, the brainchild, chairman and defender of the Un-American Activities Committee. He won his House seat in 1946 promising to root out the Communists in government and colleges. He was shown the door two years later. Apparently, voters saw enough of his shenanigans or weren't convinced of an imminent threat from the Red Menace. Canwell maintained the righteousness of his cause throughout his life. He never backed down, calling the professors a "bunch of weaklings. . . "I didn't accuse anybody who wasn't guilty as hell," he said forty years later. Never a quitter, Canwell ran unsuccessfully for public office four more times including governor in 1968. Len Schroeter, former President of the Washington Chapter of the American Civil Liberties Union, summed up Canwell perfectly. He "was like a meteor going through the sky with terrible pyrotechnics, and then gone." Canwell died in Spokane in 2002.

Clara Fraser, the only admitted communist in this story, was a champion and voice for progressive causes for the remainder of her life. She wrote and spoke publicly about the perceived ills of American society. Nothing was too sensitive, from racism to anti-Semitism, from sexism to gay rights. Above all, she spoke on behalf of American women. She was a feminist before there was feminism. In a 1992 essay, she wrote that American women were the "permanent, unrecognized undercaste (sic) of U.S. Society." She died in Seattle in 1998 at age 74.

There were few heroes during the labor conflicts of the 1940s, but Harry Bridges was the exception. The impact of his defense of dock workers in 1934 and 1948 is still evident today. The hiring hall is a permanent fixture on the docks, as well as his member-first approach to union management. Less noted was his commitment to racial equality. Workers of color were welcome and accepted in the International Longshore and Warehouse Union (ILWU). Bridges said that if he could hire only two dock workers, one of them would be Black. He led the ILWU for forty years and died at age 88 in 1990.

We're two-plus decades into the Twenty-first Century and Seattle still enjoys a reputation of a city whose people are accepting and open minded. Readers can judge for themselves the veracity of that claim, but there is no shortage of evidence to the contrary. The targets have shifted but Seattle is not immune to the nationwide climate of political derision and exclusion. Undocumented immigrants from Mexico and Central America, the LGBTQ+ community and Jews and Muslims all live with permanent targets stenciled on their backs. According to the Anti-Defamation League, there were seven bomb threats to synagogues in 2023, from Bellingham to Seattle to Tacoma. With the war in Gaza, Jews, Muslims and Palestinians are all victims of equal-opportunity hate. Exclusion and intolerance are permanently threaded into the fabric of the American heart. It's a byproduct of a country of immigrants and income inequality. India's Nobel laurate, Kailash Satyarthi, wrote that the biggest challenges facing humankind are fear and intolerance. As an eternal optimist, I both hope and believe that future generations will conquer their fears and accept people who by all rights belong in America.

Acknowledgements

Writing is hard, I tell my history students. After completing this novel, I've learned writing historical fiction is harder. I could not have survived the last four years without the assistance of numerous content experts, as well as the guidance, honesty and love of many friends and family.

In nonfiction, the facts – the time, the place, the people – are the building blocks for constructing a story about the past. In fiction, the actors are like undressed mannequins. They cannot be placed in the store window naked. Writers must adorn them with a history, a present and a future. We must bless them with accessories like emotions, prejudices and failings, all in an effort to transform historical actors into believable characters. That, dear readers, takes a team.

Let me start with recognizing those who make writing history possible – librarians, archivists and historians. Their work informed my work. I owe much to Historylink.org, University of Washington Special Collections, the UW's Civil Rights and Labor History Consortium, the Harry Bridges Center for Labor Studies and the Seattle Public Library. Thanks also to Mike Lombardi, Boeing historian; Art Storbo, Enumclaw Historical Society; and Ron Going, retired naval officer and pilot.

I am eternally indebted to those who cared enough about my story to read it and offer sound advice and recommendations over the past months. Thanks to Dwight Phillips, Sharon Phillips, P.G. Phillips, Jillian Harrington, Danielle O'Leary, Janet Cantonwine, Tom Lux, Jim Guilfoil, and Heather Miller at Historium Press. Your contributions, large and small, made this work better. Special thanks to Dee Marley, Historium Press CEO, who saw in *Unbelonging*, a story worth telling.

Finally, I want to express my love and gratitude to my family. To my daughters, Jillian and Danielle, your love and confidence in me means everything. And, finally, to Jackie, my wife of nearly fifty years, who bears the burden of marrying a writer. Your common sense, good judgement and eye for details are priceless.

www.historiumpress.com

www.ingramcontent.com/pod-product-compliance
Lightning Source LLC
Chambersburg PA
CBHW021350060726
47591CB00006B/2249